MY KINGDOM FOR A GUITAR

GLOBAL AFRICAN VOICES
Dominic Thomas, *editor*

MY KINGDOM FOR A GUITAR
A Novel

Kidi Bebey

Translated by KAREN LINDO

INDIANA UNIVERSITY PRESS

This book is a publication of

Indiana University Press
Office of Scholarly Publishing
Herman B Wells Library 350
1320 East 10th Street
Bloomington, Indiana 47405 USA

iupress.org

First Published as *Mon Royaume pour une guitare* © Editions Michel Lafon, 2016
English translation © 2021 by Indiana University Press

Manufactured in the United States of America
First printing 2021

Library of Congress Cataloging-in-Publication Data

Names: Bebey, Kidi, author. | Lindo, Karen, translator.
Title: My kingdom for a guitar / Kidi Bebey ; translated by Karen Lindo.
Other titles: Mon royaume pour une guitare. English
Description: Bloomington, Indiana : Indiana University Press, [2021] |
  Series: Global African voices
Identifiers: LCCN 2021013227 (print) | LCCN 2021013228 (ebook) | ISBN
  9780253057853 (paperback) | ISBN 9780253057877 (ebook)
Classification: LCC PQ3989.2.B3516 M6613 2021 (print) | LCC PQ3989.2.B3516
  (ebook) | DDC 843/.914—dc23
LC record available at https://lccn.loc.gov/2021013227
LC ebook record available at https://lccn.loc.gov/2021013228

O nyola bona bam bese.
To my beautiful Orange tree.

So I went, dancing on my way.

—ABIOSEH NICOL, *The Meaning of Africa*

MY KINGDOM FOR A GUITAR

–1–

There are many ways to tell this story. One way is by going back in time, to several centuries ago. During the serene hour following lunch, a page slumbered in a siesta on the ship's deck. He had surrendered to the lulling of the waves, drifting along, pitching and rolling with the heaviness of the humid air, gradually lowering his eyelids. He had unfastened the neckband to his ruff, which hung like a large white butterfly alongside his chin. The quiet hour. Even the crew was half asleep. No one noticed the brown line of a coastal strip between the blue of the waves, the green of the trees, and the gray of the sky.

But the local inhabitants, they had sharp eyes. In the distance, amid the sea mist, they caught sight of a foreign flag. A ship of that size? It was a shock and an equally exciting surprise. They were eager to get to know these men who had learned how to make these kinds of machines. They would surely be able to have a discussion with these inventors, share important secrets for the common good. From one intelligent group to another. Because they, too, were in possession of treasures. For instance, they knew the plants that could heal and those that made you invincible. They also knew the kinds of sophisticated rhythms that could transform the most formidable enemies into languorous dancers. Had these foreigners heading to their coast ever heard of such knowledge? They grabbed hold of their paddles and pirogues and headed out into the bay. They would be sure to start off with the customary greetings: they held to a strong practice of mores and knew very well that long before engaging in conversation a foreigner is thirsty and needs to recuperate from the rigors of his journey. We need to let them come and take a seat, offer them something to drink, and then introduce them to the leaders. Within the forest, the drums had sent out the message of an impromptu and extraordinary arrival. The leaders had already begun to adorn themselves in ceremonial attire. Standing looking outward, their sense of pride was apparent in their physical bearing.

Back on the ship, upon hearing the shouting from the main deck, the page opened his eyes. He slumped into the crumbled cakes soiling his black-and-white doublet and caused his guitar to fall and break a string. The top man reported:

– Some dark forms! No . . . Looks more like skiffs! Who's that heading directly toward us? They look like pins!

Friends or enemies? The captain was in command. The quartermaster bluntly shouted out orders to the harquebusiers as the local inhabitants advanced between the demanding efforts of their paddle strokes with welcoming smiles. They had brought with them banana leaves to fan their visitors and water jugs filled with coconut milk and fresh water that had been prepared by their wives. Back in the village, the chief donned his best costume. Not far off from the vessel, suddenly catastrophe broke out. Shots were fired and bullets came down on the approaching men like a lethal rainfall. Some fell immediately and were swallowed up by the waves. Others, screamed out, bewildered, and tried to turn around while fighting against the current, asking themselves, *why*?

From his hiding place on the deck, out of sight from the captain and the men trying to get away, the page looked on, appalled. He watched as the sea swallowed up the bodies of these men who, a moment ago, had been smiling. These people seemed welcoming. Was it a given that their souls were black? Unsettled by what he was seeing, the page's heart began to bleed. He hadn't left his mother, his sisters, and his family behind to witness such a horror. He wanted to discover the world, meet people, and learn, not watch men destroy each other long before they'd even had a chance to exchange greetings. He thought about his younger sister, who had been in tears, enraged because she wasn't a young man and therefore would never have the chance to take off to the Indies. He was now unsure he'd ever make it back home to tell her about the lamentation the sea carries within its waves. Tears trickled down his face. He was afraid to want for courage. His sister would not be proud of him. He discreetly wiped away the tears as the pirogues, saved by a moment of grace, managed to recede into the distance.

The page's fingers gripped the neck of his guitar.

The trouble having passed, the caravel carefully cast its anchor at a distance from the coast. From the arches of the sky, the darkness of evening suddenly fell. The page stood paralyzed, stilled by the thoughts of the events of that day. He kept seeing images of the men drowning, whose last gasps he believed he could still hear in the Atlantic night. He always believed deep down he should have become a priest or a monk. He loved the peace of mind he experienced from the words of God. Without him, he was lost. He looked within, trying to find the words to comfort himself against all the violence he had seen.

– Help me to understand the real meaning of all of this, dear Lord.

As an idea came to mind, he slowly released the firm grip he had on the neck of his instrument. A few hours ago, lives had been sacrificed; whether or not they had been devils or animals, a sacrifice needed to be made as a gesture of reparation, for what had been taken away and could never be replaced.

– My Lord, who are the savages?

For a moment, he imagined climbing onto the edge of the vessel and, after a short prayer, letting himself fall into the dark waters. But the Lord would never pardon the infamy of a soul that would have decided its own fate. The page looked around him. He felt helpless, but then remembered he had his guitar, the sole reason for his presence on board. He would tell his shipmates that he threw it overboard to make amends for what had happened. And if they didn't understand, at least he would have the satisfaction of having taken action. He examined one last time the instrument he had received from his father. Nothing was dearer to him than his guitar. He offered it up on behalf of his fellow men, men of all countries, who, because of harquebus shots, had been denied their humanity. The instrument took flight into the damp night air before falling into the water. The page imagined his guitar taking on water from the sound hole, becoming heavier and heavier as it spiraled downward onto the seabed.

But he was mistaken. The guitar his father had gifted him dated back to the days of the page's grandfather's time, when people believed things that were well made were never destroyed. The guitar had no intention of dying. In its fall, the guitar had landed on its back and the water's current aided it in getting to shore, resisting the waves by the strength of its varnish. And it all paid off because in due course it shored up, whipped but all in one piece, filled with sand, salt, and algae.

History never did say what next became of the guitar. Was it discovered by fishermen, having been caught within their nets? Did it create a big surprise the next day when it appeared at the ceremony honoring the lives of those who had died at sea, killed at the hands of foreigners? Was it taken back to the village and placed in the home of the miracle-maker so that he could decide whether it should be safeguarded or, on the contrary, reduced to nothing by throwing it into the fire? I would like to imagine that the next day while a child was playing on the beach, his heel brushed against the guitar and he was overjoyed when he discovered a ruff inside. He removed the sand and the algae, cleaned it up, repaired it, and then hid it, as one would an injured person who remained mute after having traversed years of adversity . . . And from one hiding place to another, from one child to another, from one bequest to another, and from the fifteenth century to the twentieth century, the legendary instrument found its way to become the well-guarded secret of my father's family, to whom he would entrust it at the time of his departure from his native Cameroon. Not as far back as 1472 this time, but rather in 1950 . . .

−2−

Another way to go about this might be to tell the story of all that was never said: I would re-create the story of a man and his family. I would pronounce the words I imagine they would have used and place my own words within the interstices to try to understand why life brings us from one continent to another and never takes us back, how a painful exile can be transformed into a benediction by seizing on the opportunities that come your way as new paths on which you confidently walk toward what is possible and grow.

On that day in the middle of July 1929, heavy rains fell on the village of Akwa, a small fishermen's village between the Atlantic Ocean and the equatorial forest. The whole village was used to the din of the water lapping against the calabashes, the cisterns, and streaming down from the roofs. The rainy season lasted for about six months, including two months of warnings and two months of farewell tours. July was smack in the middle of it. You woke up with the rain, and you went to bed with the rain. The long days of solitude went on for one hundred days, without ever stopping. So no one paid particular attention to the earsplitting screams emanating from the pastor's house on that Monday morning. His wife was bringing their eleventh child into the world. To help her courageously get through the delivery, a midwife with knitted brows stood by her side.

– Stop screaming, she snarled. Contractions are normal when you are about to give birth. You're not going to keep on screaming because of that, are you, especially not with the eleventh child?

The midwife took hold of the newborn at the very moment he glided into life and verified he had ten fingers and ten toes before administering a few necessary taps on his buttocks that would make him cry at the top of his lungs, thus making it clear that they were working.

– I know you can't believe you're actually here. You're asking yourself, where am I? But you need to breathe, baby. Find your rhythm.

The only mission the little one had was to survive in that moment, which meant to escape the fate of very young children who fell into death's web and were carried away by Mami Wata into the depths of the ocean. He had just come into the world near the Wouri estuary, and he was going to have to swim with all his might to shore, to escape the currents, recover his breath at the edge of the river, and stand there contemplating the world and its movements until the day would come for him to take his place. The pastor's wife was called Magdalena, and her baby's crying was drowning out the intensity of her belabored breathing. She barely had the strength to say a little prayer to ask God to save his life. She had already lost several young children and didn't want to have to go through that again. She would never know the outcome for her newborn. She drew her last breath and thus never had the chance to place her hand on her little boy's head. Was she the person who named him Francis? Had it been agreed that he would be called Franziskus or Frantz? As a result of the more recent German occupation, Prussian first names were flourishing in the country. The little boy had a first name that began with F, like his father, Fritz. Francis would survive the unjust law that condemned so many children to an early death.

He began to live, and breathe, and move his fingers and toes as his mother passed on. There he was, motherless, at an age where his memories were nothing but a shapeless mass in a humid zone, forgotten by the soul. So alone, and so soon. And so it was his father, a pastor in Cameroon, who would come to leave a mark on his childhood memories. A pastor for whom it was a point of honor to tend to his church flock long before his own children. Destitution was nevertheless also present within his own family. Francis would come to know it all too well. His whole life, he would recall how hungry he used to be as a child. But for Pastor Fritz, there was no greater or more important service than that which was due to God. Francis would go on to assimilate, at great cost to himself, that devotion to the Almighty—the selflessness and the self-sacrifice. It was better to learn to manage on your own when you were a child growing up in Pastor Fritz's home. It was better to count on aunts, cousins, sisters, and the ladies at the market, who sometimes showed great kindness by setting aside a little something for the little one who came by . . . After all, children during those days, weren't they all more or less raising themselves?

The girls learned the everyday tasks from their mothers, aunts, and cousins. Cooking took hours: you had to go and buy the vegetables, ready to be cooked, then sort through them, trim, shell, peel, and cut. You had to catch the chicken cackling out in the courtyard, slice its neck, drain and clean it out, and rid it of its remaining fuzz by holding its skin to the flame. Then you had to cut it into pieces and prepare a marinade in which it would sit for a while. Before all that, you had to be up at the crack of dawn, while the house was still sleeping, and go and fetch the precious water you would carry on top of your head, with your hands fully extended to keep it in place, your stomach tucked and your back straight . . . When you were not cooking, you were cleaning. And when you were not cleaning, you were braiding your little sister's hair or getting your own hair braided by one of the older girls, exercising great patience as you simultaneously shelled the grains that would be used to prepare the next meal. Being a girl was not a life; it was a maelstrom of chores and obligations. The boys, they learned about the world in the streets, on vacant lots, in the forests, and on the banks of the Wouri River, where they would collect stones that they would skillfully ricochet off the water's surface. The housekeepers who would come to do family laundry by the river would raise their heads and send off these annoying boys with a few well-chosen words.

– What are you doing here splashing us? Shouldn't you be over there attending the White man's school?

Because the obligation to learn to read and write was widespread, like hot pepper in a cooking sauce, children, especially the boys, were required to go and sit from first thing in the morning till the end of day to learn all the beautiful things Europeans had written in books. The pastor had already adopted the Christian faith and the Protestant church service. More and more families were converting to the practice of attending school. In their eyes, the teachings would complete what the children had already been learning: the heroic exploits of the ancestors narrated to music and dance; the legends and proverbs that sharpened the mind; the skills for hunting, navigating, and fishing; the art of planting and cultivating herbs that heal and those that can harm; the art of bantering and being able to one day seduce; the art of giving birth to a family; and all the secret know-how that men transmit to men and women to women. Francis preferred to skip classes and hang out with fellow truants rather than attend elementary school. They enjoyed doing anything but learning to read and count. Oh happy days! In school, the teacher was as severe as a prison warden. Outdoors the wind caressed their cheeks, carried their voices, and stirred the trees' foliage. When one of the housekeepers took the little rascals to task, they would just take off and hide elsewhere by the estuary. They hid in mangroves at the edge of the lagoon and in abandoned boats on the beach. And there they would hold council.

> – Me, when I grow up . . . when I grow up, I'm going to come back to the school and give the teacher the same thrashing he gave me the other day. When I grow up, I'll have polished, very shiny white shoes. When I grow up, I'll have a huge watch like this and a car, big like that. I won't need to drive it myself because I'll have a chauffeur, wearing a hat and gloves. When I grow up, I'm going to go see if the White man's country looks just like what's written in the books.

They knew nothing about the world beyond the games they played, the meals they hoped to eat, and the estuary that connected to the ocean. They played at making flutes from the leafstalks of the papaya tree and ran around naked, even during the downpours that bathed them as they went by. They played at turning their faces to the sky and leaning back far enough so that with their mouths wide open the rain could generously slide all the way into the depth of their throats and quench their thirst for life. That was all they knew. From the other side of the ocean, they learned about the Gauls, all the French departments and administrative centers, Victor Hugo and the flight made by a certain Saint-Exupéry, who went on so much about it that he even wrote a book about it. Before the Gauls, Hugo, and that other shameless one, they knew nothing more about the sea beyond the turbulent rip current of the Atlantic Ocean. Their fellow countrymen would head out to the ocean aboard pirogues from which they would cast their nets to catch fish and shrimp. And shrimp were never in short supply. There was always enough to relive that miraculous catch. The Portuguese explorers, who had been rerouted on their way to the Indies, had been struck by the incredible concentration of shrimp in that part of the world, so much so that they had named these very first shores they had come upon Cameroon—*Rio dos Camarões*—the River of Shrimp.

When Francis came into the world in July 1929, Fernando Pó's expedition was already four centuries behind him, the Cameroonian pages from the

Bismarck court had long been dead, and the English and the French had become the "protectors" of the country. Francis would prick up his ears and listen to the songs from the rainfall. In the same way he grew up listening to Bach and Handel because he had been ordered to immerse himself in this celestial music by attending his father's Baptist choir rehearsals. He was, on the other hand, forbidden to listen to the man living in the neighborhood who could be heard, at night, playing all sorts of bizarre instruments. All sorts of things were said about that man: that he knew about plants and herbs, as well as how to create magical melodies by plucking the keys from a little instrument in the shape of a box, whose sounds apparently could bring those on their deathbeds back to life. One note created the wind; another, the sky; a third, the moon; and the following, the sun. If you plucked several keys of the sanza at the same time, drops of rain would begin to fall, and if you plucked those two over there, those two keys that made a strange shrill sound, then the man and the woman were born, followed by all their children. It was far too strange to actually be true. There must have been some kind of magical stuff mixed in there.

Fritz forbade his children to go near the musician's house.

– I better not catch a glimpse of you near the medicine man's home, you hear me? His music is not good for the mind. You can hear the evil coming from it.

You had to take a huge detour to circumvent his place and establish a distance between the sounds coming out of that home and your own ears. Francis never did get far enough away from those sounds. Despite all efforts, notes from the sanza would escape the medicine man's fingers and, against all odds, enchant Francis. Yes, he could confirm that there was magic in that music because he was totally under its spell. But he was mindful to never say a word and carefully tucked away that sweet elixir in the recesses of his mind. In the first place, he was going to have to grow up, live, and learn to think for himself as best as he could.

He watched and listened.

All the grown-ups would say that the country had truly changed since the Europeans announced they were the rulers.

– Why did these people come and use force to settle here all while claiming that we were the savages and that they'd come to help us change?
– Since they have been living in our country, they keep going back and forth, dressed in their beige cotton shirts, and their domed hard hats, and in trousers far too short for grown-up men. You can see the color of their body

hairs. You can see their calves so white they make you think of *bakala ba wuba*, chicken legs. When you dare to look them in the eye, you realize their eyes are as pale as the sky.

Francis observed their demeanor. He imagined himself, in turn, creating a protectorate somewhere in the world, in some rich, fertile, foreign land. Being an adult, and better yet a master, allowed you to do quite a lot of things: wear a beige uniform, don a watch, have shoes on your feet, and give orders. *Do this! Do that! I said: "Right away!"*

When I grow up, Francis told himself, *me too, I'm going to be White, I'm going to give people orders, and they'll obey me while I sit upon my veranda* (he loved the word "veranda") *and drink fresh lemonade, beer, or French wine. When I grow up, that's what I'll do, too, for a job: be White.*

In the meantime, he was on the opposite side of the fence, invisible. He was only a child to whom adults gave orders and the occasional flogging. Francis liked neither his schoolteacher nor his uncle Eyango nor his older cousins, Léopold, Simon, and Amédée. His teacher was too quick to punish, applying the ruler to your hands or humiliating you with the dunce cap. His uncle and adult cousins had this specialty they called the *mbomboto,* a kind of walloping with a powerful punch to the top of the head, as though you were being banged into a door. In the 1930s and 1940s, it seemed liked adults had come together and agreed to treat children like that: give them a good thrashing so that they learn the right way to behave, the right attitude to adopt.

So Francis decided to leave those heartless adults behind and go live with his favorite aunt, Maa Médi, who was always lovingly tickling and cuddling him and bringing a special little something for him to eat when she came to visit the family. Maa Médi lived a few miles away in another village to which Francis had never been. But it was decided: he was leaving. Of course, he had no luggage, no personal items, no shoes, only an *ebuba* tunic and his short pants. He spent most of the day walking, with a determined stride, to get to his aunt's home. No one was looking for him. No one knew he had even left home. No one had the time to realize he had disappeared. He was a child, heading toward the heart and maternal arms he had chosen. Later on, he would similarly choose to walk toward his destiny. He finally reached Maa Médi's home, situated in another fishing village on the coastline that would, over time, expand to become a part of the city of Douala. Meanwhile, Pastor Fritz was carefully tending to his flock . . . In the courtyard to his home, family members, men, women, and children came and went in no particular order. His wife was no longer around to organize the visits.

Within a few days, however, some people began to express concern.

– Have you seen little Francis? Little Francis has disappeared. *Nu muna é ndé o wèni?* Where could the child have gone? Was he taken away by the *bebey*, the tides?

Because that's what the family name for this little *Bantu*, this little man, means in Douala.

– Could it be possible that the water took the child?

Pastor Fritz prayed to all the gods he knew for his son.

– Oh, Great Almighty Ones, whether you are from Germany, France, England, or Portugal, because in the past Portuguese explorers did make it all the way here, I beseech you, please return my baby boy to me.

He prayed for quite some time before news got to Maa Médi's village:

– The little one is safe and sound. He's living with Auntie Médi.

Fritz got down on his knees and gave thanks to God while Marcel, the older brother, went to fetch the boy from his aunt. Francis had been feeling quite at home, and so leaving felt like he was being yanked away. He returned home, held in the firm albeit tender grip of his big brother.

His brother was determined to not let Francis out of his sight. They were fifteen years apart. He was going to take charge of him like a father. To begin with, Francis was going to be returning to school. Skipping school was over.

– You must learn everything they teach, you hear me? Show that you can be diligent. Come first in your class. You have to know everything they know and go even further because this is how you're going to become somebody later on.

But what did it mean, "to become somebody"? When you are six, seven, ten years old, the verb *become* takes on the monumental dimension of a philosophical question. So life consists in *becoming*? Francis preferred to put that kind of question out of his mind. He looked up at his big brother, took a deep breath, and agreed. He decided there and then he would always follow in his footsteps, just as he had placed his hand in his following his little runaway escapade. Marcel became his role model. At school, his big brother had left a beaming bright trail behind him. He had never given his schoolteachers, otherwise quick to punish, reason to use the black whip: the boy left them all speechless with admiration, stunned by his exceptional mind, his ability to grasp concepts as others might juggle six balls all at once with great dexterity. By going to the school his brother had attended, Francis encountered all the teachers who were still in awe of his brother's intelligence.

– Oh, you're Marcel's brother?

And perhaps they were thinking "the unbelievable Marcel" or "that outstanding boy." Pastor Fritz and his wife had girls among their eleven children, but the boys, especially because of their "understanding of the world of the White man," were going to establish the family's reputation.

– Pastor Fritz's sons, they are so intelligent! people would say.
– They say the pastor's sons are very clever.
– Extraordinary abilities, those kids!
– Who? But of course, Pastor Fritz's sons!

The news traveled from one mouth to another, from one set of ears to eventually a whole household, from the household to the church, and, finally, spread to all the houses in the courtyard. When Marcel would eventually leave to study medicine in Europe, swarms of total strangers would gather round to bid him farewell. As though his incredible mind was somehow indebted to them for his success. As though something about who he was allowed them to recover a sense of pride that had been stripped away by the colonial administration. Because you have to remember, or at least try to imagine, what it was like growing up in those times. The dice had been thrown by a handful of European leaders gathered around a table filled with a bunch of maps in Berlin in 1884 who had decreed:

– Let's divide up this territory amongst ourselves! According to the explorers, they are in need of everything over there: a real God, real schools, real hospitals, and even classical music. Indeed we're not suggesting that they're waiting for us to get on with their lives, but who would be stupid enough to reject the gift of such advances? We will bring real happiness so it is only fair that we require their resources in return. It is said that their forests are full of amazing animals and rare plants, and their subsoil is brimming with minerals and precious stones. We will make them build roads and railroad tracks to transport these to our ships. In so doing, we will also provide them with work. Let's go gentlemen, let's take our rulers and pencils to delineate the borders of these countries and see who gets what amongst us . . .

This was the period during which empires were consolidating according to their fleets, military force, and distant possessions. No one questioned what would become of the minds, ways of life, cultures, and imagination as a result of the collision foisted upon these people by the imperious European civilization. Marcel, like Francis, was born after the famous Berlin conference. The world their parents had known when they were growing up was now starting to regain its footing from the effects of all that had been imposed upon them. It was up to the young people now to learn how to live in this new era, without betraying their ancestors . . .

The eldest in the family had distinguished himself remarkably at school. Some even considered him exceptionally gifted. One teacher made a plea on his behalf for him to receive a grant because at that time in Cameroon it was impossible to pursue further studies beyond a basic education certificate. Marcel received the grant and would need to leave for France—*mbènguè*, Europe, in Douala language—to take advantage of this stepping-stone that had been unimaginable in the past. While new avenues would open up for him, he would have to leave behind everything he had learned. Before letting go of Francis's hand, Marcel gave his brother instructions, always the same ones:

– You must work hard in school, you understand me, little brother? Do the best you can. You must be the best. You promise me? You must know everything they ask you and go even further. You promise to work as much as you have to, you promise me?

Francis wiped his tears. His heart was heavy. He was just starting to feel really loved.

– *Émbè muléma!* Harden your heart, his brother insisted, be courageous.

Marcel also made a gesture before leaving: he entrusted his little brother with a guitar. Oh yes, amid the immense destitution within the family, this object existed, and the beloved big brother passed it on to his younger brother, as a treasure. Where had it come from? For some months, Marcel had been making some money, working as a nurse's assistant at the health clinic. He collected the bandages and helped to position patients in one way or another. He helped mothers, who stood in line at the entrance to the clinic, to reposition their children on their backs once they had completed their visit. It seemed he might have a real ability for medical procedures. Perhaps he took on more important tasks. All the same, Marcel didn't earn a lot, but what he did make allowed him to improve his family's life. Pastor Fritz made sure there was food on the table for every meal, and perhaps sometimes got secondhand clothing when clothes were worn out, but he certainly hadn't amassed the kind of money to afford a musical instrument.

Yet, there Marcel was in possession of one just as he possessed his body parts and his intelligence. The instrument had always been there, hidden in a corner of the house where their father never went. Although their father suspected an instrument of the devil might be under his roof, he let it be. So long as no one played it in front of him! Because Pastor Fritz had espoused the rigid Protestant morality that did not allow for music but within the walls of the church, and only hymns, "classical" music, were worthy of the Almighty. On the rare occasion that his father was not home, Marcel would pick up the guitar and take it outside to take a closer look at its details in the sunlight of the courtyard. He would remove the old fabric it was wrapped in and run his fingers over the grooves of the varnished wood and awkwardly try to strum a few chords. The rest of the time, the guitar stayed hidden, enveloped in the shadow of its own mystery. As he was about to leave the country, the future doctor promoted his young brother to the role of guardian to watch over the guitar: to keep an eye on each of the six strings and nurse the cracks and swellings that might appear due to humidity.

> – I don't know how we came into possession of this instrument, Marcel said. What I do know is that it comes from afar. Safeguard it preciously; it is our only treasure. If every so often you get a little twinge in your heart because we're not together and you miss me, make sure our father is not in the house, then take it out from its fabric case. If you strum a chord, I will feel it. This way, the neck and the chords of our guitar will bind us, the music will allow us to reach each other even if we are far away, you understand?

Francis listened and tried in vain to understand the strange phenomenon his brother was talking to him about. Until the day that . . .
But that part of the story will come much later.

Francis didn't like going to school, but he had given his brother his word. He couldn't disappoint his brother, or his father, or, as a matter of fact, all those who were ready, because of jealousy, to bring down the reputation of intelligence that hung like a halo over the men of the house. He imagined that even from a distance his big brother was keeping an eye on him. So he decided to buckle down and do the work. He learned arithmetic and algebra. He appreciated the accuracy of numbers. Their metronomic rigor provided him with certainties amid all the questions he had about life. Arithmetic allowed him to enter into a comforting world in which doubt was absent. He also learned to read, and it was like a dazzling light greeting a walker coming into a clearing in the woods. God knows it was dense. You absolutely needed a machete to clear a path for yourself. But once you had your instrument in hand, you could keep on walking ahead and discover the marvels of equatorial flora. Francis immersed himself in words, bathed in verbs, played like a dolphin with language, emerging and gloating, drinking in everything his eyes fell upon. He filled up with ideas and worlds, imagining as far as the center of the earth and well beyond the sky. Balzac, Chateaubriand, Jules Verne, Dumas, Maupassant, and many of their peers, including Antoine de Saint-Exupéry, became his best friends. Life was a dream.

Misfortune interrupted those literary dreams on the day he received a letter from France announcing horrible news: his big brother Marcel had been conscripted as a nurse in the war that had exploded in *mbènguè*, in Europe. Because some grave scenes were being played out on the European stage, Germans sought to occupy France. Such a thing could not be allowed to happen. The brothers and allies of France, the members of the empire, were called on to help. Francis watched men leaving, designated as *volunteers*, to go and help the mother country. Families were shaken up. In church, prayers intensified. It was like an electric current going from one body to the next. Francis reminded himself, *Émbè muléma!* Be courageous! He was but ten years old, and his whole being was riddled with fear at the idea that he could lose the one person who was most dear to him; to ward off the fear, he armed himself with knowledge. *If I succeed at school, Marcel will come back. God will see that I've been good. If I am first in my class, he will not die in the war. They will let him come home, and we will be together again.* Gone were the days of skipping school and the joyful vagabonding along the river's edge. Gone were the days of making flutes from papaya stalks that had to be shaped quickly to create sounds before they came undone—the flutes barely lasted a day before they withered and less so during the dry season! To quiet his anxiety, Francis studied diligently every night, his open notebook illuminated by the street lamp in the neighborhood. Sometimes, in class, he would turn his head toward the window nearby. His gaze would follow the flight of a seagull lost in the city. Had the fishermen had a good catch? Would there be lots of fish? Shrimp? And those men, who had gone even farther away, would they return safe and sound? He would forget where he was for a while.

On Sundays, he would always listen to the cantatas his father made his devoted flock sing. He also heard the low-key melodies the medicine man—that lost soul—made with his sanza, he who had not merely followed the religion of the White man, who ignored—poor fool—what he risked forever and ever. Despite his father's orders, Francis couldn't help being moved by all those sounds, sacred as much as pagan. How could you ward off the melody of a song that penetrated your whole body and got into your veins rather than the reasonable pathway of the brain? One day, a parishioner from his father's church gave him an instructional manual on how to read music. A book for him to keep, all for himself! So enthusiastic about having a gift of this kind—one of the rarest he had ever received—he began to teach himself to sight-read music and relished in doing so. He discovered for the first time the mystery and love of the musical notes and the pleasures of the organ. He practiced writing the eighth note, the whole note, quarter notes, and half notes on scores he would chart out in the sand at the beach. In his eleventh year, he would experience his first moment of glory.

The school principal announced that General de Gaulle was coming to Cameroon, to Douala. The purpose of the visit was to thank our leaders for supporting Free France, and also to ask them to send additional men to help in the war effort. He would also be visiting a school, and our school had been chosen. And I would lead the choir! I had to get all the kids in the class to sing before the general. Me. They chose me! I had to choose from among the songs we had learned the one I wanted to have the whole school sing. We would have a rehearsal session. I got up on a chair to have a full view of the whole choir. I was afraid to fall. I pulled from my pocket the well-trimmed rattan baton I had prepared and I was lucky: like a miracle, the very fact of holding it helped me. I felt I was the conductor of an orchestra. I opened my arms and saw all the pupils looking at me. I forgot all about the principal and teachers standing there. Later on, when I grow up, I want to conduct orchestras. I will make choruses sing, and everyone will applaud . . .

The general did come. I can't recall what happened. It felt like a dream. I believe all the same that my baton helped. I recall that afterward, right afterward, everyone was speechless: the general came up to me. He was so tall I had to really strain my neck to see the top of his kepi when he was standing next to me, and I was already standing on a chair. The giant general shook my hand. He shook my hand. He leaned over and said:

– Congratulations little man.

But he didn't rub his hand over my head as if we had hunted porcupines to-
gether. No, he gave me a good ole fashioned handshake! The same great general
of all the French people, he shook my hand. I decided to never wash my hand
again. I was going to keep that strength General de Gaulle had imparted to me.
I would never ever wash my hand again. At least not the next day. And not the
day after that. And perhaps, not the following day, either. Too bad. I would
manage. One day, with the strength he had given me, I would be the conductor
of a full orchestra that would travel all over the world.

Years went by. Young minds became imbued with the words and colors of a
world far away. Brains organized themselves into cupboards with shelves and
drawers where all the new material was stored. Within hidden shelves were
kept proverbs, legends, tales, recipes, and the skills that boys and girls should
know how to do, and had been learning. The Douala language was nimbly
hidden in those drawers when a teacher approached a group of kids in the
playground. Whoever dared to try to speak *patois* in the playground was
immediately called out: the child was singled out and he or she would have to
wear the dunce cap.

– Here in the French school, we speak French! No one has the right to speak
anything else.

The brain developed, body parts lengthened, and the heart beat faster. As
the months went by, Francis gradually left his childhood behind. He began
to think about the future. Like his brother Marcel, his goal was to obtain the
basic education certificate and go further. Like his big brother, he hoped to do
really well and shine so that he could also get a grant that would allow him to
go see *mbènguè*, the White man's country. He wanted to discover the country
where men strut around in beige cotton suits. He wanted to see and touch the
famous snow he'd read about in books, but more than anything in the world,
he wanted to finally reconnect with his brother when the war was over. He
wanted to be with him, place his hand in his, once again, feel protected by
him, and advance, fearless, on the path of life. He hadn't had enough time
with him to feel that he was loved . . .

Francis was sixteen when the liberation of Paris occurred. His beloved
brother's return was announced, and hope impatiently compressed his heart
and held it up like the pistil of the clover tree. When Marcel finally arrived
with a medal pinned to his chest—for his military exploits in the ranks of the

Free French Forces, he had received the French Legion of Honor—Francis swooned with enthusiasm. His big brother would unfortunately not stay home for very long: his medal earned him another grant for further studies that he planned to resume. His dream was to become a doctor. Francis's heart dropped and was shy of failing him when he heard the news.

> – *Émbè nyolo! Émbè muléma!* his big brother repeated, again, after only a few weeks back home, harden your heart, be courageous. I'm leaving again but I'm waiting for you, right? Work hard and you'll get a grant too. We'll see each other in *mbènguè*.

It would take five years of patience and hard work, without ever seeing his brother, before Francis would finally have his turn and be given the famous grant to study overseas. The day before his departure in early September 1950, the young man went into a boutique to purchase a watch, which he considered indispensable to his new status in life. But the store owner snapped at him. He had entered the boutique without first wiping his shoes on the doormat.

> – Will you kindly do me the pleasure of leaving right away? You are lucky I don't make you clean up all this mess before I let you go!

Francis left the shop, humiliated.

> – Can you imagine, he would tell us many years later, I had the money? I wanted to buy a watch and give him some business. And in my own city, in my own country. Without people like me this man would be out of business. I was thrown out like a dirty rascal because I had not wiped my feet on his doormat!

Once he arrived in La Rochelle, he would spend half of his grant money on a watch. Too bad if he would have to skip the evening meal for several weeks while he waited for the next check to come in. His bracelet watch adorned his wrist as Francis walked haughtily on the port at La Rochelle, dressed in a pair of beige trousers and a white shirt with sleeves rolled up. Years later, after my brothers, sisters, and I were born, he would buy himself an even more beautiful watch: an Omega. Payback? His childhood humiliations were, however, meant to be behind him.

Francis prepared to take the plane and meet up with his big brother. He was elated. He was going to board an airplane for the very first time, a remarkable machine that truly impressed him. While he was preparing his belongings, he hesitated to take the guitar Marcel had asked him to keep. His big sister criticized it as a harebrained idea: why would you want to bog yourself down with it when there is so much to discover and so much to deal with! In the end, he left the guitar with her. But Francis had barely taken off before he began to regret not having taken the time to stress the importance of the instrument to her. The words only came to him once the airplane was flying over the forest:

– I'm begging you, please take really good care of it, he uttered, as if his sister were sitting right next to him. This guitar is all we have. I'll be coming back for it.

In his final moments before leaving, Francis tried to hide his anxiety, which had him in a grip. He smiled to put on a good face. He held on to the imminent joy of seeing his big brother again.

Unfortunately his excitement would be short-lived: the time spent with Marcel would come down to a mere few hours before he would have to leave him again. The newly certified medical doctor aspired to practice back home among his own people as soon as possible. When Francis met up with him, he was already packing up. Embarrassed by how little time they had together, Marcel offered his little brother a copy of his thesis on sleeping sickness: *"Le vainqueur de la maladie du sommeil, le Doctor Eugène Jamot (1879–1937),"* which had allowed him to graduate from the Faculty of Medicine in Paris with honors. Summa cum laude—for a national from a French Overseas Territory, that was a real triumph! At least that's what members of the jury thought, proud of themselves.

– Here, this is for you, Marcel said, to show you how far we owe it to ourselves to go, we who have had the opportunity to study. As for my departure, don't be angry with me, little brother. There's so much that needs to be done back home. We'll meet up again later on. Now you get on with your studies and, when you're finished, you come back home too. And then, we'll stop following each other around from one continent to another. We will be back together forever. Until then, don't be afraid and everything will go well for you.

They hadn't seen each other for six years. Francis's heart sunk. Was it a curse? Was he destined to be alone, always alone, no matter where he went?

Among the people present at the airport in Douala on the day of his departure, was the woman he would marry. My mother, Madé. Neither he nor she knew that the gods had already planned to weave the yarns of their destinies. They were even farther away from the idea that one day I would be here too, re-creating their story many, many, years later ... To be honest, it wasn't my father that Madé came to greet but rather another family member. She had dressed up for the occasion, as was customary in those days. Airport style, as people would say. It was purely by chance that she would make eye contact with Francis. She recognized the pastor's son. Was he also going aboard the huge airplane bound for Europe? Wasn't he a bit young to be making that kind of journey? Wasn't he afraid? Wasn't his family concerned about letting him go like that, so far away? He made eye contact with her as well. Recognizing the young lady gave him momentary relief from the anxiety that had been compressing his chest like an invisible corset. He recalled the few times he had bumped into her during the last few months. His heart would get carried away in her presence, and he couldn't understand why. Seeing her gave him mixed feelings of joy and regret. He might have talked to her. He should have. As for her, she hid her feelings, but a thousand thoughts coursed through her mind like shooting stars.

We lived in the same neighborhood, but I went to a girls' school and he to a boys' school. Like all the girls my age, I had so many things to do that it was very unlikely for me to meet him. The boys played outside, took off on expeditions, made traps for little animals, climbed up mango trees, would go and sneakily spy on the local madman, the one they claimed had an evil spirit, who fabricated unholy musical instruments and whose songs undoubtedly conveyed curses. We were never to let his music reach our ears! As for us girls, we went to fetch the water from the well, crushed and ground the manioc, and would go through the laborious process of preparing and cooking each meal. We were also bathing and watching over the younger girls from the different families, and from time to time when there was a little spare time we would grab a book to do a little bit of studying. So in the end, I only really came across him on Sundays at church.

The pastor was known for his poverty, a positive sign in the eyes of everyone, proof of his integrity. His children, however, they were renowned for their intelligence, which was unanimously considered to be exceptional. The boys and the girls alike. Eleven of them in all. That was without counting those who had died at a very young age. The pastor's eleven children were all very beautiful, but him ... Him! For me he was even more beautiful than the others. I had noticed his long fingers and his smile, which was so sincere. Sometimes, at church, we would stare at each other. He would turn around. His eyes would stop when they got to me, fixated for a while, then he would resume his position. I would suddenly become so hot I would feel embarrassed. I was afraid everyone would notice. I would look down as soon as I could.

One day, I was busy crushing pepper on the stone slab. I was holding the smooth roller and rotating it in a rhythmic motion when I heard a joyful buzz coming from the main street. My mother gave me a nod of approval to go see what was happening. I ran out. Pastor Fritz's son was wearing short pants and an ebuba, a matching tunic. He was walking barefoot. Several of his classmates who were escorting him were praising and applauding him, singing about him, sketching out dance steps around him and whistling . . . They were say-ing that the pastor's youngest son had swept up all the school prizes and that there weren't enough friends to help him carry all the books back home. They also said that in addition to being an excellent pupil, he was a good classmate, which was why everybody was celebrating him. I kept looking at him. I had often seen him studying at night, a notebook on his lap, lit by the streetlamp. I kept looking at him and my heart began to beat really fast.

The plane took off and disappeared into the horizon. Madé's heart sunk. Perhaps she was saying to herself on her walk back home: Pastor Fritz's son is gone . . . Pastor Fritz's son is gone . . . Pastor Fritz's son is gone.

Like a litany.

He was the last one in his family, whereas in my family, I was the first child, the oldest of three girls. My father was a land surveyor. I never fully understood what kind of reality that word really covered. All I knew was that it was enough to say it to command respect. People would say, "Mr. Géomètre," in the middle of a sentence. The word gained even more attention because it was pronounced in French: impossible to find its equivalent in our language. All my friends knew to take the word seriously, at least as much as if my father had been a schoolteacher or a nurse. His name worked for the White people in gob'na, the French administration. Every morning he went to work perched on his bicycle. On his path, elderly folk would nod in admiration.

– This man succeeds in providing a regular income for his family. And he gets around thanks to the only steel machine in the neighborhood. Without falling! He shares in the janéa, the authority, alongside the White men. His daughters wear sandals. In his home, you don't only eat the local food; you get to eat bread and butter.

There were no boys in the family, but thanks to his work, thanks to his bicycle and his long trousers, thanks to his white buttoned-down shirts that looked nothing like the neighbors' ordinary tunics, thanks to his polished shoes, which I took care of each day, we were respected, envied even. No one knew how he had managed to get such a prestigious position among White people. And no one knew that he couldn't wait to get home and take off his shoes and those long trousers and slip into a simple pagne at the end of the day. He would sit for several minutes in the penumbra of his bedroom while I massaged his sore feet. My mother would prepare a basin of lukewarm water into which he would plunge his feet and express a great sigh of relief. In silence, I took my time to massage his feet, waiting each time confusedly for a gentle touch, which never came. In the evenings, he would slip back into trousers to receive supposed family members, coming sometimes from considerable distances to discuss problems of the greatest importance. According to a mysterious form of arbitration, he would offer a bank note, some coins, a meal, or a place to sleep. Similarly, during the rainy season when buckets of rain would be coming down, causing people to stop and seek shelter beneath verandas, ours was always crowded. Many hoped to get a glimpse at what the interior of Mr. Géomètre's home looked like. We would offer everyone a sugar cane cube or some coconut milk, but our mother maintained both doors and Persian blinds locked to keep the mystery intact.

– Now that's how respect is earned, isn't it? she would say.

I was the oldest daughter. His prestige bounced off on to me and kept the boys at a good distance. The very idea of pointedly smiling at the-daughter-of-Mr.-Géomètre, of speaking to her in public—approaching her!—required courage. My sisters and I had to be irreproachable, heads held high, just like our father. At least for a long time we thought he was irreproachable, until the day a young lady came to our door, carrying a baby in her arms. She sat down on the ground by the veranda and declared that she was prepared to wait for the bicycle man to come home. To my mother's horror, our father set up the young lady under our roof and all of a sudden introduced her as our stepmother. I came to realize that the bicycle was not only being used every day in the service of the French administration. For the next four years, five boys, one after the other, restored Mr. Géomètre's manhood while my mother, my sisters, and I, we retreated into humiliating silence. I was finally able to distance myself from this war on position in the family some years later when I received the only grant that would ever be awarded to my family to study, despite the fact that I was a girl and thanks to being the eldest.

–3–

That was how the pastor's youngest son and the land surveyor's oldest daughter both wound up in France—of course, not yet together. That would've been too easy. He was studying in La Rochelle. She was in Coulommiers during a terribly cold autumn. She, like he, had also gone through the parting ceremony, airport style, with at least fifty people in attendance. Elderly aunts, practically disabled, adorned in ceremonial dress had even made the effort. And so many of the faces were unrecognizable to Madé. On the jet bridge, she had hesitated to turn around. She hadn't wanted them to see her crying. The wind had breezed through her lightweight clothing. She would leave behind friends she met every morning before dawn at the standpipe. Their sleepy conservations were often fragmented because of the physical demand, leaning over the pump, their necks bent beneath the weight of the enormous bucket of water that was to serve the entire family. She left to her friends, sisters, and close friend, already promised to marriage, the numerous tasks she used to carry out before heading to school. She left her mother and her exhausted smile. She left behind the fragrance of *foufou*, made from manioc; the *ndolè* meat-fish dish; the taste of young green avocados wrapped in skin that was almost black; and the little dried shrimp, *dibanga*, used to enhance sauces. She left behind *sao*, with its purplish skin and smooth aftertaste, cooked on a bed of hot ashes, and mangoes, eaten with your whole mouth, whose fibrous strings got stuck in between the teeth. She left everything behind. To stop herself from crying, she tried to *panè muléma*, "suspend" her heart, as her mother had advised her to do. *Attach it!* her friends repeated to her, jealous of her good fortune. She was leaving to go study and would have to make her family proud. Succeed above all else and in every way possible.

I arrived in Coulommiers in the evening, on a scathingly cold autumn night. I remember the smells, and how foreign they all were to me. The kerosene that was close to the airplane. The talc powder the flight attendant was wearing, who leaned over to me in her navy-blue cap to kiss me on my forehead, kindly wishing me good luck. My arrival in this foreign city gave me quite a shock, so much so that I was shivering upon entering the boarding school, and the staff was concerned for me. I had come because I had succeeded at all the exams that allowed us to have scholarships. And as a result, I was among a handful of students lucky enough to get to study in France. Yet I had never seen so many White people before. My jaw tensed up as I tried to hold back the tears, but the first smile that came my way caused them to come pouring down, and their erratic flow didn't stop until the wee hours of that night, amid the backdrop of regular breathing coming from my roommates sleeping in the dormitory.

One account of this new life would be about how cold the water was, the wake-up calls at the crack of dawn, the long hours of studying in the winter, the rare outings chaperoned by the Sisters, and the wild laughter, despite everything, because you only get to be a young girl once in your life.

All too aware of my family's huge expectations that weighed so heavily on my shoulders, I didn't even dare to have personal ambitions: I had to get my baccalaureate—the first in my family—then return home so that they could find me a man who would take the risk of marrying an "educated woman" who was capable of standing her own ground. I did not fail in my mission. I sat and passed the exam for which I had been sent. But I did not go back home as planned. My father, following a rather surprising reasoning for those times, wanted me to continue with my studies. What was he imagining for me? Even today, I still have no idea. Diploma in hand, I left Coulommiers and went on to study science in Paris.

In La Rochelle, Francis did not spend his time strutting on the port with his beautiful wristwatch. That was an idealized image. Most of the time, he was sitting in the back of the classroom in the Lycée Eugène Fromentin, where he was in boarding school. And when he was not in class, he was working at the library. He even studied using a pocket light in the evenings, secretly, while others slept. His classmates were amazed by his literary knowledge. He could quote whole passages from the great works, which he knew like the backs of his hands. He was brilliant, very intelligent for an African. He studied not only to become one of the best but also to distract himself from thinking about *mboa*, home, his home country. He loved this region: the ocean reminded him of his native city and comforted him, yet the moment he took his eyes away from the books, he was often overwhelmed by a wave of the blues.

Occasionally a friend would invite him to the family home. They would come and pick him up in a car, and Francis would take note of the names of the villages as they went by: Loulay, Villeneuve-la-Comtesse, Saint-Étienne-la-Cigogne, Doeuil-sur-le-Mignon. He enjoyed their sonority, and the spellings fascinated him. As he took pride in learning about everything, he would wonder during the journey: Do we say la Charente or les Charentes? Is it like la Flandre, in the singular for the Belgians and in the plural for the French? And as a matter of pride, he would never ask his classmate but was frustrated not to have the answer. He was warmly welcomed, sometimes as the distinguished guest in the home. He would be shown the blue room or the yellow one in which he would sleep. A hint of discrete ordinary flowers would decorate the wallpaper while fresh flowers were placed in a vase on the night table. Francis would recall the bougainvillea and hibiscus flowers back home. It would never cross anyone's mind to go and pick them and make bouquets. He discovered this particular refinement and appreciated it. The bed was high and comfortable. He sat on it and felt the flexibility of the mattress, ran his feet over the softness of the warm sheepskin spread on the floor alongside his bed.

– Pierre, his friend's mother explained, used to lie right here on this same bedside rug when he was a baby. He used to have ringlets just like yours! It was a whole drama to get him to stop moving around when we wanted to take his photo!

In the family photo album he flipped through after dinner with "Mrs. Anne," he spotted the famous picture of his friend, who had been chubby, blond with hair as curly as a sheep, bare bottomed, and an arched back with laughing eyes, looking directly at a point above the camera.

During dinner, they would ask Francis lots of questions. They would all interrogate him, express surprise, and make comments and comparisons. The questions were of the utmost sincerity, a real momentum of interest. But the same questions would resurface each time he found himself under the lights of the projectors, and he couldn't help but think he had to do the dance again, *my tap-dance number.* He had to tell the tale of Africa! He hadn't rehearsed that! What did he know about Africa? Africa was huge, even if you were to limit yourself just to French Equatorial Africa. *I only know about the country where I'm from. And even so, my home is by the coast.* He couldn't bring himself to admit his ignorance. So he pretended he knew far more beyond the forest, where apparently the landscape dried out and the herbs turned yellow and gave way to the bushes; areas where the men didn't have the same stocky physique as in his region. He also pretended to know other countries, and their customs and practices, while in truth, the information all came straight from the *Larousse Encyclopedic Dictionary.* He had good table manners and was admired. He was somewhat jealous of his friend Pierre, whose mother, with her handsome profile and elegant chignon, knew how to make apple tarts that smelled so good. It triggered a feeling from deep within, and he was overcome by a longing to have a mother, especially as he had never known his own mother. That feeling would however soon disappear when he realized how much he was appreciated and delightedly doted on.

After dinner, back in his room, he was embarrassed by the sound the piping made when he washed his hands and brushed his teeth. He was afraid to disturb. It took him a while to fall asleep because his senses were alert to the surrounding sounds, which he distinguished poorly given the walls were thick and the windows sealed airtight. He would go over in his mind some of the expressions gleaned at dinner: "*entre chien et loup*" (at twilight), "*rester Gros-Jean comme devant*" (left holding the short end of the stick), the latter, in particular, he had never heard before and immediately made a mental note. He would be sure to use it in the future to show just how cultivated he was. The world could be so kind when there were no more classes to master or fears of any kind to have. He would be sure to explain to his brother how happy he was and how well he was adjusting. Finally, he drifted off to sleep with a smile on his face.

The next morning, he was the subject of quite a fuss. Hesitating between "*vous*" and "*tu,*" Pierre's mother spoke to him in the third-person singular.

– Had he had a good night's sleep? Does he take coffee or tea?

Being polite, he didn't want to ask if they had hot chocolate, although that was really what he would've preferred.

– Does he like his bread toasted? Butter? Salted or not?

Francis carefully observed the behavior of his hosts and adapted accordingly. On another occasion, while he was the guest in another classmate's home, he had come to the kitchen dressed in his pajamas. He walked in to find the entire family fully dressed for the day. Humiliated. That was a heck of a lesson.

An afternoon outing was planned to visit the Poitevin marsh. He found himself in a rowboat, amid the calm of the undergrowth. The air was impenetrable, the pace slow, with the gliding of the oars stirring the duckweed. Time passed like dripping honey. Once back in his room, he realized that the light stinging sensation he had felt on his calves were mosquitoes that had traveled up the length of his trousers. Overcome by nostalgia he burst into muffled tears and was unable to stop himself. It felt like an eternal mourning. He furiously scratched the bites, which eventually formed patches that, in turn, itched him even more. His hosts had insisted, in the most affectionate way, that he should feel right at home. But for a while it just didn't work. He was all too aware that he was not home. All he wanted was to miraculously find himself back there, in his real home, in the thick smell of the river hearing the squealing bats at dusk, slapping his forearms, shoulders, and legs, amid the mosquitoes' early evening serenade. He would give anything to be able to take in the aroma of a *foufou*, manioc, seeping from the pot. The abyss of all his yearnings pulled him in irreparably. Taken aback by this disorienting experience, he did his best to talk himself through it. He didn't want his hosts to hear him and think he wasn't happy.

Madé would also be overcome by melancholy, get caught in its enormous grip, without warning. She couldn't do anything about it. Her life in Europe was all too recent. "You're giving up too soon," her more seasoned classmates told her. All it took was a rainfall for her to see people running for shelter. The rain made her long to experience *her* sky, *her* water, which would be a downpour, whole barrels of it, for days on end, but it would never stop people from going about their daily affairs. Sometimes, the simple gesture of turning on the tap would trigger it all. She would watch the water gushing out as if, instead of a miracle, it was the most natural thing in the world. She would go back to being the daughter of Mr. Géomètre in the quiet of the kitchen. The one in whose home, according to my father, you could have bread and butter . . . but who, no matter what, would go to the standpipe every morning to fetch water.

My parents were about to meet for the first time. They would bump into each other by accident, on Boulevard Saint-Michel, having jostled each other unintentionally. Surprised, they recognized each other and smiled. He invited her to have a drink in a café. Disconcerted, she refused. (He was relieved because he actually didn't have enough money.) They stood talking instead on the sidewalk. How is your father? And yours? And your mother? And your father's second wife? Yes, I heard . . . And your sisters? And Mr. So-and-So's sons? All of a sudden they felt very close, experiencing a similar feeling of estrangement and solitude: months that kept accumulating without ever going home, never really knowing what was going on over there; while also enjoying being here doing almost exactly anything they wanted to do, without being under the iron rule of parents; feeling adjusted to happiness in this new world to which they had first arrived, terrified, and were now beginning to feel quite good about. I would like to imagine the conversation went silent for a while and that their hearts were beating fast. They simply didn't know what else to say. My father suddenly became aware of how beautiful his future wife was: her doe-like profile, her almond-colored skin dotted with a thousand almost stylized freckles. And that he was so stunned.

A picture of her comes to mind.

Against the light, her skin appears uniformly dark. In broad daylight she surprises everyone: people are struck by the density of the freckles that stud her arms and legs. "Freckles" is not exactly the right word: each one of them was a beauty spot on a dark shimmering ocean. Her face also carries the legacy, thanks to which wrinkles and fatigue lines meld by means of a visual effect into a skillful pointillism. So much so that she still looks like the young lady she was around fifty years ago. In her class picture, she is sitting in the first row, in a white smock, wearing sturdy leather shoes. One of her shoelaces appears undone. Her mouth hints at a shy smile. You first notice her hair, which is in the shape of a crown on her head. Her cheeks are forever childlike. A nose not flattened but rather flattering, amazingly so. And finally, her wild eyebrows and the gray liquid gems of her eyes. The number of people who must have thought, "Eyes to drown in." How many got lost in them? Men, in great numbers, must have fallen under the charm of this splendid mélange. Like flies. A unique specimen in her family. As though she came from a foreign country. Even in Douala, many wondered. *That child has very fair skin. And those dots all over her face, she is the only one who has them.*

Where does she really come from? Later on, I would hear guests, who were visiting at home, ask her the same questions:

– Pardon my indiscretion, but where do you come from? Polynesia? Madagascar? The Caribbean? Are you American? Tahitian?

Then continue gushing:

– Oh, yes? Oh, really? From Cameroon, like Francis?

But no, there was no stopping on the sidewalk in the Latin Quarter. It was not yet time. Madé and Francis would have to wait a few more months, possibly two or three more years, before they would meet. And it wouldn't be in Paris either. But that's a whole other story.

Francis would be awarded his high school diploma from the Lycée Eugène Fromentin in La Rochelle and head to Paris to register at the Sorbonne to continue further studies. He had the allure of many students from the African colonies, whose mere presence—it's new, it's rare!—made heads turn. He was constantly being stared at. Impossible to go by without being noticed. People were curious: they would ask questions, and he didn't know how to deal with them so he pretended to be comfortable and act casually about it all. After all, he hadn't stolen his place: he had worked hard to get it. He preferred not to concern himself with those who were egregious, who were bothered perhaps by his presence, who would ask, Why, when we have built everything in their country, are these Africans still here taking advantage of France's generosity? We have so much to do ourselves to get back on our feet after the war. To feel more legitimate, Francis thought about the deputies coming from the overseas populations of French West Africa, French Equatorial Africa, Togo, and Cameroon, sitting on the benches of the French National Assembly since 1946, and of his glorious brothers, among whom the Senegalese, Blaise Diagne, were the first to sit in Palais Bourbon in 1914. That was the year Marcel was born. Francis saw that as a symbolic date!

Being a rarity was not all bad. Francis realized that his refined French impressed people. He played it up. The range of his vocabulary was cause for surprise, his lengthy, sophisticated sentences with relative and subordinate clauses. Truth be told, he had taken quite a liking to the French language and had a great time speaking with precision and turns of phrases for the pleasure of arousing admiration. *Can you believe he said "Gros-Jean comme devant"* (left holding the short end of the stick), *"à fleurets mouchetés"* (with kid gloves), *"sorti de la cuisse de Jupiter!"* (thinks he's God's gift to mankind!)? *And did you hear him, practically no accent. It's extraordinary . . .*

Francis was enjoying himself. He was a grown-up now and had put the "giant General" of his childhood back in his proper place. By his use of the language, he was gradually transcending the painful memories of colonization. He was leaving behind the era during which his country's national anthem began with the detestable verses:

> "O Cameroon, birthplace of our ancestors. Once up a time, you lived in bar-bar-ism, tintintintintiiiiiin . . . Little by little you are leaving behind your savagery . . ."

He was now a student in Paris, proud and loud, wearing his good fortune like a banner across his shoulder. He still worked very hard, but he had learned to take the time to live and have discussions with fellow classmates.

They were quite full of themselves, those new African kings in Paris. West Indians, Americans, Reunionese, Senegalese, students, artists, writers, and workers of all kinds mingled with them. Seated in a café in the Latin Quarter, they would enjoy their drinks while discussing *the situation*, and on the terraces, not far from the Sorbonne, students had swank. Like film stars, they were particularly mindful of their haircuts that were styled with hair pomade, with the part in a position that had been carefully thought through. The middle part was more American. The side part was also American but more American pastor. The shape of the glasses was equally important. Round or rectangular would yield different effects. The rest of the outfit had to also be immaculate: impeccable pleats in the trousers and two-toned moccasins always well polished. They would be seated with their legs slightly apart, wielding the language of Molière, without reserve, and repainting the future in its ideal version.

They imagined themselves holding leadership positions once they returned to their home countries. They would restore the dignity of their forefathers, those enthusiastic local inhabitants, who had confidently taken off in the middle of the waves to greet foreigners coming from afar. *We need to preserve this ancestral value: the sense of hospitality, an interest in others . . .* Everything got mixed into their conversations. They took on the political issues of the day. You could feel that they really wanted to do battle with the French politicians, propped up by the Empire. They were immediately fired up at the slightest evocation of the arts, cultures, and histories of their home countries. They couldn't get enough of those discussions. The Senegalese students were holding their own up against the Ivorian students, who believed that they had quite a lot to say to those from French Upper Volta . . .

They would get together and join the African student association in Paris, anti-colonialist student initiatives, the Association of Catholic African Students in France, the African Democratic Rally . . . Meetings would multiply. A certain Cheikh Anta Diop took on a haughty tone as he evoked his original ancestors from ancient Nubia. Communists, Catholics, progressives, and Third World thinkers were all in attendance.

In reality, while these classmates from the amphitheater sat at terrace cafés declaiming, doing their best to appear completely laid-back, they were feeling quite good about themselves. The mere perspective on the buildings that surrounded them amazed them. Before coming to France, they had quite simply believed that White people did nothing, that they were more than happy to just go about giving orders to other people. *Later on, that's what I'll do, too, for a job: be White,* Francis used to tell himself as a child. But the buildings, erected everywhere in the city, lined up one after the other, with so many floors, apartments, stairs, passageways, mezzanines, clearly a man's hand had to have been involved to raise them all the way up to the sky. These students would open their eyes wide when they crossed men dressed in suits or overalls, women cinched into their suits, so preoccupied they could barely spare the time to say hello: they were nothing like the administrators they knew when they were children, who would stroll along in their stately manner, lording over everyone. At times, certain students would accompany the ladies, attracted to their poise and intelligence. It was quite something. *Oh, these two ladies are good friends.* They had never met blond women before nor spent time with them. The smooth hair flowing almost to the ground, the blue of their irises, that skin so pale next to their own, the pulsating veins so transparent in their arms, those lips so thin, and that accentuated nose. These male students found these ladies charming and gave it all they had in trying to sweet-talk them.

– I am the son of a chief, you know?

The ladies were never too sure whether to believe them. Sometimes, they would quite simply burst out in laughter.

– Son of a chief? What does that mean?

– In my country, I belong to nobility.

Among the young ladies present, some would perhaps go on to become the wives of ministers or even the president. It never crossed anyone's mind back then. These young ladies dared all the same to sit with these men and laugh and smoke and have meaty discussions in which they held their own, suited out in stylishly posed berets and smart trousers, which they wore unapologetically. People weren't accustomed to seeing mixed couples, who, by their very presence, surprised, provoked questions, and confirmed that it was possible.

All while they strutted their stuff in style, the students pursued hearty debates and discussions. Given the general was able to free France from German occupation, they argued, he ought to quite logically reconsider France's relations with the African countries, by finally making them free to govern themselves. The ladies agreed with them.

– When are we to expect our independence? It certainly can't go on like this. The country's not doing well. We need to be able to get out from under this, stand on our own two feet, use our own hands and feet and our intelligence!

– But of course, it's obvious. This idea of Empire makes no sense at all. It's time to emancipate these people. Colonialism has gone on for far too long. They are more than capable of managing themselves by themselves! You are our equals!

– It's time to put an end to all of this! Independence! Independence!

Francis wondered how best to respond, torn between Marcel's injunction to put his studies first and do his very best and his own desire to be in on the action. Even from a distance, he really didn't want to betray the commitment he had made to his brother. He also knew how much he owed to France, aspects of which he had discovered by chance through words starting with his dictations as a schoolboy. In his head, he was playing the tune of a hesitant waltz. On campus when he wasn't about to crumble under the amount of work he had to do to get the highest marks and impress his professors, his ear was cocked, listening out for everything that was being discussed. He would attend the meetings of the newly created Black African Students Federation in France (FEANF), the umbrella organization for a number of smaller associations, but stand in the back of the room. When the debates got heated, everything would get stirred into the mix: the will for African independence and the fight for African Americans and civil rights, the dream of a return to a lost paradise, and the desire to turn their backs on the past and have the present guarantee a renewal. There were those, on the one hand, who were fired up to fight for their liberty and believed that the struggle had never been and therefore never would be an easy one and then those, on the other hand, who wanted to maintain status quo and kept reminding everyone that the scholarships they had been awarded had come from the very people they were now criticizing and that instead of biting the hand that feeds you, we should take hold of it and advance together.

Francis was torn between the two militant movements. Violence was not a part of his temperament. For a while now, he had been keeping a diary for those times when some of his most painful memories would emerge. In France, he had made some sincere friendships that he could never have imagined as a boy. But he was not going to share the wounds from his past with those new friends. Hadn't they also been children at the same time he had been? So he unburdened himself of the unpleasant memories by writing about them. It was a way for him to get rid of those wounds, definitively. *Although it isn't written anywhere, there were areas reserved for White people, separate from those for Black people. There was more than a distance between them and us. Some of them took advantage of this situation and revealed the worst of themselves. Others were truly humane. A schoolteacher would look at you a certain way and you'd be living in fear of the worst punishment. Sometimes that same schoolteacher would turn around and speak up on your behalf before the administration and even get you a bursary. I saw tears of joy when I got the results for my basic education certificate. What was truly painful was the fact that you just never knew what to believe, what to expect. The situation kept everyone feeling tense, Blacks and Whites alike. So I would go to my father's church to get some peace of mind. I prayed in my own special way, without words, just letting my heart open up. I would leave feeling at peace, and to put it all behind me, I would burst into peals of laughter.* He would say next to nothing about any of it to anyone. Not even—or so little—to us, his children, who would only become a part of his story many years later.

His body slumped over his desk, his head slipped on to the page. He had fallen asleep on an open book when, in the middle of the night, the telephone rang. He jumped up. Feet dragging in the corridor, an angry and exhausted knock on the door:

– Hey! Cameroonian! It's for you!

Who died? Overcome by anxiety, he rushed to the phone to avoid keeping the caller waiting.

– It's me, Marcel announces in a desperate voice.

In a rushed tone, he explained without explaining much.

– I have to go away for a while. They're looking for me. You, you do not know me. We're not from the same family. There is some confusion with our names. If you've written things down, get rid of them. And burn all my letters. Do not join any organizations. Nothing. Not a one. Don't get involved in anything; do not take any risks. *Émbè muléma*, be courageous. And do your work, that's all that matters. Work is freedom. I'll call you as soon as I can.

Francis hung up the phone, shaking, suddenly realizing that history had somehow penetrated into the courtyard of his imaginary family home. So this was where his big brother was, back home, involved in the movement, while he, Francis, had been asking himself how to gradually go about it. How far to go in getting involved? And why hadn't he warned him? Was it to protect him? From what kind of grave infraction? And why hadn't his big brother done what he had demanded of him—to follow the straight and narrow, regulated by calm and wisdom? Why had he crossed the line?

The next day at the Sorbonne, while he was going about from one class to the other, Francis got lost in his thoughts. Up until then, whenever he was walking through the university grounds he was always admiring the sculptures and murals in the amphitheaters. He would imagine the prospect that one day, when he was finally gone from this earth, his very own bust would be skillfully sculpted in white marble, in remembrance of his contribution to humanity. But on this day, he was tormented with worry. This was where Marcel found himself now, and he had been thinking his brother was solely devoted to his patients' sicknesses. He was, in fact, in danger, forced to disappear and hide in the bush. What was really going on with him, what could he have possibly done to provoke the wrath of the authorities and force him to disappear in this way? For Francis, a wound had just reopened after the phone call from his brother: it was just one long story of expectations and frustrations. The last time Marcel had guided him, he had held his hand on his return home from Aunt Maa Médi's place. He had been quite young back then. Since that day, Francis had learned to stand on his own two feet. Didn't he now realize that it was for his big brother, above all else, that he was studying and trying so hard to relentlessly advance, for him that he was doing all of it? For his brother, who had insisted that he be perfect in everything he did? That same brother, who demanded nothing short of excellence from him? Hold his head high, and make the family proud. And now there it was, that same brother had announced to him, almost in a whisper, that he was in the opposition movement, among those who had stepped outside the norm and were looking for trouble And why was he giving him so little information? Marcel had gone back home, crowned with his medical degree, full of faith in mankind, full of hope for the future. Was he no longer devoted to that cause?

To ward off the frustration and anger, Francis decided he needed to go his own way. He applied and received a scholarship to study in America. And so he took off, a free man, to study journalism. At the end of the day, his family didn't seem so pressed to see their cherished darling. He might as well take the liberty of going even farther away, as far as the New World. *Let them take care of themselves over there, with their politics!*

He left Europe behind and went to New York, where he would experience full-scale glitz. It was a breath of fresh air, so thrilling that his lungs were too narrow to take it all in. To begin with, he couldn't get over how lively the city was. It felt like drums were beating all day and all night. He almost twisted his neck and fell over trying to get a glimpse of the top of the skyscrapers. Here, too, man had really made use of his imagination to erect all these great wonders! He began his studies with the nervous excitement of a timid person and finished up determinedly passionate. He had discovered the magic of the voice through a transistor radio and was convinced he had found his calling! His stay in America would come to satisfy him far more than he had ever imagined: he became a radio reporter and would go about weaving his way in wherever he could, holding his microphone to whomever had something to say. This was the period of tape recorders with magnetic tapes, when interviews were edited with hairdresser scissors and rolls of Scotch tape. He enjoyed playing the role of sound wizard. The experience with this New World gradually unburdened Francis and freed him of his fears and reserve. He let go of the books and got out and met people: professors, researchers, scientists, lawyers, and human rights activists. The list of names included John, Matthew, Ray, Kitty, Sidney, Winifred, Mickey, Ellen . . . Blacks and Whites alike, who didn't seem to know much about his continent and expressed great curiosity in asking lots of questions: *Tell us about your country, Africa.* Once again, he found himself in the role of ambassador for this country called Africa. He shared the fondest memories of his childhood and kept hush about the experiences of the bloated stomach, which would have betrayed a starving preacher's son. He told happy stories of the everyday life he missed, perfumed with the aromas of the dishes he loved: plantains, sauces made from *ndolè* leaves, the *ngondo pâté*, the *ekoki pâté* with palm oil, chicken in the sauce— *wuba na ngond'a sengéti*. The memories got his mouth watering and brought tears to his eyes.

One night, friends dragged him into a basement club where he discovered a scintillating scene in which trombones, saxophones, and trumpets were playing off each other. A piano player, a drummer, and a bass player completed the scene. They were accompanying a singer, cast in a strapless dress, whose seductive voice brought the scattered notes together masterfully. He discovered jazz and the clubs where the public participated in the performances by beating time, snapping their fingers, clapping the chorus, and daring suggestive dance moves. Something of that distant place called Cameroon was there, in its depths, and made his inner chord reverberate. The velvet voice of Ella Fitzgerald moved him. Louis Armstrong's grainy, cheeky sense of humor gave him a real jolt, while the Cuban sound of the cha-cha-cha basically turned his heart inside out. He felt more alive than he had ever felt. The liquid power of the music ignited him, as if it had penetrated directly into his veins. He marked the beat by shaking his head from left to right. *No, no, no! It's so good! To die for.*

But he would also bring back some bitter memories that would serve as a reality check, for America was far from finished with its history of racial segregation. There was still so much to fight for: to begin with, the freedom to be one's self. Don't ever forget: *be courageous.*

One day, after having carefully verified that there were no explicit signs prohibiting him, he walked into a bar. He was badly in need of something to quench his thirst. It was scorching hot. Upon entering the bar, the atmosphere was notably tense, and he felt a strange compression in his chest. Without a word, the expression on the clients' faces said, *You are not wanted here, Negro.* He hesitated, undid his tie, then approached the bar and perched on a bar stool at the end of the counter.

The barman looked at him, stared him down from a distance with his arms crossed on his chest. It was one of those places you would see in the movies where the waitress, with her apron and matching headband, goes around from table to table, refilling coffee to clients who request it. Rays of sunlight shimmered between the blinds and streaked the piano keys, the tiles, and the imitation leather armchairs. Francis, in turn, looked at the barman for a few minutes before placing an order for a glass of 7-Up. The barman screwed his face into a smile. *You want a girl's drink? A bit of sugar will do you good, nigger? Can't you have a real drink, like us men? A beer, a whiskey?* Francis placed his jacket on his thighs, doing his best to put on a brave face. The barman eventually turned away to prepare the order and then sent it sliding down to the end of the counter with one forceful swing of the hand. Francis caught it in the slide and sipped the splashes that were on his hands and shirt. Laughter punctuated the moment. The lemon bubbles exploded and tickled Francis's throat. As he bent down to pick up his jacket that had fallen to the ground, he narrowly missed his glass, which had been thrown against the back wall by the man, filled with rage, who was sitting right next to him. The glass smashed into a thousand pieces. Someone said, *This way, no White man risks drinking from a glass that this monkey just used!* Roars of laughter resounded in the bar.

What do you do? Fight? Go and complain? To whom? As though he were in a bad dream, Francis walked slowly toward the exit. Outside, he found himself relieved in the blazing heat of the American summer, the last bubble of 7-Up stuck in the back of his throat. Again and again, he had to learn to harden his heart.

The end of his American exploits would coincide with the completion of his studies. He was excited at the prospect of going back home. But the news about the state of Cameroon was not very good:

– Stay where you are, the family told him, your brother has put us all in danger.

He had not seen his family for such a long time and those new orders plunged him into great distress. This family! This family that didn't understand him and that he himself no longer really understood! Still, he wanted to remain loyal. He owed that to them: that was what he thought and what he kept telling himself. Although he lived far away, he was forever tied to the banks of the Wouri River, like an umbilical cord. The news from his country saddened him, made him feel helpless and confused. He had not been home in years, but since they were asking him to reroute his travels to France, he was going to have to do so. He took advantage of his last days there to take in everything he could of America, immerse himself as much as he could in this country to which he had come a young man and was leaving a new man, a journalist, proud to be who he was. He saw himself being all at once James Brown, Martin Luther King, and Sidney Poitier. His body no longer trembled but rather stood firm with his heart eagerly fluttering in anticipation of that great moment in his life. At nighttime, he would sometimes think about how lucky he had been and wondered why the celestial compass had seen it fit to expand the scope of his existence as far as to the other side of the Atlantic. Like a great cat, he was gathering momentum from within, getting ready to make that great leap onto his most prized prey. He wanted to jump as high as he could, grow, as much for himself as for all those behind him, who hoped that the earth would one day turn in their direction.

The gods threw him a final challenge one day that led him to do a news story in Minnesota. Who did he meet there? History has not left an account. On the other hand, it does say that he almost fainted when he turned on his transistor on the evening he arrived there: a melodious guitar tune plunged him into a powerful emotional state, so much so that he beat his very own record for holding his breath for the longest time. When the Bach Chaconne ended, the radio presenter pronounced the name of the virtuoso guitarist— Andrés Segovia. It was as though a flame of lightning had descended from the sky and struck Francis right in the head. The impact was profound. The guitarist was of Iberian origin, and Francis had just listened to his performance. His Cameroonian polyphonic childhood reawakened at the speed of light. Everything suddenly appeared before him at once: his father's Baptist choir, the scores from his very first sight readings, and the used strings from that old instrument, hidden away in a loincloth in the family home. In line with the searing intensity that flooded him, he made a decision: he would no doubt become a journalist, but he would also learn to play the guitar. Seriously. He wanted to someday be able to play as well as this artist who had just raised all the hairs on his head so much so that his heart was "suspended."

Then he went on to do something that had become a rarity for him: he began to pray.

Back in Paris, Francis bought a guitar lesson book, guitar picks, a footrest, a metronome, and, of course, a guitar. He had returned from America penniless. On completing his studies, he had earned a degree but, quite logically, lost his status as a grant recipient. The guitar purchase nevertheless seemed essential. Until he could retrieve the old instrument left in his sister's care, he wanted to immediately learn how to play. Hadn't Marcel told him that the neck and strings would keep them connected, forever? *If you strum a chord, I'll feel it . . . This way, the music will connect us, even if we are far away from each other . . .*

Learning began slowly. The instrument proved rebellious, even surly. Strumming a few chords was one thing, playing was a whole other story. Still, right from the beginning Francis tried to compose, to pay tribute to Segovia, a piece whose title had come to him right away: *Un été près du lac Michigan.* He had no idea where the notes came from. Perhaps he just seized upon them as we do with words that surround us, to make sentences. He composed music that was truly unique to him and that carried a mix of inspirations, among which, the wind filled with the rain from the *Rivière des Crevettes* and the crystal clear voices his father brought together in the choir. Onto his sub-Saharan identity he grafted Lusitanian and Prussian chords. Everything came together on the instrument and resonated in the overture from the same body. Using his thumb, he tapped the soundboard and could feel the pulse of the trees. He was gliding, taking off and allowing the power of the gods' spirit to traverse his whole being. All he had to do was pluck a string to find himself at a bird's-eye view, skimming the peaks before an immense green vegetation, with variegated greens and browns, a real chlorophyll dream. Here, the roof of the world was green, deep, and infinite, like the sea.

Francis gradually took on other instruments. He explored the banjo, the balalaika, and the ukulele. During the daytime, he was a journalist, and after his interviews and reporting and the long stretches of listening and editing, he would turn to his music in the evenings. The guitar was still resisting him but he was determined. He wanted to be able to play what he heard. He let the nails of his right hand grow so that he could better pluck the strings and learned the American approach to reading music, following the letters of the alphabet. When it came to his musical education he was leaving nothing to chance.

In time, he was able to improvise as an orchestra musician in the clubs of the Parisian underground scene on weekends, which also provided a way of making ends meet. When he played in that setting, according to what was requested, he took turns passing for an African, a Cuban, or an American. Francis's life felt somewhat bohemian, had a kind of southern bohemian groove with the Parisian morning strolls. It wasn't too bad; in fact, it was rather beautiful, inviting him to greet midnight at the door without worrying about what tomorrow would bring. No doubt, he was slowly learning that happiness comes with a carefree spirit, which makes it easier to let go of whatever might weigh your heart down. He was earning a living and that was all that mattered. He was living as he could, in garret apartments and at his musician friends' homes. He somehow made ends meet, from a news report here, a gig there, between reality and a kind of blasé attitude, making the best of the six thousand kilometers that kept his family at a distance, happy for the lightness Paris afforded him.

As for my mother, she was much too well behaved to go out exploring in the evenings. At most, she went to the university restaurant—the place, she reasoned, where it was possible to have that unlikely encounter. A life well calibrated, of her own choosing, for which a nun would have absolutely nothing to reproach her. Books and only books. Family honor. The mission. Unlikely to find her in a Parisian underground nighttime scene where the melodies of the world and the comedies of charm and conquests played alongside each other. Madé would never want to have word get back to her family that, in one way or another, she had "behaved scandalously." I have no idea what she was feeling when she went to bed at night and her body awakened to the prospect of novel desires, and she had no idea to whom to direct those feelings. Did she look in the mirror at times to try to understand what the word "beauty" might mean? Did she ever gently caress her own shimmering dark skin? I can say no more: we're talking about my mother, undoubtedly the most discreet zone on this earth.

Until the day when.

-4-

In the Parisian basements, in the rooms at the university residences, in the backrooms of cafés, tongues were wagging. The previous generation had paved the way: Black students even had a magazine in which their own image was being reflected to them. This monthly magazine, *L'Étudiant Noir*, was overseen by Martinican students and had launched in Paris in 1935, spearheaded by Aimé Césaire. The Senegalese president and poet Léopold Sédar Senghor and the Guyanese poet Léon-Gontran Damas had notably each once contributed poems and articles. Senghor and Houphouët-Boigny were now deputies sitting in the National Assembly. Despite his big brother's injunctions, Francis attended meetings and signed up with the Black African Students Federation in France (FEANF). After all, it wouldn't do any harm to listen to what was being said about the changing world, and he would be taking advantage of a concrete aspect the federation offered: the vacation summer camps. He was now twenty-six years old. FEANF's conference had made a point of addressing the former African student body, reminding them that they had a responsibility toward their communities and encouraged them to not forget that the African people were watching and judging them. FEANF engaged in a number of activities during the academic year, and during the summer period they organized vacation camps in Saint-Martin-d'Ardèche and Menton. Some would choose to participate in the vacation camp in Menton. While the journey to the region was long, it was joyful. At one point or another, the driver would stop for breaks during the night. The young people would wander off into the open countryside to relieve themselves, occasionally getting their legs pricked by nettles. The girls would wait in line for the toilet at the gas station. Afterward, they would shake themselves off, smooth out their wrinkled dresses, then hop back up into their seats and get lulled by the steady movement of the coach. In time, some would fall asleep in the stiflingly warm compartments, even if the thunderous snoring of Atangana and Mbaye would amuse and, in the end, exasperate everybody.

From August 17 to September 16, 1954, FEANF organized a camp in Menton on the Côte d'Azur in collaboration with the *Ligue de l'enseignement*. Inspired by the Madagascans in Castellane, the participants staying at the Hotel des Îles-Britanniques wanted to prepare their own menu and do the cooking. The leaders' report also highlighted that FEANF had organized sport and cultural activities. It was important to remain accountable for how the contributions made by the territories AOF-Togo and AEF-Cameroon were being used.

In the early hours of the morning, exclamations woke those who were still sleeping:

– Look! Look over there!

The mirror effect of the sea drew everyone to the windows as the sun took over the skies, gradually intensifying the cerulean brightness. They were blown away.

Many had no idea how to respond to the prospect of being able to fully relax without the weight of studies or the eternal responsibility for "good behavior." Here they had a chance to forget about it all for a while: the glaring judgment that hung over them, at all times, that menacing presence that followed them from the day they had been awarded scholarships and that would follow them all the way back home. Francis stretched out his legs as he listened to the monitors give instructions and divide the students into groups of threes for the rooms. He slid his suitcase under his bed, hid his journal under the mattress, and carefully put away his guitar.

My mother was still back in Paris in her room, preparing for her departure that night and would arrive the next day. Nineteen fifty-four was well underway and my mother and father would soon be meeting each other. Did he even know her first name? How would he go about pursuing her?

On the morning of her arrival, she did not go to breakfast: she had not slept all night and was resting in her room. He was not expecting her anyway. He had no idea that Mr. Géomètre's daughter was right there, close to him. Two whole days would go by before she would finally hear the sounds of the guitar chords in the evening air. It was coming from the boys' quarters. An upbeat melody that made your whole body feel good. A song in *their language*. When the singer stopped, all the girls applauded him out in the hallway. The musician walked out of his room followed by ten boys who had been crammed in there with him. He was given a chair and invited to play again. He sat down, thought for a moment and then began a new tune. When he raised his head, the most beautiful girl from Bahia was standing in front of him, in the second row. The most beautiful girl from Menton, from Coulommiers, from Paris, from New York. The most beautiful girl from Douala was there, right in front of him. His whole body vibrated. He would have lost his ruff had he been wearing one. Her? She swallowed and tried to maintain her composure. Despite all her efforts, she batted her eyelashes. Fortunately, her friends didn't take notice. There was a crowd, which made a reunion somewhat difficult. When the recital came to a close with the final applauses, everyone headed back to his or her room. Shaking their heads in disbelief, they agreed:

– He's right to be singing in Douala. We need to preserve our languages. Let's not have them take that away from us as well.

Some people kept singing the refrain, humming along what they hadn't understood. Nighttime eventually quieted the noise. In her bed, Mr. Géomètre's daughter's eyes were wide open. Francis waited to be sure his roommates were fast asleep before pulling out his journal from under the mattress. That's it. He had to write to her. His heart was inflamed. He scribbled a few lyrical words in the pale light of the moon. The words came in the form of poetry. He wished he had the talent of his elders Senghor, Césaire, and Damas. He quoted them all the same and kept on writing, one line after the other, trying his best to calm the intensity of his feelings. A night of ecstasy after such restraint. A strangely powerful night in which he could already see himself in a photo, holding his beauty.

I had signed up to the federation without really knowing what I was doing there. A friend I was living with convinced me to do it, suggesting that at least from time to time, we might be able to relax and talk about our country with other classmates. I would subsequently learn that there was a political dimension to the organization, but I didn't care: I was neither a socialist nor a communist. I had never really even understood what the difference was between them. On the other hand, I really longed to be able to speak to people who could understand that life in France was very hard for me. Although I was long past my first school year, I still didn't know—I had never really learned—how to protect myself from the cold. As far as I am concerned, once you know how to dress and what shoes to wear in a country to protect yourself from the cold or the heat, then that's it: you belong to that country.

Thanks to the federation, I got involved in cultural activities during the school year. We would learn and visit various cultural institutions in Paris, like Notre- Dame, Chaillot, les Invalides . . . la Tour Eiffel, we visited from the ground because we didn't have enough money to go up the tower. But it was already magnificent from that angle. We would also take walks in the parks or in the Bois de Vincennes. The boys would improvise soccer matches or we would play volleyball together. All the girls would remove their shoes to avoid breaking their heels in the grass. The federation also organized a stay on the Côte d'Azur. I can still recall our arrival in Menton after an overnight coach trip. The light was so bright that my eyes hurt and I wound up having a huge migraine that kept me in my room for two days. Once I began to feel better, I felt like I was breathing differently, more deeply than in Paris. It was hot, really hot. It was great!

At Îles-Britanniques, I shared rooms with a Gabonese girl and a Senegalese girl. We spoke a lot about our home countries. We had so much in common! The Senegalese girl—her name was Ndeye—and I, we would braid each other's hair. I liked waiting for her to finish by twisting my neck to place my head in the right position. When I was much younger, I was never patient. I was always being reprimanded because I wouldn't stop moving on the stool. With Ndeye, on the contrary, recalling the patience we had had to learn very young, I really wanted to prolong it this time. Make the patience last. While Ndeye would separate my hair into chunks with the tip of the comb, I saw a palm tree by the window. Oh yes, the magic of the vacation was also about the palm trees in Menton, I loved watching them sway just like back home! It made me feel so good. Marie-Thérèse, the Gabonese girl, was always laughing very loud. I would notice the marks under her armpits already at breakfast. I hated the smell of her sweat, which would bother me even during the night. But she had the most fantastic laugh. It felt so good to hear someone laughing so heartily without worrying whether it was going to bother X or Y, or if we were going to be given those glaring looks that were sometimes shot our way on public transportation and in public places. Oa pula duta l'am? What are you looking at?

With Marie-Thérèse and Ndeye, we talked about cooking and shared recipes from our respective homes. I remember that after those conversations I was always feeling nostalgic because to be able to eat those dishes, you had to wait for someone to go back home and bring back the ingredients. Those were rare occasions. At times, I would have a serious longing to smell the aroma of mion-do, sticks of manioc, or taste some ngondo on my tongue. It would bring tears to my eyes. But it was also good to be able to talk and share those challenging moments, and especially share it with girls, who, like me, had grown up fetching water from the well every morning. We promised each other that later on we would be sure to visit each other once we were back home. "You'll come and visit me in Senegal? I'm inviting you to Gabon. You have to come, okay? You promise you're going to come?" We talked, and talked and talked, and talked some more, for hours and hours . . .

And it was during that trip that I saw Pastor Fritz's son again. During that vacation I learned his first name: Francis. It was a wonderful surprise to bump into him again. But in truth, we didn't see much of him. It was beautiful weather, there was a bit of wind, the sun was really strong, but that didn't seem to matter too much to him. He didn't come out much to go walking with us. He would spend whole days locked up in his room playing guitar or writing. When I asked what he was writing, I was told: "A book. He's writing a book." I burst out laughing. I wasn't the only one to have that reaction: the idea made us all laugh. "A novel! A what? About what?" We had so many different experiences, so many different ideas to share about the world, our home countries, this country that had welcomed us and its civilization, the joy of living here and the difficulties of being accepted, about our dreams for the future. We wanted to have discussions all the time and felt a kind of urgency to talk about our lives as African students on scholarships. Everyone saw Francis's project as nothing more than a farfetched if not outright ridiculous idea. A novel, that was something we had learned to respect in school. How could anyone who was born in Douala begin to think for even a second that they could one day possibly become a Victor Hugo, Balzac, Stendhal, Zola, or Rousseau? The very idea of it struck us as an absurd conceit on the part of an African man! How pretentious, for those who knew that our ancestors, the Gauls, they may have passed on to us a gift for music and words but certainly not a talent for writing.

Writer. Francis loved writing. He had tried to convince us all by reminding us of our elders, Senghor, Césaire, and so forth. Indeed, we did speak about them with the greatest respect, but for most of us, the very idea of writing struck us as huge, far too ambitious. Our elders had paved the way for us in a certain way, but to take a leap like that and believe we could be like them or compare ourselves to them, that was a giant leap to make. A giant leap. Francis didn't let our taunting get to him. Some nights he would take out his guitar and sing songs he had written, and we would eventually all join in together, even those who didn't understand a word of Douala. I loved that. Among us, no one seemed to notice his talents but me. I admired his talents for writing and playing music. To be honest, he had my heart racing away. Like on those Sunday mornings at worship. Sometimes, in Menton, our eyes would meet and he would hold his gaze just long enough to let me feel that there was something there. But what exactly?

I was shy. My freedom made me shy. That vacation was for all of us a wonderful space of freedom. There was limited supervision by a few monitors, and for the first time there were no supervisors, no professors, and evidently no parents to restrict whatever we felt like doing: no chaperone to control our every movement. Yet we still displayed remarkable reserve, held in the grip of this invisible authority behind which each member of our respective families was holding court: "When you go overseas, you will conduct yourself well. O bè so muna bwam! Behave yourself!" It was in those days when a-girl-who-respected-herself knew exactly where she should not cross the line. We were feeding our minds and keeping our bodies good and quiet. Marriages were being decided between families almost four thousand miles away such that the relationships between the boys and girls that we were back then, distanced from the decision centers, yes, those relationships were tinted with romanticism. And the marriages that took place because there had been an "accident" were for the most part rare.

That vacation was tremendous. I hadn't felt so good for such a long time. As I didn't see much of him, I thought of him quite a bit. Very often. I would think of all the things I would say to him when we would be alone together, just the two of us.

Don't give anything away; don't give anything away. Her heart was thumping so loudly that at nighttime she was afraid her roommates might hear it. She knew something was happening to her, just like she used to feel on those Sundays back at Pastor Fritz's church. He was always turning his head to look at her. And now the pastor's son was making her head spin. His name is Francis. She didn't dare to say his name in the depth of her heart. Her name is Madé. When he had learned her name, he had taken it as a positive sign: Madé reminded him of Médi, like Maa Médi, his beloved sanctuary. Seeing her again like this might just be pure luck, but he decided to see it as a divine blessing. They would each come face to face with one of the most important events in their life: the prospect of happiness, right there, all of it, with the rapid pace of a beating heart.

How did he ask her to marry him? Did he look her in the eyes and in a nervous voice propose to her? Did he offer her a flower, a bouquet, a gift, a ring? Did he improvise? Did he offer her a finely crafted note in which each word had been carefully chosen? Did he write a piece of music, something he had composed for the guitar? Did he get down on his knees? Or had he chosen not to use words at all, and rather have her read the intention in his eyes, see into the depth of his heart and his open hands, just how modest and sincere he was? She obviously never did say. This was kept in the secret drawers: those for which parents alone possess the keys. They know what is hidden in those secret spaces, and one day they choose to leave and take them with them. Mum's the word!

There is one thing I do know with absolute certainty: they had to come up with all of it on their own. Choose how they would give themselves to each other and commit to a life together. Because there was no one around to forge the way for them: *When you go overseas, you will conduct yourself well!* No further instructions and a world of habits and customs to create all on their own. A long list of memories to piece together. Before they left, no one had thought to write it all down on paper like this: In the event that you want to marry, you should understand that the process does not only concern you. You need to confide in an aunt or an uncle. Make sure whomever you choose is very close with your mother. Open up your heart to this person and be honest, sincere, and passionate, so that person will be so convinced of your feelings that they will, in turn, go and talk to your mother. Your mother might be upset at first, even if her whole life she has known that one day her son would come to demonstrate his qualities as a man and a great person. Once your mother is convinced, she will, in turn, wait until evening to talk with your father. Darkness will make it easier for her to say the words, and the warmth of the bed will help to sweeten the announcement. The next day your father will call on one of his brothers for what will then going forward become a matter of business—or rather, the matter of Business—for the whole family. Using a trivial pretext, you will have to then go and visit your girl's father. Return home without having said a word. Go back with a delegation. Go back another time with a gift. Express your appreciation for the range of the assets, weigh in on the risks of the union, acquiesce, reflect, go back again, further define, and make an offer. Time, fabric, and drinks . . . That's how a man gradually gets to take the hand of a woman in marriage.

But alone in a major city, in this great country so far away from everything, where you yourselves were Christopher Columbus, that the writings of your future husband were precisely trying to document, in this country, my dear mother, you and my father, how did you get engaged?

They had just finished eating and singing. It was a relaxing evening and everyone was just lying around looking up at the stars. Some of them—especially the girls—got up to go clear the table. She had not moved. She was incapable of making the slightest gesture because he was in the room. Everyone was chatting and the evening was winding down. Soon enough, people started wishing each other a good night. Ndeye got up from her chair and invited my mother to join her. Madé took her time getting up, brushed off her trousers to give herself an air of composure when suddenly she felt a hand on her shoulder and without a word was led outside for a walk. There they were, right next to each other, alone in the world, as if everybody else had been held back by an invisible wall. She had no idea where they were headed and she was so overcome that she had a difficult time breathing with ease or even seeing where she was going. So she followed my father's footsteps and kept pace with him. He hesitated: "If one day, it's possible . . . If you and me . . . If our families approve . . . will you? Will you accept? If I ask you if you want to become . . . If you like me enough . . . If we have a roof . . . If I promise you the moon, the sky, the stars, kids . . . And earn enough . . . Will you accept, if I ask you kindly, will you accept if I ask you sincerely to become the woman I will cherish for the rest of my life?" She nodded her head. His smile said far more than words. They were engaged, these school kids who had fallen in love at first sight. They had been destined to be together and finally committed to each other, hand in hand, with their hearts beating at the same cadence.

Life resumed after the vacation, but Francis's rhythm was soon turned on its head. When he tried to reach out to his brother Marcel to get his advice on how to go about everything, Francis learned that he had returned to his position as a doctor in the city. What about all the problems he had? He didn't bring it up, and didn't so much as even mention it. Francis didn't dare to ask questions. With regard to the major event of the upcoming nuptials, his big brother suggested Francis talk to one of the uncles and then to the girl's father for the initial negotiations. And so while my parents were living in Paris, family members were meeting on their behalf back in the home country.

> – Hello, I am Mr. So-and-So from So-and-So's family. We're originally from Such-and-Such a village. We carry the name of So-and-So's ancestors. One of our sons is over there in *mbènguè*, Europe. Went to study. He met one of your daughters over there . . .
> – Of course, come on in, sit down, can we offer you something to drink? Thank you so kindly for your visit, which is a great honor for us. We are from family So-and-So, we are from Such-and Such-village, we carry the name of So-and-So's ancestors and the daughter of whom you speak is indeed in *mbènguè*. Went to study. She met a man from your family. What's his name again? It seems to us that they are at the age where they can marry, isn't that right? Oh! Thank you! You brought us a gift? But you shouldn't have . . .
> Thank you ever so kindly for this thoughtful gesture. Would you like to have something else? Can we offer you another drink? Aren't you very hot? Are you comfortable? Have you heard the news that this year there will be even more shrimp than ever on our coasts? Yes, every day the fishermen return with their nets full, very satisfied. Our wives are happy . . .

The conversation would go on like this, long, meandering chatter in the most audacious convolutions. On both sides, they each knew that the aim was to marry two children whose union would seal the connections between the two families, but tradition dictated that you take the time and dance around the heart of the matter for a while. As for the two primary parties, they would have to wait until the end of this long, endless discussion, without losing their patience. So be it.

Did the negotiations take a long time? I can easily see my parents wisely waiting to officially become engaged before being seen together openly out in public. I can imagine that my father lived at the university residence in Antony and took public transportation to go and meet his beloved, when she got out of her classes. They would go walking together and then he would accompany her back to the girls' residence. During their strolls, they would stop in the park and sit close to each other on a bench. In the beginning, her shyness made it hard for her to know what to say, whereas for him being with her made him quite chatty. So talkative, that after each meet-up, he couldn't remember any of the topics he had gone on about.

As they would have to gather the necessary documents and complete administrative forms, Madé and Francis soon became more involved with their wedding preparation. On the day they finally got an official date, they came out of the town hall in the fourteenth arrondissement, all excited, and announced: *It'll be taking place right here! In a few months!* They took a few steps back, suddenly impressed by the building's architecture, and then looking on at the kids playing in the public garden, before you knew it they were discussing how many children they would have. Francis's count soon used up his ten fingers, and despite my mother's alarming shouting, *No! No! Stop there! You're crazy!* he kept on counting past fifty. He had a good laugh at his own joke! I can imagine he had her sitting on his lap—no, impossible, certainly not in front of everyone—I can imagine he took her hand or placed her arm in the nook of his elbow while walking, and without looking directly into her eyes, he said, while trying not to have his voice quiver, *Madé, mulema'am, na tondi oa.* And I think it's best not to translate these words so that they remain enveloped in their glassine wrapping.

They are so beautiful in the photo! He is wearing a black suit, a bowtie, and a French-cuffed white shirt with G clef cufflinks. She is wearing a long dress made from taffeta and lace, the cut highlighting her tiny waistline. A veil is positioned in the lower part of her hair and extends to the floor in a long train ruched in a ball at her feet. A single braid, decorated with little white flowers, forms a diadem around her head. They are smiling at the camera, smiling at life, smiling at each other, she rather timidly, he with determination.

I love looking at this picture in the first page of the family photo album. Over time the album has slightly faded and turned an off-white shade. At times I tell myself that one day, magically, the pictures are going to take on their characters, and change places, bringing together the different people according to the secrets they share. But each time I open the album, the pictures remain intact with the scalloped edges coming unstuck from some of the photos. Whenever I've had the occasion to sit and flip through these pages with my mother, she always asks the same questions and makes the same remarks:

– *Her, I can't remember her name. Suzanne Something or other . . . And I have bumped into her over and over again. It's quite something when your memory starts to go. Here are my bridesmaids. They were well put together, weren't they? We were missing a ribbon for one of the dresses, the seamstress had to buy another one. Not exactly the same shade of pink. When the ceremony was over, I threw my bouquet, but the one who caught it never did get married . . .*

Oh him, we never invited him. He was one of those who just showed up,
claiming he knew we were getting married and had no intention of missing it.
I found that somewhat brazen and I was especially worried there might not
be enough seating for everyone at the restaurant afterward . . . We had made
the reservation in a Chinese restaurant. In those days, there weren't so many of
them and it was considered unusual and quite chic to dine there. I'm not sure
I could name one thing that was on the menu if you asked me. In fact, I'm not
even sure I ate. I was just so emotional on the day it was impossible for me to
eat anything. We danced and danced! Now, that I can remember really well.
At some point, I even took my shoes off because my feet were hurting so much!
We left three days later on our honeymoon, and while we were away we were
burglarized. All our wedding gifts were stolen. All of them. Every last one.
Regardless, we can truly say that we started out with nothing; no one ever gave
us anything. What little we had, we bought ourselves . . .

They each slipped their wedding rings on their fingers, leaned over the registry at the mayor's office, and signed the marriage certificate. They smiled at the photographer and then a series of photos were taken: they posed with their witnesses; they posed alone; they posed exiting the town hall; and then in the garden, in front of the town hall. There were all these elegantly dressed Africans: the women in high heels, their hair relaxed and pulled back into chignons at the nape of their necks; the men in three-piece suits or in tuxedos, patent leather shoes, satin cummerbunds, and some were even wearing top hats, all leaving the town hall in the fourteenth arrondissement on August 14, 1956! I can still see the mayor, his deputy, the court clerk, and the municipal staff, and outside, flabbergasted bystanders. And who knows, the garbage man wielding his broom with small wooden bristles, in the gutter across from them . . . You didn't get to see an event like this every day.

She was twenty-four years old and he was twenty-six. Fifty years of hope conjugated. My parents were still students. Today, no student would dare have the kind of ambitious dreams they had projected for themselves back then. All she had to do was complete her studies and he his journalism training and they could buckle down to the grandiose project of all young educated Africans in those days: change the world! She wanted to work at the Pasteur Institute and, following her illustrious predecessors, discover the vaccine that would put an end to the scourge of malaria. As for him, he wanted to become an international correspondent in order to raise awareness and mobilize the forces of a new continent, full of hope at the dawn of independence. They also planned, like in the fairytales, to have many children.

In the hope of realizing their dreams, they set aside their wedding gifts in my father's room at the university residence in Antony, in the outskirts, south of Paris, then took off for their honeymoon in Menton. They would spend three days at the Hotel des Îles-Britanniques, which was more than a luxury for them at that time. Grit your teeth. Shrug your shoulders. Creative people start out with nothing. The space in their room was really narrow but they didn't care: they were together every day and every night, getting closer, touching and caressing each other. On their wedding day, two years had gone by since their first meet-up at the FEANF vacation camp. As a married couple now, they could finally give way to the physical desires of the body.

Here, too, as in every other aspect of their lives in Europe, they would have to explore and discover because they were far too inexperienced to speak openly about physical love or the sexual attraction they felt for each other. I can imagine that in their intimate life they gradually abandoned the modesty and reserve. The young bride would go and consult with a doctor, who would explain how to space out as much as possible the births of their future babies. First, she wanted to get her degrees! With her head low and her cheeks flushed, she listened to the doctor. She felt so far, so very far from home. There was not one woman in her surroundings to explain what a young bride-to-be ought to know before getting married. She would have to learn all about this new life on her own. Her husband was no less apprehensive, even if boys generally have a little bit more experience. In the end, he bought a book on the mysteries of married life by a certain Doctor Bovet, *Le Mariage ce grand mystère*. One evening after getting in from work, he pulled it out from under his napkin and placed it on the dinner table, next to the bread, without a word, as though it were a trivial object. Initially, his young wife didn't go near the book. After a quick glance at the cover that evening, she moved it and placed it on a shelf. Some time passed before she would open it, which she would only do once she was alone. She would read it and cringe at times. She would boost her courage by recognizing that doctors were absolutely in the right to talk about all of it. The book finally made its way into the couple's bedroom, on her husband's bedside table. Eventually he too would refer to Doctor Bovet's book and appreciate having access to written words that helped him better understand his feelings and learn how to go about honoring his partner. However, neither of them would ever speak about what they had read.

Years later, I would come upon the book, hidden in the second row of the bookshelf, where I had noticed the red cover with the title in the middle and a white background. I leafed through a few pages and was taken by surprise at what I saw. I wondered how it was possible that my parents, who were so distinguished, always smartly dressed, could ever have found themselves together without clothes. And I would decree that such a thing was quite simply impossible and that even if doctors might have studied a lot in order to qualify and practice their profession, they could still make mistakes. In addition to the duty to propriety and unflinching dignity, a veil of modesty made it impossible to openly address "relationship questions." Even in private.

One question kept gnawing at Francis. His family had not been able to come to the wedding. He understood that they couldn't all have attended, but his brother, his beloved brother, why hadn't he made the journey? *The airline tickets were too expensive*, Marcel had been terse in explaining, leaving the wound of their estrangement, already glaring, to deepen even further. Francis heard the same answer from the rest of his family, which led him to suspect that they were hiding something from him, as you might with a sick person you didn't want to trouble with further worry. He still hadn't forgotten that urgent phone call he had received on that now famous night, when he was studying at university, and the warnings pronounced by the same brother who had this time been conspicuously absent on the happiest day of Francis's life, because of a purported costly flight.

His big brother had clearly come out from hiding since he was practicing legally and even intensely with all the consultations, vaccinations, and operations at the free clinic that he had set up. Francis wondered what price he must have paid to make that comeback, because he suspected his brother was still involved in the politics to which he was deeply devoted and against which he had paradoxically warned his younger brother. Francis remained gripped by worry. Marcel was not the kind of person to abandon his convictions. Was he being pressured? Hard to imagine. Marcel would not be Marcel if he gave up fighting, however discreetly, so that the voices of those who sought change could finally emerge and be heard. How long had it been since they had not seen each other? While Francis kept on writing his articles and the ballads that came to him, he imagined his brother filling pages with his critical reflections on the country's land-use policy. Francis wasn't sure whether his

brother was right or wrong to get involved, to write, to resist. He was caught
in a quandary: his big brother was right because the status of a protectorate
country made no sense whatsoever, but he was wrong to be so outspoken in a
time when the risk was imprisonment.

He was sure of one thing: he missed Marcel terribly. In the evenings, he
would try to soothe his sadness by practicing guitar. The instrument continued to challenge him, but he now knew how to put together a number of
chords and was determined to master each chord, each note, each nuance,
driven by hope—to one day become an international concert performer, like
Andrés Segovia, *Émbè mini*, work those fingers!

–5–

Francis began his professional life at Sorafom, which would later become Radio France Internationale. It was a French-language radio station broadcasting news, educational programs, and, at times, some advertising, to distant regions of the empire. These vast, diverse geographic regions were featured along with the different expressions of their cultural practices. Officially a journalist, Francis was well suited to this radio station and took to the work like a duck to water.

A month after the wedding, in September 1956, he was at the Sorbonne attending the first Congress of Black Writers and Artists. He was excited to be in the same room with his elders, in the flesh—Léopold Sédar Senghor, Aimé Césaire, Frantz Fanon, Richard Wright, Jacques Stéphen Alexis, Jacques Rabemanjara, Amadou Hampâté Bâ, and so many others—holding his microphone and Nagra recorder up to them, thrilled to be listening to their comments. Texts by Claude Lévi-Strauss, Jean Rouch, and Roger Bastide were read. Magnificent and profound declarations were made from the podium. Yes! The Black man is worthy! And yes, a thousand times yes, he has a role to play on this earth! Hearing it said loud and clear had never been done before and felt legitimate and powerful to the aching hearts of the children from Overseas France and the colonies.

Madé, for her part, had resumed the new school year at the training center. On the same evening that my father came home fired up by the conference at the Sorbonne, she would timidly announce that her school year risked to be interrupted. She was expecting a "happy event." Nothing but great intense feelings in a singular day! They held each other for a while, then my father rushed to the concierge's office to use the phone: he wanted to announce the good news. And perhaps finally clear everything up. Since no one had come, as was customary, to celebrate the happiest day of his life, he would be heading to Cameroon as soon as he could to have a good talk with his brother. He would be making the trip with his wife and future child once he had the funds. The distance from his home country could not go on like this forever. In any event, *I don't plan to live in France for the rest of my life: I want to come home, I want to help, get involved and contribute, I owe this to all of you. I will be coming home as soon as . . .!* While he waited for that day to come, the suspension points would multiply.

In the meantime, microphone in hand, he began to explore the world, starting with his own continent. On March 6, 1957, the Gold Coast became Ghana and broke free from British colonial rule. In African circles, Parisian as well as international, it was an immense moment of exaltation. A new world of reason and harmony was in the making. My father was sent on assignment to Ghana, which had just begun asserting its independence in different terms. He was seduced, hesitant, returned to France, and immediately wanted to return to Ghana. The exalted speech made by Kwame Nkrumah, the prime minister and future president of Ghana, convinced him to give it a go: he was going to stay for a few months. He wanted to be a part of bringing about the first radio programs of a free Africa. And why not live there one day with his wife and children? Why not consider *going back* to this brand new country that was young and open to his competences? Why not imagine the possibility that *going back* did not necessarily mean returning to his native region or to his country of birth? *After all, no one seems to really be waiting for my return in my home country.*

From Europe he was able to spread his wings. He was beginning to feel good no matter where he was because he was able to do the things that interested him. In France, gradually, without yet truly analyzing it, he was feeling at home. As for Africa, she belonged to him. He knew he was the son of an immense land, including the one situated several thousand miles from his place of birth. Kwame Nkrumah used the term *Pan-Africanism*, which immediately appealed to Francis. Make it so that all African countries become one! He felt himself a member—Ghanaian at heart. His own country, Cameroon, was not yet there. So Ghana became the example: it was possible, we could have sovereignty, invent something else, a new country; who knows, maybe even a new Eden? He wanted to contribute to its edification by working to realize these great ideals. It was a joyful and exhilarating time. Francis spoke English, like the Ghanaians, and felt like he was coming into his own and seeing more clearly where he rightfully belonged.

> – Ghana, do you realize that Madé? Kwame Nkrumah, this incredible visionary! What an opportunity! Everything is finally possible for us. As soon as we have found a house, as soon as I have saved enough money, at the end of the school year, I will send for you. We are going to experience something incredible!

Our mother encouraged him, happy as always that he was happy, smiling despite the fatigue and the weight gain of her first few months of pregnancy. Men and women's experiences of time are completely different. He left. Months went by.

While Francis was in Accra, his older brother Marcel was in Douala, working very hard for the liberation of his country. He decided to openly campaign alongside those who were fighting for independence. History was gaining momentum. The example of Ghana had emboldened the people of numerous African countries. Everywhere on the continent people were outspoken and the fight was on for change by all means necessary, whether through official party channels or underground organizations.

At the end of 1956, the Legislative Assembly of Cameroon replaced the Territorial Assembly of Cameroon. In April 1957, Cameroon became a United Nations trusteeship territory under French provisional supervision. The following month the deputy and president of the council, André-Marie Mbida, was designated prime minister of the first government in the history of the country. He immediately took steps to put an end to any unconscionable or offensive behavior on the part of the settlers. The posters "No dogs, no Blacks" had to be taken down in the White neighborhoods, and any acts of racism that were committed could lead to the perpetrator's expulsion. It was time to speak to each other as equals between the different communities.

This said, progress toward new expressions of freedom was far from a straight course. Within the Cameroonian ranks, opinions diverged, parties dissented, and a small resistance army led an underground operation in the bush, which would subsequently be subjected to a severe response by the French military command to what was considered and presented to them as a terrorist rebellion that needed to be put down. Back in Paris, the military violence being practiced in Cameroon was barely covered in the news. Yet the debates, deliberations, and discussions had been going on for years among a population who had suffered at the hands of the Germans, then the English, and then the French, in the hope of holding the reins of their own destiny. It was left to the leadership in the military to make the decisions that needed to be made in the distant territories. And while the real fight for liberation was going on in 1956, a year and over three thousand miles separated those dark days from the happiest day in Paris for my mother who, in June 1957, would give birth to her first child, my older brother, Marcel Eyidi Jr. Marcel, like my father's big brother; Eyidi, like the forest, in Douala language. He had, following tradition, the first name of *mbombo*, the beloved namesake, and the dark green colors of the dense equatorial forest. An absolute homage. My father was present at the delivery, at least in the way you could be in those days, when the midwife came and finally announced, after hours of your pacing back and forth in the corridor, that it had all gone well.

– Sir, you have a magnificent little boy. You can now come and see your wife and your baby.

Oh! The overwhelmed expression on the father's face when he discovered the miniscule face in the cradle! And the proud exhaustion of the mother who had overcome the pain to reach the welcoming shores of maternity.

But Ghana couldn't wait, no more so than the longing to believe that an extraordinary country was about to be born and that you might be able to make a contribution. A few days after the great emotional moment of the beginning of fatherhood, Francis was off again. In Paris, my mother had to contend with the labyrinthine challenges of everyday life. After spending the summer taking care of her newborn, she enrolled once again at university: she wanted to complete her studies. But she kept questioning herself. Would this now become her life, married to an absent husband and father, who was always on the road? Or would she have to join him in that new Anglophone country that she knew nothing about? And why live over there when her own country, *mboa'a su*, was waiting for her, where her mother, her sisters, her cousins, her aunts, her uncles, and a whole tradition of welcoming newborns and lavishing attention on mothers would provide full support and familiar settings. She felt alone but refused to admit it. She was adept at quieting her malaise by keeping it at a good distance. She learned to transform her moods into a formidable smile of dignity. My whole life, I would hear my mother answer politely to whomever questioned her worrying expression:

– All's well, thank you, and you?

And she would offer her gracious smile as a gift. But she had worries.

They had decided I would be the first in our family to graduate high school. I did not fail in my mission. I had sat and succeeded at the exam for which I had been sent. Then I took on further studies. I continued to complete the silent agreement between my family and me. So why didn't they keep their end of the bargain over there? They hardly ever called and wrote even less. They only made themselves known when they needed help: financial help from the one who had settled in mbènguè, *over there, and was surely living well. They told themselves that I was living the high life, buying beautiful shoes and dresses. Couldn't they even have imagined that I might actually need help? My scholarship was rather meager and my husband had just begun to earn a living and we were about to have two children.*

Fend for themselves, that's what they would have to do. There was no other way. They had to show themselves as being exemplary all while getting on with it and taking care of themselves on their own. They had to contend with times when there was not much money and hesitant landlords who, at the mere sight of them, suddenly no longer had an apartment to rent. They had to celebrate alone and from afar, the most joyful moments as well as the most despairing ones: marry without their family, mourn without being able to pay their respects, re-create here where they were, vigils so they could feel a part of the community, and despite everything, give life without the precious presence of their older more experienced siblings . . . And they didn't have the right to express their exasperation, except discreetly in silence and in the secrecy of the bathroom where no one could see or hear them.

Of course they did wonder whether they would *go back*. After all, they had come here on a mission: to learn and take everything they found inspiring in the West to share back home with everyone. They were doing an apprenticeship. They were here to take in the air, to understand ways of seeing and living. They would take back culinary recipes—quiche lorraine, roasted pork with green beans, boeuf bourguignon, le pot-au-feu, French fries, tarts, crepes—and the grains that could give birth to new plants unknown back home. They would bring with them the habit of eating fresh bread every day and drinking wine. They would also return to the annoying experience of having uninvited guests drop in along with their cronies, the way things were done in that country, where people routinely interrupted you in the middle of whatever you were doing. *They think they're back home, they just show up like that, without even calling. How irritating!* They didn't realize that they were actually in the process of putting down roots. Time was taking care of connecting them to this new land where they would be docked for a long time. It hadn't been planned this way. Life had quite simply caught up with them and tackled them by offering children along the way that they would try to raise as it was done here and would have been done over there, teaching them the values from their own country of origin. Introducing us to all these flavors we would grow to love: *miondo*, sticks of manioc, and the *ndolè*, the *ékoki*, and *ngondo* paste and the chicken with *wuba na ngond'a sengéti*. Palates were fusing and a new world was coming into being . . .

But we're not there yet. For Madé would have to keep up the pace. She had to learn to be a mother and a student all at once. Without a nursery or a nanny, she didn't know what to do about her classes when her friends were not available to take care of the little one. My father, who would be home between every two or so overseas trips, suggested that she had close family back home who could keep the child until she finished the school year. It was 1958. Despite her efforts, she had spent the year missing classes. With a heavy heart, she decided to entrust her son to the family. She took off in the month of June before the official summer vacation, having otherwise decided that her exam performance didn't warrant her waiting around. Too bad, she would just have to take them again next year. The airline ticket swallowed up their savings, and she indebted herself to bring gifts back for everybody, making sure not to forget anyone. She would have to put her full weight on her suitcase to close it! It had been eight years since she last saw her family.

Stepping out of the airplane, she wobbled ever so slightly, caught off guard by the heat and humidity. She had completely forgotten how dense the air could be, how it could stick to your skin like a mask. She held her baby tightly and descended the jet bridge carefully. Once on the ground, she was so overcome with emotion that she wanted to get down on her knees and give the ground beneath her a heartfelt kiss. It was nighttime. She noticed about ten or so faces behind the waiting area window. They must have come as a delegation, as they had done when she had left. Her heart swelled as she whispered to her son:

– They are all here to welcome you, my child, because you came into the world. They have all put on their best outfits for you. *The lion is wearing his most beautiful shiny mane and the panther has put on her prettiest dress.* The whole forest is waiting for you.

She was inspired by the lyrics to one of my father's songs, whose words had come to him in French and for which he had begun to compose with the guitar. Although lately he didn't have much time to play guitar, he did take it out of the case from time to time and strum a few chords. Madé could feel that her husband was nostalgic for those days when he used to run around the city working by day and playing by night. She realized that some time had passed since. They had become parents, happily although with a "but"—she still needed to complete her studies. Indeed it would mean that she would be separated from her son, but they needed to earn money to feed him . . . She went through customs and the health checkpoint. She had had to get vaccinated against yellow fever and cholera, which were real concerns in the city following the floods. She also had had to remember to bring Nivaquine to protect herself and her baby from the mosquitoes. *Get vaccinated and take protective measures before coming home. Don't the mosquitoes in this country know who I am?* She waited for her luggage and finally piled everything onto a cart before heading toward the exit. Those in charge opened the suitcase that contained all the gifts, and the green-eyed officer was surprised by the variety: lingerie, plastic dolls, hairpins, headbands, pens, socks, shirts, cologne . . . He stalled and seemed to want to get a gift too. She hesitated. The baby began to cry. Then he let her go.

Finally, all the formalities were behind her and before her stood a group of people, some of whom she had a hard time remembering, especially the elders. She found that everyone had changed. She didn't know what to say. One of her sisters took her son from her and Junior immediately began to cry. She had no hope of consoling him because they were soon embracing and hugging her too. She finally burst into tears. How could this overwhelming sense of relief possibly be put into words? How could she express the intense joy of seeing those who you have missed so much? Life suddenly took on a new palette of colors, vivid colors, so many more contrasting colors than Parisian pastel. Don't ever go back! She wouldn't have the courage. Stay here, in the warmth and affection of her own people, feel the air passing through her quivering nostrils, welcome nature, the dance of the mosquitoes around her calves, close her eyes knowing that the world, her world, was right here, and that it would not disappear in the morning should she inadvertently fall asleep. She felt great relief and a sense of peace came over her. She was in the right place, finally, *at home*.

She slept next to her baby beneath the mosquito net. The next morning, she was awakened by a familiar sound coming from the courtyard. The women were grinding the manioc in preparation for a big welcome meal. In the next few hours the family size was going to expand: women, men, and children were going to be pouring in to visit with Mr. Géomètre's daughter and take a close look at the face of the eldest-who-lives-in-Paris, to see what might have possibly changed and taken on the color of *mbènguè*.

Still in bed with her son cradled in her arms, Madé took her time to slowly shed her state of slumber and open herself up to take in the rhythm of the life around her. In no time, a downpour could be heard on the roofs in the neighborhood and she smiled recognizing the familiar sound.

Flashes of memories came flooding in: the pitch-black early mornings when they came together as young girls at the standpipe . . . The sand in which they improvised acrobatic hopscotch . . . The smell of manioc fermenting . . . Mothers with a baby on the breast or a little one asleep straddled on their backs in the heat as they went about getting things done . . . Breakfast of concentrated sweetened milk and cocoa powder that was diluted with boiling hot water . . . Peanuts roasting that were then forgotten and wound up burnt . . . The salads you needed courage to go and pick in the back of the garden, afraid to have a snake cross your path, the *bekoko ba ti*, the freshly gathered lemongrass leaves, soaked into a soothing concoction for bedtime . . . Slapping your skin to chase away the mosquitoes . . . The patient and determined work of the ants, in a single file doing long distances in search of spoils they would carry to worker ants . . . The impromptu visits, elderly folk treated with great respect . . . Time for the women among themselves, braiding hair, preparing meals, and being patient . . .

In the bathroom, the water jets had spotted the cement walls black. Madé rediscovered the habits of her youth when she used to repeatedly gather the liquid in the palms of her hands and then splash it all over her body. She sloughed her skin with a *sissako* before quickly rinsing off. Running water had still not been installed. She had completely forgotten about this kind of complication over the last eight years. Junior woke up and confidently reached his arms out to his mother, who put him on the breast right away. Then it was time to leave the back of the house and make an appearance up front. To Madé's great surprise, about ten to twelve people were already there, seated in rows against the wall in the living room, waiting to see her.

– We've come to share your reunion with your home country. What a pleasure to see you again! You haven't changed! And your son, how wonderful, he's so handsome! He is so lively, smart, kind, calm, fidgety. It's a boy, that's good. Your husband's family must be very happy. What? He is one year old and he's still not walking?

– Come on little man, you know that we don't like lazy folk here? You have to get on your own two feet to learn about life!

– Bring more kids next time. Yes of course we're expecting more, what do you think? We have always known you, we watched you grow up before you went away to study over there in *mbènguè*. We always knew that one day you would become a mother. We knew you would make us happy this way. You remember us don't you? Here is Uncle Rudolf, Uncle Jean-Noel, Uncle Isidore, Uncle Boniface, Uncle Fête-Nat, and also Auntie Edna, Auntie Josephine, Auntie Paula, Auntie Solange, Auntie Agnès, Auntie Marie-Bénédicte, Auntie Grace.

They all felt obliged to give their Christian names and keep the conversation going in French, at least those who had a mastery of the French language. On the contrary, she felt obliged to answer them in Douala to show them that she had not betrayed her origins. In fact, she kept it close to her each day in her heart and in her mind. Right under her tongue. The country was there in a blended flavor that lingered on her taste buds. She had tried during all those years to cook like they do back home, as much for the taste as the pleasure and nostalgic feeling. And God knows it was a challenge trying to get all the ingredients: banana plantains in hot oil, crushed pumpkin seeds . . . As a matter of fact, she would try not to forget to take back a flat plate slab and a stone pestle: she didn't want to use the mixer anymore; it was noisy and made the baby cry. She wanted to adopt her mother's ways, the way she moved her wrist in a quick, rapid, regular motion, which allowed the foods to progressively grind down and readily blend into sauces.

Members of her husband's family showed up and announced that Dr. Marcel had gone off into the bush, to the village, to take care of patients who were expecting him. He couldn't have done otherwise. Not to worry though: he would be back in a few days, with more than enough time to see her—to see them all—and take the time to have a meal and a good talk together. She nodded. So be it, once again medical urgencies couldn't wait. Madé had come over alone as the first to face the families. Her husband was traveling and would join her later on. There was a striking resemblance between both brothers, far and above the distances, it was their capacity to be present without being physically present, bringing the whole family together while they themselves kept everyone waiting. Madé knew about this all too well. Time and time again, she was playing the waiting game when her husband would be called away on reporting assignments.

In the meanwhile, she was going to enjoy being coddled. Her position as the eldest was still hers for a few more hours, and she had better seize on it now rather than later, assume it—to arbitrate conflicts and decide what had to be done. She had noticed that her mother lived in the house as though she were in a trench camp: the second wife appeared to have fully established herself as hen of the house. As for Mr. Géomètre himself, she saw him yesterday at the airport, aged and emaciated. He had become quite ill from what seemed an incurable disease. Apparently he only left the house on special occasions. Holding his daughter in his arms must have been one of those rare occasions. She was truly grateful. However, she would rarely see him during her near three-month stay. Mr. Géomètre was no longer gloating and remained bed-ridden, curled into a position that left very little hope, while just outside his room his wives were sizing each other up and down, wondering who among them was going to gain the upper hand once the old man had passed on, who would reign over the house and come into possession of the small plot of land on which they all lived. The walls of the building were beginning to crack far beyond what was visible to the naked eye. My mother despaired at the idea that this gray life was falling further into even greater sadness, the color of misfortune. Her parents were born poor and, despite the glory days of Mr. Géomètre, it was highly probable that they would return to that state in their later years. Unless their eldest child managed to provide for their needs as they retreated from society.

Yes, she knew she also had a responsibility to pay for her father's retirement and help her parents to live out the end of their days. And she was the only one capable of financing the needs of her elders. That was what was expected of her, because everyone knew she had to be living the high life in Paris. Unlike her, her sisters hadn't lived overseas. She would absolutely have to finish her studies, find a job, and earn a good living. When she closed her eyes, she could foresee the trajectory before her, what she would need to do for years to come. Give back what you had received. Prove yourself worthy of this gift. Take action in favor of your family and community. And beyond yourself, think about your country, about the development of the country. The idea of all this responsibility suddenly weighed on her shoulders. She consoled herself by playing with her son's chubby hands and feet; his little feet were so reassuring and delightful.

The rainy season came on at record speed. After the reciprocal visiting among family and friends during the first month, the second month would be about sending out invitations once again and finally the farewell visits. It was important to see that it all got done in advance because, before you knew it, September would be around the corner, summoning them back to endless snow. Dr. Marcel was back from his consultations in the bush, but unfortunately Francis announced a setback and had to postpone his arrival for two weeks. So the brothers would miss each other once again, with one arriving while the other was packing up to take off. This was an undoubtedly deliberate maneuver on the part of destiny, aimed at postponing the face-to-face reunion of the two brothers in accordance with the Greek calendar.

I may as well say it here and now: they would never see each other again.

Hope would rise in my father's heart, to hold in his arms the one person who had been his model and a beacon from the very beginning, but that day would never ever become a reality. Politics and its setbacks would lead his beloved brother from the palaces of power all the way into hiding in the bush, then into the darkness of prison walls, admired by those who resisted, reviled, on the contrary, by those who aimed to bring down any possible hope of change. Marcel was living in a time where the mere act of speaking was perilous for those who had the courage to say what they thought. The prospect of freedom made him tremble with rage.

There were quite a few of them, like Marcel, who shared the idea that the country ought to be governed by those who were born there, on that soil. That it was time to pass the baton. And that violence was not necessary to make that happen. Others opposed that idea and they were not only French. Within the local population, some already considered the possibility that they might be able to acquire auxiliary positions and the accompanying glory, power, and recognition.

Madé wasn't sure she wanted to have that kind of a discussion with her brother-in-law. She preferred not having a full grasp of politics and was particularly afraid of what was going on. Upon his return from the bush, Marcel

visited her and focused on lavishing the bride and her firstborn in endear-
ing terms. To which he added his medical review as a pediatrician and was
delighted to confirm his little nephew's good health. No political issue would
be raised. His sister-in-law had enough on her hands as it was: *let's talk about
France, Paris, vacation* (because vacation was hardly an idea here; this notion of programmed rest was quite simply unheard of) *and the studies* she
would have to resume in the coming year. How was she planning to approach
it? He encouraged her, fully aware that women were still a rarity in the field
of knowledge and that all abilities would be useful for building the country,
when the time would come to heal the wounds left by colonial bloodletting.

> – We need women like you. Do your best in your studies and finish well . . .
> Try to get the best grades on your exams and come back to us when you've
> graduated. Look at little Marcel! So young man, you are my namesake, my
> *mbombo*? What an honor! Grow a little bit and I will teach you about medi-
> cine. Your mommy will prepare the pharmaceutical potions while you and I,
> we will get our patients to drink them and get well!

She perked up at the idea of her own relevance. Her brother-in-law knew
just the right words to boost one's self esteem. But of course she would complete her studies with honors and return home haloed with distinctions.
She would then open a laboratory, analyze the blood of her compatriots,
and—between the diaper changes, breast feedings, microscopes, and blood
platelets—eventually become Marie Curie or someone who came pretty close
to resembling her. At no point did Marcel address political concerns with her,
which did not prevent Madé from thinking, like so many others, how very
impressive he was. She understood that her brother-in-law's encouragement
went far beyond the family circle in the Bona Kou'a Mouang neighborhood.
Yes, educated women like her would have an important role to play in the
development of their nation. Because the Cameroonian nation was going to
be established, that was what Marcel said:

> – One day, we will—soon—hold the reins to this country. It is the logic of
> history. But will we do things as well as we should?

That was exactly what he said. Years later, my mother and father would tell
us about this uncle, who had been a doctor, and he would become a legend.

> – Your uncle was a renowned surgeon, graduated first in his class from the
> Faculty of Medicine in Paris—in those days, believe me children, you had to
> go for it. He had to really be unbeatable . . .

Surgeon and headstrong and a political opponent . . . And deputy and prisoner . . . It was my mother who would explain it to me, in a hushed tone—when my father was absent—because it was a hot-button topic:

– It is said that the great surgeon died from a purported cerebral hemorrhage in circumstances that were never made clear . . .

This last part of his biography would always be kept quiet. Not hidden, but hushed because it was too difficult to talk about. And like all children, we knew intuitively that it was best not to ask too many questions, because talking about it could only cause pain and reopen wounds, a gulf of silence, too great a sorrow. What remained was this emblematic and onerous figure of perfection. With regard to studying, this uncle would incarnate a myth that was to serve as an example, generation after generation, all while agreeing to never question the dark side that others—researchers and historians—would know better than us.

So later on, I would avoid the illuminating talks, I would sidestep the conversations people would try to pursue with me—*Do you know what became of that man who was well known in your family? Did you know that he was not only a doctor but that he had also given his energies to healing minds and souls, raising them toward an ideal, before the Cameroonian government had sawed his legs off in a cell, the kind of torture that is the same the world over, for all rebellious heroes hungry for justice? Torture. Do you know that this is the word that should be used to explain how that "accidental death" came to happen? Do you know that the disappearance of your uncle was the consequence of the horrific hours where one human being's abuse of power brings together terror and pain to take down another human being?*

Instinctively, I would avoid the topic, without ever taking into account that analysis, and focus on the sunny side of my family that welcomed light and protected my heart and my thoughts from the grips of memory. Try as I might, as much as I did avoid it, one day I would find myself finally questioning this model and trying to understand, by turns with words and with my imagination, why they spoke so rarely about him, or why they only spoke about his exceptional qualities—a model of work ethic and devotion—skillfully hiding the other part of him, the part that had dreamed and had had faith in the future, the part that revealed his convictions and that had cost him his life. Was our father afraid we would wind up taking our militant uncle as a model, follow in his footsteps, and discover a cause of our own to engage in with the risk of putting our lives in danger?

After the screaming and the tears, after the pain, silence covered over the story of this uncle, and I am piecing it together here in my own way by guessing and making it up with some difficulty and errors, surprised to still come upon historians or respectful former members of the underground resistance movement, more informed than me, about connections between my family and the great history of the country. They know the brilliant trajectory and subsequent casualty of this person. They know his memory has been buried in the darkness of the dense forest . . .

That summer of 1958, the brothers crossed each other without ever meeting up. Another moment in which, like two broken lines, their paths came close then separated. My father was in Douala when his brother would take off again to devote himself to other patients in the rural villages. I can't be sure if he was there strictly in his capacity as a doctor or if he was also using the occasion to participate in secret meetings by the resistance movement, fighting for independence, sheltered beneath the thick foliage of trees. They wanted to change the world so that each person in the country would be better positioned to make the most of their lives. The fact remains that the big brother felt the distance, and his little brother could not hide his disappointment.

For my future parents, their return date to France was set. As the departure date drew near, Madé tried to convince herself that she was making the right decision leaving her baby boy in her family's care. Sisters, cousins, uncles, and aunts each offered to take turns to protect and ensure the safety of the little one that the student-mother was unable to manage alone: there would be more than enough hands to take care of the baby while she completed her studies. *Do you hear me my little munchkin, I'm not abandoning you. We'll be back together in no time, you'll see.* My mother and father finally boarded the plane, leaving behind their little Marcel Jr. Madé could neither eat nor drink during the flight back to Paris: during six long hours, tears poured down her face; all her thoughts, every fiber of her being, was directed toward her baby, her first-born of only fifteen months, who she would not be able to see for a whole school year. They could keep on saying that *things were better this way,* but she alone knew what it was like to experience that kind of separation. *Na ndé é.* So be it.

In September, Madé remained indifferent to the brightly colored changing leaves of autumn and to the delighted smiles of city dwellers returning from their fully paid vacation time. She barely took note of the distant news

of a tragic death: Ruben Um Nyobè, the general secretary of the Union of the
Peoples of Cameroon, a banned party, forced into clandestine operations and
who, for the last six years, had been demanding independence. Um Nyobè
had been killed in the bush during a battle with the French army. After his
death, they proceeded to disfigure his body, dragging it on the ground for
nearly four miles, to the horror of the population. As an example. As a warning to those who imagined they could put a stop to the direction of history
that they would pay dearly. My mother knew nothing about this supposed
"terrorist," nor about the "communists" the administration wanted to destroy. She was completely ignorant of the fact that September 13, 1958, was
marked by a scarlet stamp of gravity, a moment in the history of the country
whose importance would be denied by the authorities, French and Cameroonian, for decades to come. To protect his sister-in-law and guard his family
against eventual reprisals or harassment, Marcel had refrained from telling
her anything about it. Because he too was participating in these movements
that those in power were fighting against. And those in his family who shared
the same family name were also in danger. Nope, during the month of September, my mother only saw the face of the director of the training center,
who gave her an ironic glance as she signed her name in the registry.

– Your results were not particularly impressive last year . . . Isn't it time you
thought about making a serious choice between pursuing your studies and
having a family?

*Wait, you'll see, I am twenty-five and I have all the time I need to study now
and I am going to prove it to you.* That's what my mother said to herself when
she courageously resumed her courses. Husband, nowhere around: he was off
to Ghana and busy discovering America. Family, no one around: they were
far away, taking care of her darling Junior, who never knew what to say to her
on the rare occasions she had him on the phone and his maman blurted out a
little cry, followed by a confusing silence. He must have been asking himself,
who was that woman who kept losing her voice in the crackling phone wire.
Madé herself felt increasingly miserable after each phone call. Her fellow African classmate Fanta taught her to knit with wool, and she made a long red
scarf with which she hoped to, according to her various mood swings, either
traverse the winter wearing or use to hang herself. She said nothing about her
dark thoughts to her beloved husband when he would come home for a few
days. She just let nature take its course. It felt so good and tender curled up in

bed, with his warm arms embracing her waistline that she just forgot about
the world.

– It'll be a girl. We already have a boy. So, next it's a girl. It's logical.

My mother had just announced she was pregnant for the second time and
for a moment was disconcerted when Francis burst out laughing. It was the
beginning of 1959. She decided to take his huge guffaw as a sign that he was
on board.

– You think it's funny?
– To be honest, no, but how do you want me to take it? I'm laughing at myself. I got the impression recently that you had a kind of clunky walk. I was
asking myself—I'm ashamed to admit it—has she gained weight? And even if
you had, you know you will always be beautiful to me. And, in fact, it is the
tiny creature, not even two inches yet, that has already taken over your body
and imposing its will!
– It'll be a girl, she declared.
– I would be so happy, but you know it's a fifty-fifty chance.
– Yes, but I can feel it's a girl this time. It'll be a girl. My God! How am I going to go about organizing myself? Next summer, after my exams, we'll be
going back home to pick up Marcel. He will only be two years old when his
sister comes into the world.
– Don't listen to her little creature, okay? Your mother is wondering what
she's going to do with you . . .
– No, that's not it all! What I'm wondering is what I'm going to do about my
studies. I have to finish, you understand?
– Okay! We'll see in due course . . . Don't worry too much. Kids take nine
months to come into the world until otherwise proven, so the little creature
will see the day sometime in October, worst-case scenario in September.
There's nothing to stop you from finishing the school year and getting your
degree . . .

They both fell silent. Francis was tickled pink by the news, while she kept
her thoughts to herself, having a hard time imagining how she was going to
manage to finish the school year with a protruding belly. The director of the
training center might very well send her home for good when she learned
Madé was pregnant. How long could she hide it from her? She would have to
manage to complete her courses regardless of what was going on and be able
to understand them without needing too much help. She was certainly appreciated among her classmates, but would they go as far as to give her the time
to share their knowledge? She was immediately discouraged. Things should

have happened in a different order: first get her degree, then go and get her son, and, finally, settle down with her husband and child in Paris or Accra. That was the image she had had in mind for all of this. As for my father, he was masking his feelings with a playful tone, but the additional responsibility was worrying. He was going to have to feed all these little ones. And there was no way they were not going to literally have bread and butter on the table.

At the beginning of the following year, when he would return to Ghana to continue his mission of setting up a radio program, he would need to really make a decision about the future this time: *Should we, yes or no, settle down here?* This question would gnaw at him during his whole life: stay or go back home, or live somewhere else again. What was best for his family, what was the best choice if he took into consideration what was good for his community and, even more, for his country? These major questions offer a broader perspective and, at the same time, weigh heavily on the shoulders of the smaller destinies of each person compelled to answer them.

It was like that in those days, Francis. One could hardly have been born by the *Rivière des Crevettes* in the year of the Great Depression without having to one day confront the feverish anxiety of ambition that far exceeded your original status in life. And, moreover, having the brother you had, who raised the bar so high, it was impossible to imagine getting over it without the help of a pole. And yet you dared that leap, and you managed to get to the height you aimed for, above the bar, so much higher than you had ever imagined.

On his return to Ghana, Francis would go up and down, roaming the alleyways of Accra, carrying these questions across his shoulder. He would decide long before everyone else, intuitively, that President Kwame Nkrumah's plans seemed more like a lure: indeed, Nkrumah dreamed of a united Africa but imagined that he alone had the power to lead. Francis anticipated that the "father of the nation" would one day transform into a dictator and take the country in a different direction, one Francis would not want to have anything to do with. He went back home.

Going back home that year meant returning to Paris. My mother felt reassured and let her belly, which was up until that point constricted by worry about the future, finally fully relax. As luck would have it, the school doors were still open to her and she could pursue her degree. She would finally become a laboratory technician. My father and she went out to a restaurant and celebrated her success. On the radio, Sacha Distel was singing *Scoubidou,*

bidou, ha. Things suddenly began to lighten up. Just like that, after a rainy spring, summer finally came: the Parisian chestnut trees flourished with beautiful dark green leaves. Life was smiling at lovers, and happiness kept inspiring new ideas, flowing and bouncing around in my father's head.

His Ghanaian experience inspired him to consider his first book project: it would be about radio broadcasting and the extraordinary opportunity it provided to accompany the development of the whole African continent. He immediately embarked on composing an essay, writing day and night while my mother, literally floored by the sluggishness of her pregnancy, merely enjoyed being able to breathe the same air as her beloved husband.

In the tiny apartment in Sarcelles, the keystrokes and carriage returns of the typewriter regulated the pace of the days. White paper and carbon pages kept flying in and out of the typewriter, my mother lounged around, and life had the flavors of the sweet indulgences of *calisson* from Aix and *bêtise* candies from Cambrai. On the eve of July 14, the little creature whose name was Fanta turned her nose up at history by showing up three months in advance. Her feet, her hands, her face, her body were all—miniscule. My parents were so afraid to lose this tiny little person. Years later when our mother would tell the mythic tale of our different arrivals on this great Earth, I would eagerly ask her:

– She barely weighed as much as a hamster, isn't that right Maman?

Why a hamster? That's what comes to kids' minds . . . Six little months of vulnerability immediately placed into the warm protection of an incubator, and the experience of a team of doctors and pediatric nurses all approved by my parents. My parents, who were basically holding their breath the whole time, hesitated to share the news back home, and surprisingly it was Marcel who would happen to call.

– It's a girl? You see little brother, your wife was right. And you are lucky that you are in Europe. A premature baby, born at six months, would have had no chance of surviving back home. You're right to stay where you are . . .

That intuition that he shared with his baby brother and those strong feelings that bonded the family together had prompted that phone call. But he had also reached out to convey these subliminal messages, for which he alone knew the secret codes. He would not encourage my parents to come back home because major changes were on the horizon, which might very well lead to great social upheavals. The hope of the great moment of independence was on the horizon, but the counterpart to this ultimate joy was a looming threat that people were making every effort to disregard.

– News about Little Marcel, *mbombo*, is very good, the older brother confirmed, wanting to end the conversation on a high note. At only two years old, he is already a great soccer player who knows how to score a penalty and that, I can tell you, his uncle feels in the tibia. Everybody loves him and is taking very good care of him. Be sure to tell Madé for me.

That evening, still emotional from the birth of his second child, my father returned alone to Sarcelles. His wife was also alone in a hospital room, while the baby was alone in an incubator, fighting for her life. Sitting in front of the door to the apartment, Francis was greeted by Fanta, Madé's friend who had been waiting. She had brought a plate of food, prepared as it would have been back home, for her friend.

– Back home, we do this when a woman is pregnant: the day she becomes so big that she can no longer see her feet, the other women come together and prepare the meals.

Recognizing her kindness and her patience, my father welcomed her inside. He told her the great news and they shared the meal, both eating pensively without saying much but rather formulating silent prayers so that the gods would save the baby girl's life.

———

We were still students when we got married: everyone from our generation did it like that. Luckily, a few weeks later Francis began earning a living. We were able to move into a much bigger apartment, which meant I no longer needed to clear the table of my textbooks and notebooks for us to share a meal. We were living on the outskirts in Sarcelles, in a building that I was not particularly keen on. I didn't understand why neighbors barely greeted each other. Every day you were coming across the same person in your building for whom you held the door. You ran into the same neighbors in the elevator, even got off on the same floor, exchanging a few words, usually about the weather. In this country, people talk a lot about the weather.

– Oh my God, it's freezing! Oh my, oh my! It's pouring down, it's horrible! Oh my God, it's stiflingly hot! But you must be used to it, right? Isn't it like this in your country? It must feel good to you, the sun . . .

Or people just looked straight ahead, trying to give the impression that he or she was not really there, although standing right next to you. A whole year went by like that, with meteorological commentary, and by the end of it you never really got to know each other any better. There literally had to be a catastrophe for you to find yourselves coming together on the sidewalk, looking on at an apartment in flames, shaking, hoping to God that the firemen managed to control the fire before it was too late. Once or twice, perhaps, a neighbor might knock at the door:

> *– Hello, sorry to bother you, might you have a bit of salt ... or butter ... an egg ... some flour? I thought I had some left and it's a bit too late to try to head to the shops to buy some. I'm so very sorry to put you out like this ...*

I would smile listening to the unnecessary charade, then a few days later I would knit my brows when they would come ringing the doorbell to return the egg. I had given the egg willingly: I didn't expect to get it back. Or rather, I was hoping the little shortage might have been the perfect opportunity to possibly have a different kind of rapport going forward. A friendship? Never really feeling sure about how to go about things with my neighbors, I never dared to venture beyond the apartment to the one in front of me or even next to me. So much so that when I really did need help, each time I had to manage it all alone. In those days, men didn't know how to give a hand with babies. It was always up to us women to change diapers, apply talc powder, diaper pins, all of it was meant to be natural to us. Our neighborhood seemed sad and, over time, gloomy to me. Then, as it always is in life, things evolved and changed. Francis came back from Ghana, disappointed.

> *– Make me promise to never get involved in politics, he insisted bitterly.*

Thanks to half of our savings, we moved to Paris into an apartment in the fifteenth arrondissement, rue Ernest-Renan. The other half of our savings was used to buy my mother's plane ticket. She was to bring back Junior and spend a few weeks with us. When they arrived, she was holding his hand at the airport. He didn't recognize me. He even stepped back and began to cry when I wanted to take him in my arms. I felt so terribly ashamed and hurt that he had forgotten me. It was September of 1959. He had not seen me for a year. My own son, afraid of me!

The following days would become more joyful. Maman would discover Paris, her eyes filled with wonder. She couldn't get over how much there was to see, every day, in the streets Ombwa tè wanè! Ombwa tè! *Look over there! Look! She couldn't get over the fact that people had built all these buildings. Nor why they had decided to enclose the roots of trees in asphalt and grills. When she would express awe out loud, passersby would look back at her and she in turn would look back on at them with curiosity. She loved Paris. In the beginning of November, before her departure, I had the hardest time trying to convince her to leave me her faux fur coat we had bought together. I had tried to explain, insisting that it was in anticipation of the winter. Your brother had begun his first year in nursery school. I wanted to continue another year in my specialization. This way I would be able to open a laboratory once we moved back to Douala. But the nanny lived far away, outside of the city, and so it was decided that she would keep little Fanta with her during the week. We would only see Fanta on the weekend, after a long haul on public transportation.*

School for Junior and for me during the day, then taking care of him in the evenings, picking up my books and notes after dinner, and finally going to pick up the little one on weekends . . . It was a real challenge juggling it all.

The moment your father went traveling on assignment, I could barely keep up the pace. The family kept asking: "Why?" without having a full understanding of things. When Francis would call from overseas, the simple question "How are you doing?" made me burst into tears. In the end, I decided to have little Fanta stay with me. I told your father: "If my kids aren't going to recognize who I am because I'm studying instead of taking care of them, then I'm quitting." We both finally agreed. I would put my studies on hold, with the intention of resuming them much later.

But of course I was far too busy to ever go back to school. In any event, it was like that during those times: the men went to work and the women took care of the home. As the years went by, I let my own plans disappear. I, who had always wanted to become the next Marie Curie or Pasteur, I became a mother doing her best every day to stay on top of everything. With all five of you, I didn't have a minute to twiddle my thumbs.

Several years later—I was perhaps about six years old—I was watching my mother get ready in the bathroom. She was wearing a little black dress with three eyelets on the collar, trimmed with a black ribbon with rhinestones. A light woolen cardigan covered her shoulders. Her legs were molded into designer nylon stockings, and her feet were doing all they could to adapt to the shape of her triangular-pointed, patent leather stilettos. Her relaxed hair was styled into a chignon. She was not known as a researcher in social circles but rather as a wife who accompanied her husband on a special evening out for his very first book-signing event. She stood before the mirror in the bathroom trying on and hesitating between different jewelry that I was passing over to her one by one. I was surely learning, without realizing it, how to become a woman. I was sitting on the edge of the bathtub with my feet on the bidet, observing every gesture she made, as I always did when my mother and father were getting ready to go out.

– Maman, can I have this necklace when you die?

She laughed while I looked on at her.

– Did I really hear what I just heard? Do you realize what you just asked me?

She perfumed herself, left the bathroom, and turned off the light. Distracted, she had suddenly forgotten that I was still in the bathroom. I stayed there a few moments in the darkness, absorbing the trail of her fragrance. Had she similarly left her professional ambitions behind to evaporate gently into a dark corner of her memory? Did she have any regrets? One day, she stopped hoping to earn a living based on a professional career choice. Later on, she would try to learn stenography to become a secretary. She would also learn English using different methods, Atlas, Assimil . . . For the moment, she spent her time trying to get her little brood to stand on their own two feet. After all, what do ambitions mean when the walls are solid, the ground beneath you is firm, and the man brings home what is needed to pay for the roof over your head and put food on the table? Isn't that what we call a family?

Following a conference where Francis had been a speaker, a man came up to him.

– I find your ideas very interesting. So you believe the radio can have an important role in the development of third-world nations?

The terms *third world*, *underdevelopment*, and *non-aligned countries* were increasingly circulating at the time.

– Yes, Francis most certainly responded. The radio is, to my mind, a simple and fast way to allow Africans to get informed but also to learn, to get an education, because there are many African nations where listening and retaining what has been spoken orally is an integral part of our education. Furthermore, it is precisely culture that makes each nation unique. It's also the image of oneself that each country proposes to the others. An artist's creations bring greater visibility to his or her country, gets it on the map. Thanks to broadcasting, it then becomes possible to promote the artist's production. Gradually, thanks to the artists and broadcasting, you create a desire— listeners want to learn more about the artist's country and people. You can attract tourists to that country. Commercial exchange becomes the next logical step. At first glance, culture doesn't appear to have a real connection with money, but it can really help a country to develop economically . . . You know, I've written a book all about radio broadcasting in Africa. It's called *La Radiodiffusion en Afrique noire* . . .

As he was expressing his thoughts, he began to realize that he had found the key he'd been seeking, somewhat confusingly, over the last several years. Held back by his big brother, who had ordered him not to get into the political arena, he wanted to, however confusingly, find a way to contribute. He wanted to, in one way or another, take on the challenges for the future. The Congress of Black Writers and Artists at the Sorbonne had made a mark on him. As a participant, he also wanted to draw inspiration from it.

The man proposed a meeting.

– Let's continue this discussion, why don't we? I get the feeling you could be extremely valuable in an organization that is looking for people precisely with your profile . . .

My father would go to work for UNESCO and, with his position, have an office with a view, a touch-tone telephone, a swivel chair, and, in the adjacent room, a secretary. He became an international civil servant in the department of public information. He was attracted to the mission of this important organization and to the worldwide ambition in the aftermath of the war that had given birth to these international organizations, to make the world a better place and create a peaceful planet. As for his role, he was in charge of accompanying the development of third-world countries by supporting their cultural politics and their broadcasting network infrastructure. A dream job. So the year ended on a high note, with him signing an amazing contract that secured his family's financial well-being. I can imagine my father coming home to announce the news to his wife that he was now *somebody*, within a world-renowned organization. What a huge leap from the young boy, running around naked playing in the rain with his buddies, to this office space with a secretary! Lessons that would be told by the glimmer of the streetlights on the imitation leather armchairs where visitors would sit! He himself couldn't believe it. Little bursts of pride would come over him like shooting stars. Before heading home, he would do what men in this country do when they have some great news to share: buy their beloved a bouquet of flowers. He would also stop by the local Félix Potin convenience store and pick up a bottle of champagne.

> – For an occasion of this kind, you should certainly have a brut, sir, the shop-keeper suggested.

Francis carefully made a mental note of this information along with a thousand other little details about French *savoir-vivre*. Madé and he were going to celebrate in a befitting manner. The good life was about to begin, the life his family back home had long ago imagined they were already living. The year came to a close with all of them in good spirits, thus allowing for a certain degree of comfort and reassurance.

For the first time in his life my father bought a Christmas tree. Marcel Jr. hung the garlands and the balls, bunching them together one next to the other as children do, unable to step back and appreciate the image in its entirety. He climbed on top of my father's shoulders to place a glittering star at the top of the tree. On the radio, Toni Rossi intoned *Ave Maria* in a high-pitched voice.

And in this little corner of the world, in Paris, in an illuminated apartment in the fifteenth arrondissement, while snowflakes tempered the buzz of the city, my family welcomed the famous magic of Christmas. My mother cooked a meal of roasted turkey with chestnuts and fried banana plantains, which gave an exotic flavor to the near traditional menu. After the meal, my father played a few chords as he looked into my mother's eyes.

> – *E titi bu so biala ba mwéngé mwama, o bon bunya* . . . (It is pointless to try to understand the lyrics to my song today, the words that would allow me to say just how beautiful you are, oh you, my flower, so beautiful . . .)

Smiling, Madé joined him in the refrain. Junior, in his little kid voice, also sang along in Douala. During his year in Cameroon, he had heard more Douala spoken than he had French. At the end of the evening, four people appeared in the picture: a woman whose gracious smile called to mind a doe, a baby snuggled in her arms, a man with a satisfied expression, and a child of two years looking up at him. The man had just placed the apparatus on the tripod. He clicked on the self-timer before rushing to stand in front of the camera. The flash went off. Time stopped.

There was not a shadow of a doubt that happiness was captured right there in that moment.

−6−

January 1, 1960, it was official: France's trusteeship was finally over. Cameroon was independent at last. This new liberty was presented in the news as though it had been a gift on the part of France: independence wrapped up in pretty paper, a Christmas present, because when it was all said and done, it had to turn out this way; and of course the people very well have the right to govern themselves. Those who were better informed about the reality of the situation, they knew only too well that this decision had been far from a given. This revolution had only been made possible because of the fact that men and women wanted it with their whole heart and soul and believed that, in one way or another, the pages of history would finally turn.

Some people also knew that the new leader of the country, Prime Minister Ahmadou Ahidjo, was nothing like his predecessor, André-Marie Mbida. By way of a subtle political sleight of hand, Ahidjo had been placed in the highest office and would soon show, through his actions, how he intended to maintain solid connections with the former colonial powers who had now become his friends. Too bad if he would have to use military might to trample on the ideals of his own people and have his country wait in the antechamber of the big world players. Isn't it the driver of the vehicle who decides whether to use the brakes or to step on the gas?

In the immediate, the official photo received applause and the population dreamed of a beautiful tomorrow. Did my father remember that day when the general had shook his hand when he had finished conducting the choir? Did he recall that huge, wide hand in which his very own had disappeared, brown like a *sao*, a sour plum in a pool of milk? Did he feel like *un ami de France,* as they liked to put it in the newspapers, he who had already developed solid friendships in France? The event was historical. The orators followed one another onto the podium: a representative of the United Nations, followed by a representative of France, then the prime minister of Cameroon, Ahmadou Ahidjo, who would declare:

– Cameroonians, ladies and gentlemen, Cameroon is free and independent.

The whole population was boiling hot, sizzling with jubilation.

In Paris, despite the winter temperature, Francis and Madé decided to celebrate this memorable occasion with a stroll in the Jardin des Tuileries. And before heading out, my father had a surprise. In front of the building, Madé discovered a car. Her husband had learned to drive in America and had just bought a secondhand Renault Dauphine without discussing it with his wife, as men would do in those days.

She obviously welcomed this novelty with a smile, gushed over it, and admired the sparkling bumpers, even promised to learn to drive as soon as she could. She settled into the backseat with Marcel Jr. and my sister Fanta. Francis stepped on the gas, shifted the car into gear, and listened, all smiles, to the engine roar. *I could never have imagined when I was a boy that one day I would be driving my own car in the streets of the capital of France.* He drove into the deserted streets on this first day of the new year. Parisians were recovering from the festivities of the previous evening.

While the Cameroonian people were all fired up with a newfound pride, Francis and Madé zoomed up and down the Parisian avenues, their hearts filled with joy. January 1, 1960, marked not only the day of independence for Cameroon but it was also an important day on a personal level: that day marked ten years since my parents had first arrived in France.

– Ten years, can you believe it? I would never have imagined that I would have spent ten years here, Madé murmured.

Of course not. They could never have imagined coming to France as foreign students and then one day, out of the blue, gaining the status of citizens of the Republic of Cameroon. They could finally begin to walk with their heads held high. In the Jardin des Tuileries, Junior made a dash for the pond, leaned over and almost fell in. My father smiled with the occasional fellow stroller he would come across. He rented a little sailboat and launched it into the water. He could hear his heart beating to the rhythm of the new world he had dreamed of living to see, rid of the indignity, condescendence, and arbitrary hierarchies. On equal terms, as equals. Everywhere on this planet. He would have loved to have just blended into the setting. Simply be. A utopian dream. A human without a complexion. As he watched the little wooden sailboat bobbing up and down on its Parisian ocean, he dreamed of this advent for his son. Little Fanta let go of my mother's hand. My mother raised her head and looked at her children and her handsome, smiling husband, always so caring. I would like to think I was conceived right at that moment, not in terms of the act itself but in thought, a joyful idea conceived of the mind . . .

The weeks and months following would soon confirm that January 1, 1960, that glorious day that had been anticipated for so long, would not actually open the gates to paradise. From the moment of "liberation" for the country, the whole game proved to have been rigged, the ideas about utopias were toppled, and men revealed their true faces, each seeking to take their best shot at greatness in the political arena. Within the very first weeks, a handful of slick operators took advantage of the manna falling during that historical period. Farewell to all the great ideals. Everyone suggested that they wanted to participate in the development of the country, but, above all else, what they wanted to do was to seize the important roles that would allow them to favor family and clan alike.

Certain former militant students set aside their demands and patriotic aspirations to return to the country and take up ministerial positions for a government they knew was corrupt. Others returned swearing loud and clear that they would not be duped . . . but a few months later had given in to the sounds of the famous *local realities*. There were many who stepped through the looking glass only to find themselves on the side of those who believed in nothing and were more so attached to the luxuries of public riches and the chimera of buccaneering.

As for those who believed that staying loyal to their ideals was a matter of honor, they were of two kinds. There were those who joined the ranks of the armed resistance, whose objective was to dismantle at all costs the travesty of the authorities in power. In the bush, in the mountains, they wanted to blow up fortified areas and force the government to reconsider their actions. Some would eventually disappear, having succumbed to the violence of the repression. Others would come together to form a segment of citizens holding on to hope, who still wanted to believe in the power of the law and political discourse.

My uncle Marcel was among this latter group. He chose the legal channel and was determined to argue every step of the way so that his country would change. He refused to see the extent to which the country was increasingly gangrenous with each referendum and rigged election. After all, it was not normal to see in the voting offices, one urn for the "yes" votes, one urn for the "no" votes, a third for the blank votes, and standing guard at the door, a military officer with a sinister expression. Uncle Marcel, who already held the office of national secretary to the PTC, the workers party, was now campaigning for the legislative elections. In the evenings, after a full workday of medical consultations, he would go out and give fervent public speeches, and the sincerity of his discourses would mobilize people and succeed in convincing them to support his candidacy.

On April 10, 1960, Dr. Marcel Eyidi Bebey became deputy of the Wouri district in the National Assembly. He had no political affiliations, even though it was known that he was close to the underground resistance movement, all of whom were members of the clandestine party of the Union of the Peoples of Cameroon. He hoped that by putting his convictions alone to work, it would be possible to, in good faith, offer a better life to all Cameroonians. A deputy in the family! On the evening of that victory, Francis dialed his brother and told him how much he admired him and was proud of him. That joyful spirit would, however, be short-lived because within three days two paternal deaths were announced to Madé and Francis with an early morning phone call. Both of their fathers had passed, almost at the same time, give or take a few hours' difference. The pain of these losses was immense, like a merciless bolt of lightning, crossing the Atlantic and continents. A confusing flood of images overwhelmed my parents:

– The last time I saw him, he wasn't doing so well. He never left his bed . . .
– He was always pulling my ears when I was little because I was always skipping school.
– His bicycle! I learned to ride it, sneaking out behind his back!
– I was in his choir.
– I was always massaging his feet at night when he came home from work . . .

And the realization that neither of their fathers had been able to attend their wedding, but that they had surely known each other since they had negotiated the terms of the union between the two families. A pastor and a land surveyor were now holding hands as together they entered the gates of paradise, one holding a thurible and the other a compass . . . *Let's go peacefully, we haven't forgotten anything! We will never forget anything.* During the decade away from their home country, my parents had kept the pictures of their childhood intact, as if they had been fixed beneath glass and framed.

Following these losses, Francis would have to go on assignment and Madé would stay in Paris, alone, to take care of the two little ones. My parents had organized a wake in Paris and sent money orders to Douala, with almost all of their savings. Still, Francis found himself preoccupied by the same haunting thought: *Go back home!* He wanted to feel like he was participating, like his brother, in one form or another. Indeed his job gave him the opportunity to do so: he was going on assignments, identifying artists, journalists, supporting the nascent cultural policies. But in the moment he was writing up his reports, a strange dissatisfaction came over him, more than was usual. Should he be satisfied being the man who tours the world, going from one conference to the next, writing reports favoring solutions, and be happy with this position, squeezed into a chic suit, a white shirt, a new tie, and cufflinks? Others would surely be satisfied . . . Coming home, be it from the office or another country, he had occasions to play the guitar at the end of the day and take notes on scores and melodic lines for his compositions. When he played, the instrument captured his children's attention and even seemed to calm them down. On some Saturday nights, he would head out to replace a friend behind the conga drums with a group of Cuban musicians. At times it was hard to stay on top of all of it.

> – What if we were to leave?—he launched out at my mother. What if we were to *go back home*? After all I do have two arms and two legs, even if I can't work at the beginning, I will surely be able to find something in no time. I am sure they are in need of well-trained journalists. And let's face it, it's not like we are all alone, the family can also help us!

Madé looked at him without saying a word. She didn't need to say it. They both knew for quite some time now that neither one of them could count on their family, because, on the contrary, their families were counting on them, imagining they were kicking back, living the high life in the City of Light. Francis had the impression he was sitting in the dugout while the biggest soccer match of the year was being played, and the future of the entire country was riding on the outcome.

In May, Prime Minister Ahmadou Ahidjo became president of the Republic of Cameroon. Independence had been underway for only five months, but rumors were already circulating that the new regime was heavy handed. It was best not to address certain subjects in public.

It was best not to ask why certain people were disappearing from one day to the next, or to ask how those who were dead, whose bodies just showed up and were found mutilated, might have been killed. If you insisted on talking about domestic policies, it was best to do it overseas, and insofar as possible, stay out of the country. It should not be heard anywhere by anyone that you had made critical remarks about those who had accepted to take on the difficult charge of governing an emerging nation. If you were living within the borders of the country, you had better be certain that the friend to whom you were speaking would be among the best of the lot—a man whose body might be carried out and not the traitor, who feigned the contrary—and that you were in a car that was going at record speed on a road far away from ears that overhear. In fact, it was said that it was best to keep a lid on it, even if you were far away, because all you needed was to have a family member back home—especially family—and your words could put that whole family at risk of losing their lives.

The new regime held the reins of power with an iron fist, and would not think twice about reprimanding those who made demands or repressing those who criticized. At the pace he was going, a certain doctor could very well lose precious years of his life. Although my father was not a diplomat, he nevertheless found himself obliged to demonstrate a strict duty of reserve day and night. In the daytime, it encumbered him in trying to do his job. And once his suit was off, he still had to remember that he was the brother of a political figure and that it was best—for his sake, precisely—to not talk politics. This was all the more difficult for Francis because he wished to, on the contrary, be just like his brother and have the freedom of speech to get involved and be a part of building the nation. He had to slip between the blades of a double constraint. And as it turned out, Marcel got on the phone with him, imploring him to stay right where he was and take care of the three lives he had created and the woman he had married and the music he was composing. This was what was important.

– They're all crazy, CRAZY, you hear me? Marcel said. Crazy in a way men become when they have been holding too great and dangerous a set of arms in their hands. They want the country, which is to say power, and have become allies with France to get it, with those who ought to have left it to us and who have been more than happy to pretend they have long gone. My deputy title is a joke. They had hoped to use the title to rally me into their camp and then corrupt me. We will never be able to develop this country; we will never be able to fully govern as the masters of our own land if these hands continue to hold the power. I want to fight so that the people who betray our people are punished. Democracy must triumph, you understand me? But you, no, don't come. Don't come, it's far too dangerous at the moment. Trust me on this one. It won't last forever. The situation will improve. I am engaged in politics precisely for this reason: Cameroonians are hungry for justice. There are a number of us here doing everything we can so that the power returns to the people, following the very principle of democracy. It won't last, you'll see, the situation is going to change. So promise me you'll stay right where you are for now. Please, promise me. After, later on, you can come back home when things have gone back to normal. Then we will finally be reunited . . .

The dividing line was right there, traced by his big brother, once more. Francis hung up abruptly, deeply disappointed. *When is he going to let me come home? And what does he think? That I'm going to listen to him my whole life like I did when I was little?*

He always obeyed him, as you do blindly the person who had saved you from drowning. There had never been anyone else for him. Francis didn't only have a brother, he also had a guide who made fatherly decisions. All of this he knew, felt deep down inside, and was grateful to his big brother. He could never possibly forget. He was nevertheless beginning to feel restricted by these unspoken rules from his boyhood. Shouldn't there come a time when we put an end to the seniority rights, when maturity is confirmed and you've even created your own family? His big brother, his beloved brother, his rock, his lighthouse who had lit his path all along, wasn't it now time to take a critical position alongside him? *I know he wants to protect me, he's always done so, I know. But today I want to be a member of the team and fight by his side and give us an even greater chance to win the battle. The distance gives me protection and guarantees my family's safety, but it is also suffocating me. The Parisian life is all well and good, but why must I be condemned to life in exile?*

Worried and melancholic, Francis was conflicted: what kind of life should he choose? In fact, do we really ever get to choose our life? He was afraid to slip into a comfortable place of ease (which, when all was said and done, he had earned) without ever having done battle with the troubles of the world. Sitting in his office at UNESCO, his feet were fitted in a new pair of well-polished black Derbies, he wore an impeccable shirt, and with his hair slicked down, he looked toward the sky. He would never admit it to his colleagues, but he didn't feel good in this outfit as an international civil servant. It wasn't because he thought he didn't deserve it; that was not it at all. His superiors were proud of him and he was also proud to belong to an organization devoted to education, science, and culture. What a great ambition! He was also glad to have not been appointed by his country of origin. At least he would not have to implement the policies of a nation whose legitimacy, as far as he could tell, was already coming apart.

As for his personal life, he could very well describe it in the shrill gaiety of a real estate agent: he lived in a beautiful apartment, and he owned a white Ford Taunus with a green diplomatic license plate 401K606 that impressed the mechanics at his service station. Coming to the end of 1960, his wife was pregnant with their third child. He was not too preoccupied with becoming a homeowner, although from to time he did entertain the idea.

Gradually, even while he didn't appreciate the looks he got sometimes, he was beginning to feel like he was fitting in to this society. When it came down to it, was he fitting in or slipping in? That he was slipping in or asserting himself? That he had been adopted or rather that he himself was adopting the ways of behaving, of carrying oneself, of eating and drinking, of thinking? On Friday evenings when he left the office, he would pop into the UNES-CO commissary to purchase groceries and then carefully arrange the provisions in the trunk of the car. Sometimes he would even plan the dinner, picking up some bread and cheese in the neighborhood before announcing as he walked in:

– Tonight Madé, don't you worry about a thing, I'm taking care of dinner!
– Really, *igni*, my darling?

Francis believed he was helping his wife or at least relieving her of certain tasks rather than actually doing them himself. Anyway, he didn't know how to cook because he had never had to: a mother, a sister, a cousin, an aunt, or a friend was always there to take care of everything. They now bought local dairy products and baguettes and enjoyed accompanying their meals with a glass of wine. Madé began to have consumerist dreams: a new electric Singer sewing machine, a yogurt maker, a Bissel carpet sweeper, a Moulinex coffee grinder, a plate warmer, a modern stove with a roasting spit, a drinks trolley where bottles of alcohol could be put on display—Martini, Suze, Dubonnet, Cinzano, Picon—and which she would offer as an aperitif or after dinner drink, because she had begun to do more entertaining than she had done in the past. Francis might not have noticed the fact that people were increasingly curious about him. His friends were French, American, Spanish, and Senegalese, Black and White. The pleasures of living were often ringing at the door.

He would sometimes step back from it all and forbid himself to consider settling down for a long time—forever? Definitively? No, it was not possible, not *definitively*—you never say definitively, you only go back home definitively. That's what was expected of him, that he would come and help, contribute to the development of the nation instead of enjoying a cushy life in Europe. By now he had been in Europe for eleven years. He didn't want to be perceived as cruising along, enjoying a cushy job. He had begun doing some important things in Ghana; he was continuing to do his best at UNESCO. Despite everything, he tried to convince himself that all of this was temporary and that the little he possessed could easily be packed up into two suitcases and placed in the stowage of an airplane that would take them back *o mboa*, home. That moment would come. His brother would call him one day and say:

> – Come on, it's time. There is a place for you here. The politicians have finally done what they ought to do. Our country is finally on track and needs well-trained people to lead as a driving force.

All he needed to do was be patient. He was doing quite well; he was in the home stretch now. It was just a matter of a few months.

So why was he feeling so out of sorts?

He had just come home from work and was greeted by a rubber giraffe and Marcel Jr.'s cubes, reminding him that he was already making a life for himself. Papa . . . *O m'oka na mba?* Are you gonna play with me Papa? Marcel Jr. asked. My father smiled. There, too, he had succeeded: his oldest son spoke Douala and baby Fanta's babbling already showed promise of a good accent. No one would ever be able to take his language from him: it was right here, safe and sound, living in his children. He was so happy to see them growing up bilingual. To put up a good front, he grabbed his guitar and played a new melody for his son called *Accra se mit à danser autour de Noël* that talked about the love for a lost country.

The story would continue like this: on that Thursday afternoon, Francis noticed from his office window how the sky was changing. Wasn't that a break in the clouds taking shape over there, near Montmartre? At that same moment, Madé screamed out and immediately touched her belly, which was feeling increasingly tight. I had just given her a head butt, as you do in soccer. I was about to come into the world. Francis dashed out of his office mumbling a few words to his secretary on the way. In his haste, his files were left open. He slipped on his raincoat as he galloped through the long corridor, risked skidding getting out of the parking lot, then pulled himself together and stepped on the gas. During this time, Madé entrusted my older siblings into the care of the concierge.

My parents headed to Baudelocque-Port-Royal Hospital as a beautiful rainbow erased the final drops of rain. I spent the night trying to come out between head butts, going from one contraction to the next, right up until the wee hours of the morning when, at 4:40 am, I suddenly emerged, gently, from my mother's belly and launched into life. My father, who had spent the night pacing up and down outside in the corridor, was finally called in. Apparently, I was all smiles right from the beginning. A few days later, the five of us were in a picture: Francis, Madé, Marcel Jr., Fanta, and me. I'm wearing a onesie made from quilted cotton and I'm yawning—or bawling (can't be sure, but my mouth is wide open)—in my mother's arms. My father pressed the release button then jumped back into position right next to us. The image came out in black and white in a square format, on glossy paper with serrated edges, as was the fashion in those days.

Yes, the story would continue this way, and since I have just arrived on the scene, I could describe the next four years in glowing colors. Pink, the swaddling clothes in which I came home and discovered the world from my perspective of twenty inches. I was an easy baby, who babbled from morning till night. I would cry when I was hungry; I would laugh with just about everybody; I would clap my hands or, on the contrary, shed emotional tears when my father would play a guitar chord, before bursting out in laughter right afterward.

Tender green, the delicate foliage of the spring, in the parks and on the chestnut trees on Boulevard Pasteur when, on Sunday, we would go picnicking on the avenue de Breteuil. Once we had found our little patch of green, the children would run around kicking a little plastic ball. The parents would lie on the grass and enjoy a romantic moment.

Madé would be wearing white trousers and a light twinset. In the time between when he used to whisper sweet nothings in her ears and then, she had given birth to three children and had remained ravishing. *E titi bu so biala ba mwengé mwam . . . I'll be looking in vain to find the words to adequately describe your beauty, oh you, my flower, so beautiful . . .*

Red, the glowing tenderness between these two people.

Blue and gold, the unobstructed clear sky of the month of August in Paris, when the bakery and newspaper shops were closed and the city slumbered for a while.

That would be the story of a rose-colored childhood, the kind of oral legend you come up with for friends as you flip through the family photo album.

But brown gradually clouded the picture of happiness, burning the edges of the story like the tongue of fire from an explosion. *Deputy Marcel Bebey Eyidi had been accused of treason. Weapons were found hidden away in his home. It was claimed he was most certainly instigating a conspiracy.*

The Cameroonian intelligence services had ordered his arrest. A military vehicle rolled in and parked in front of his house, and a squad, dressed in khakis, stepped out, weapons in hand. There were six of them, standing together in rows of two before their superior. The latter ordered my uncle to step outside, and failing to get a response, he had the squad break down the door. With an authoritarian stride they entered the first room, threw around the furniture, ripped off a mask hanging on the wall, and turned over the armchairs. There was no one to be found, neither in the first room, nor in the second, but that did not prevent them from throwing the mattress on the floor after ripping it open. They went into the kitchen, but no one was there either, nor in the bathroom, which did not stop them from ransacking the place, the ground floor and the first floor, perhaps to get over their rage at having to wait yet again before accomplishing their mission.

This way, doctor, it will be clear to you who is in charge, and you will stop talking up a big game. Don't go thinking you have arrived just because you were elected a deputy. You will not undermine this government. We want nothing to do with men like you, utopian idealists; your kind have nothing to offer our country. No. That is all ridiculous nonsense. We need men with force, men who decide and not men who listen to the people first before making decisions. Keep your degrees to practice medicine, but don't come filling the people's ears with all this talk about democracy . . .

Far from having the least inkling of what had been hatched, uncle Marcel had gone for a walk along the riverbank. He would often wake up early in the mornings to take advantage of some alone time. The sound and movement of the water did him well. He gave himself these moments of contemplation: his own way of praying. On that morning, he wanted to thank the gods for having obtained the people's vote that would allow him to, he hoped, make the country evolve. There was no doubt that they were going to propose he join forces with the leaders of the ruling class. Not that he was particularly attached to a ministerial role, but he believed he would be able to get things to move forward if he held the reins for a while. He told himself he had to play his part and use the education he had received to the best of his abilities.

Of course, I could be mistaken and, at that hour, while the little fish were slipping through the mangrove and the water lilies were opening up their calyces, he was thinking of his personal life and the desire he secretly harbored to start a family and make a home. He chided himself. *No, it's not possible. Life would not be easy for the woman with whom I'd share my life, and furthermore, I don't have the time, I don't have the right to start a family,* because he knew all too well the danger his long-standing convictions might eventually cause for a wife and children.

He had, all the same, loved a woman and been loved. It had been during his first visit to France, on the front lines, and she had been a nurse. The circumstances had not made it possible to get closer. And yet this was precisely what the war allowed for: to have you realize you needed to live life to the fullest right now, have the experiences you wanted to live. Whether you were Black or White. Because tomorrow was not a given. He had also loved a second time, in the last few months. He had made eye contact with a woman, a simple look, and he had understood right away the meaning of love at first sight—it wasn't something you could really explain, simply the feeling of being traversed by an electrical current. The relationship had begun somewhat shaky from the very beginning. He quickly realized that she felt nothing for him but was more than happy to have caught the attention of the famous doctor. He had spent several months telling himself things would change before finally making a decision:

– You and me, I think we're going to stop here. Look at us, we can't live like this. I don't even know your family and I think it would be cheating to go ahead and get married . . .

The woman had nodded in agreement and had not made a scene upon leaving, even though she had very much settled into his place.

Marcel left the riverbank and returned home, appeased. From a distance, he could already see the soldiers but changed nothing in his bearing. His body barely stiffened. His extreme calm impressed the men who had come to arrest him. It was impossible to know what he was feeling. Perhaps he had always anticipated that they might eventually show up and obstruct his path. He impressed them so much in his demeanor that they were mindful not to shove him. They didn't even bother to use handcuffs and let him lock the door to his home.

He was arrested on Friday, June 29, 1962. His neighbors watched the scene, appalled. The doctor was loved in his neighborhood. Men shook their heads, and women raised their hands up to the sky, fully expressing their power-lessness. They took off at full speed, and the doctor had not had the time to notice a woman, his former companion, slowly approaching down the street, a protruding round belly preceding her. That day would be punctuated with audible gasps.

His handsome face, structured by high cheekbones and a straight, flat nose, like my father's, would receive blows. He had been used to wearing his hair cut a bit short on the sides and in the back, but within a few days his haircut would no longer look like that. As someone who was in the habit of taking his time to get ready in the mornings, with a certain flair for vanity—moisturizing his body with hydrating creams, apportioning a dime-size of hair pomade before combing it—there wouldn't even be a broken piece of glass for him to look at himself. Given the temperature in the cell, his skin began to dry out and his withering fingers would run over the bedsores and wounds, gingerly feeling for his internal injuries. He would have the time to give them a diagnostic but very little water to treat them, having to choose between drinking the water or using it to wash his wounds. He had been stripped of his white shirt and lightweight beige trousers and left in briefs, practically naked in the cell.

They would do everything to make him forget that he once wore a stetho-scope and a white coat. They would treat him like an animal, placing a bucket in the center of the room to be used as a latrine, and the bucket would remain there for a week, filled with human excrement, before the door would open

violently and he would be ordered to go and empty it. He would no longer
know what kind of air he was breathing.

Sometimes the cell, already too small for one person, was crammed with
other men, and he would be at a loss as to where to place himself.

From time to time, they would come and get him and interrogate him, try
to convince him he had committed a crime that he refused to admit to. Wasn't
it true that he had been fomenting a plot with others? Wasn't it true that he
had been hiding weapons in his house? Wasn't it true that he had planned to
use his position to overthrow the ruling government and take the place of the
president? How could he wish for the downfall of a head of state, who was so
applauded by the international community, who had already taken on the
stature of the great African sage everyone had expected him to be?

As punishment, my uncle was rotting in prison. This amazing mind, this
idealist, this dreamer, this human being who sacrificed his life for the better-
ment of everyone, languished deep underground in a cell, merely for believing and having suggested that we could do things differently and by convincing others with fair reasoning.

Despite his arrest, the sick living in the neighborhood formed, for a little
while, a long line of lamentation in the hope of seeing him return. They kept
coming back each day for several weeks before finally giving up. Because, who
knows? Sometimes, people did come back because they had been expected,
because people had been waiting for them.

———∞∞∞———

– You have to come home right away. A man had just called. He said he
absolutely needed to speak with you. He didn't want to tell me what it was
about and he didn't want to leave his name. Come right away. He will call
again tonight.

Francis left his office in a hurry. He tried to reassure himself. It couldn't be
a death: Madé would have understood that right away. But then what was it?
What could it be that couldn't be shared with his wife? He knew, suspected at
least, the call could only be about his brother. But what? Had he disappeared?
Had he finally allowed himself to be convinced by the Marxist ideas of the resistance movement? Had he gone to join them out in the bush? It was difficult
to keep a healthy distance from your home country. Each time bad news just

kept coming and undoing whatever layers you had managed to create to cope with the estrangement.

– Marcel's been arrested!

By phone, the announcement from an unfamiliar voice rang out like an explosion. Francis staggered. He couldn't figure out if he was supposed to cry from shame or worry. Prison was never a possible destination for Pastor Fritz's sons. And now, the most brilliant one among them had been taken there, brought to his knees. For what reason? Nobody knew really, even if everyone had an idea. *He had criticized.* What can we do? Nothing. Bring fruit, personal items, and letters to the prisoner. And try to see him in the visiting room. If it's authorized. But who could speak with a deputy who had been arrested? Three leaders were now behind bars for "political subversion." This was what a speedy trial would claim. On July 11, 1962, three members of parliament were remanded into custody for a period of three years. As an example. *You don't criticize.* Politics was diffusing a most foul smell of terror.

Sitting, while afraid the chair might break. Laughing, while discreetly wiping away the tears that come. Admiring the landscape, while remembering those you were used to seeing back home. Appreciating a vegetable, while recalling its taste was one you loved as a child. This is how it becomes possible to create a partition in your heart: here, I like, I hope, I enjoy, I'm delighted . . . There, I'm shaking, I'm afraid, I remember, I forget. That's how you managed to bear that terrible distance for so long, a weighted distance in time and space that even migratory birds don't dare to chance. My father's heart steered clear of an oblique fissure that made him fragile, all while it strengthened him. In the way that a gash makes your face appear sadder and at the same time more beautiful. To bear his brother's imprisonment and the incredible impotence that the distance accentuated, he would focus on the good things in his heart, dote on his wife and children, and blot up all the internal bleeding. Besides, wasn't it an opportunity? At two months old, my little brother was still a newborn when Marcel was condemned, and his vigorous wailing got everyone's attention. That was what my parents would most certainly hold on to; their baby's crying that reminded everyone that the miracle of life was here and that it was good to pay attention and to accompany it every day.

Months later, beyond the Atlantic Ocean, other cries called on my father. In America, the civil rights movement was taking on an unprecedented scale.

In August 1963, an extraordinary demonstration occurred in Washington, DC. Thousands of men and women were determined to put an end to the unjust system of segregation. My father's aching heart expanded in the face of this new frontier of possibilities, his ears fed by the stirring of the crowd, and he was drinking up the words of the Reverend Dr. Martin Luther King Jr. Francis's eyes captured the images broadcast on the television that brought to mind another history still in process, like an echo of his own. He composed his first long musical piece and called it *Black Tears*, in homage to all the people of good will, everywhere in the world, who wanted the freedom to be, to speak, and to think.

For the patients of the good doctor, there was nothing they could do, the wait would be too long: three whole years before the beloved doctor would be able to return home, exhausted and wrung out. When he finally did get out of prison, the darkness of the cell had impaired his vision. The great doctor and deputy had become blind. Perhaps his eyes could no longer bear the sight of human brutality? Or perhaps he had contracted an incurable malady in that filthy cell. As with all men who believe in dialogue, he had naively believed in the virtues of the exchange and expression of ideas. He would try in vain to recover from the torture he had suffered during that long incarceration. The machinery of repression had finally won. He would never again practice medicine, nor dip his pen in ink as an editorialist for *L'Opinion du Cameroun*, the newspaper he had started.

⸻

I was five years old when the second explosion occurred. This time waking my parents in the wee hours of the morning, startled by a phone call. At the end of the line, a faraway voice announced the news. My parents immediately understood despite the crackling phone line. My father tried to ask some questions, stammering, before the receiver fell from his hands. Out came a raucous wail and then he collapsed. My mother, her eyes staring wide open, began to squeal loudly—*Ayo mba ndé éééé! Ayo mba éééé! Woe is me!*—then she burst into tears, crying her heart out, and we, the kids looking on, spontaneously began to cry, a choir of tears with no idea what was going on. My parents' world had abruptly been turned upside down.

Later on my father would get some details. They were contradictory. It was claimed that the doctor had suddenly collapsed at home while he was coming down the stairs, trying to find his way from one room to the other in his house, in the darkness of his new life. A mortal disease was said to have wormed its way into his body, climbed up the length of his leg, passed his heart, and reached his head, and wound up suddenly throwing the man to the ground. *Cerebral congestion*, that's what they said . . . Cerebral hemorrhage? Concussion?

My parents didn't believe any of the medical diagnostics. No more so than did the great doctor's supporters and all the members of his party and all the discreet or noteworthy opponents of the regime in place in the country. They knew that Dr. Marcel Bebey Eyidi had died for his ideas. He had been punished for believing that everything wasn't already rotten and that he could change the world. He had died because of the torture that men inflicted on other men, as you would accomplish a job you were asked to do: by burying your conscience at the bottom of your garden. One day, much later on, historians would calculate up to fifteen years of repression; of disappearances; of unexplained murders; of arrested opponents; of unspeakable torture; of bodies decapitated; of heads on display, bleeding before the population to terrorize those who were thinking about crossing over into the camp of the alleged terrorists. Fifteen years of resistance, prior to and following independence. So many mutilated or murdered bodies and shattered spirits!

And why all of this? This was what Francis asked himself as he tried to bear the unbelievable pain that had so suddenly fallen upon his shoulders, leaving him transfixed. Images from the past resurfaced, all muddled in his mind. There had been that day when, as a little boy feeling all alone in the world in his large family, he had left the house and walked several miles to Aunt Maa Médi's house. She was the aunt who, whenever she came to visit, always took the time and care—she was really the only one—to caress his cheeks with a gentle touch. He was so little back then. Several days later, Marcel had come to Aunt Maa Médi's door and held his hand out to him.

> – Do you realize that everyone is asking where you've gone? And me, hey, I was worried about you, what do you think! Don't ever make me afraid like that again. Come on. Hold my hand really tight, little brother, and come. From here on out, you will listen to me, you will do what I say, and I will watch over you.

He had dragged him along and taken him back, guided him resolutely and tenderly all the way back to the family home and then onto the path of life. His hand in his brother's hand cinched their pact forever. And now death had come and broken that pledge. Confused, Francis thought about all the things he had not done with his brother. He would have loved to have taken a trip with him to America. He would have shown him the New York skyscrapers and then taken him all the way on to Atlanta to show him that bar where, thanks to Marcel's teachings, Francis had been able to get out with his head held high even though hate had materialized toward him with a shattering of broken glass. Francis remained distraught when he realized that in addition to the pain of losing his brother, he wouldn't be able to attend his brother's funeral. He was advised not to make the journey:

> – The country has become far too dangerous for you, his loved ones told
> him at the other end of the line. Your brother did nothing illegal, but you
> might wind up paying, because of your name . . . We know you have done
> nothing wrong and that you have neither said nor written anything negative,
> but people tend to mix things up sometimes. They equate this one with that
> one . . . Be careful. Stay in Paris.

His brother was lying in the ground and Francis had to once more agree to stay away, even when Marcel was now on his final journey. Francis felt a blinding rage mixed with sadness. *Émbè nyolo*, Be strong! Be courageous.

Francis remained silent. Devastated.

All my life, this event is among my earliest memories, the one that returns and interrupts the crystal clear sounds of the happy days of my childhood whenever I think about the past or have recollections. I hear my mother's screams in the early hours of the morning, and the strange sadness of waking up to it all takes hold of me all over again, sending into obscurity all the moments of light spent playing with the ball on the lawn on avenue de Breteuil.

Without warning, a guitar chord is released with a pop and the playing stops. Sounds intensify then fade away: our father's wailing, our weeping as kids, in unison with the suffering that gradually blankets the house. Soon, nothing more is heard but for the creaking of steps on the wooden planks, the clinking of spoons in bowls while our mother, with a fixed expression in a series of automated gestures, serves our tartines of bread and jam and Van Houten warm chocolate milk because, *Here you go children, you have to eat.*

In the kitchen, there are five of us sitting silently together in an expression of solidarity. My younger brothers are only three and twelve months old, yet Patrick, the baby, also stays quiet, as if he somehow understood the gravity of the situation. On this morning, we do not fight among ourselves to be the first to turn on the radio. As a matter of fact, the radio has nothing to say. Outside, a trace of blue is dawning amid the clouds. Our father lies cowering by the phone on the varnished parquet floor. His behavior frightens us. We have never seen him this way, motionless, and draped in a silence that progressively penetrates every single room in the apartment.

Overwhelmed as they were by the affliction, neither he nor our mother took the time to explain what had happened. They didn't even think about promising, as is often done with children, to explain later on. *You'll understand one day . . . When you are older, I will tell you all about it . . .* But did we really need to know? We understood the essential fact: a tragedy had just discolored the blue sky in our life. I realized that the echo of death had stormed the phone cables and exploded into the handset by striking down the pillar in my life. And this echo, more than even the death, was more daunting because of its inconceivable magnitude. The sweetness of laughter, joy, and happiness were only on loan: they could be retracted. While, alongside my brothers and sister, I drank my hot chocolate in silence, a few steps away from my crushed father, the soft padding of my childhood was losing a bit of its density. My eyes were wide open and I was advancing unwillingly, yet in a most decisive step, toward the age of reason.

Years would go by before I would recall this day and revisit these images. A whole lifetime. I would have to begin writing this book to finally understand the memory of those screams. In the meantime, they were muffled by a little secret song that parents sing to their children to protect them—and to protect themselves—from what is just far too painful. A little song whose lyrics went like this: Once upon a time there were two brothers born in Cameroon, in the time of colonialism, who would later on discover the New World of Independence. Fifteen years separated them. They were nothing without each other. They had the good fortune to pursue, one following the other, higher education in Europe. They both had the ambition to serve their country and that is what they did, each in his own way. The elder brother came back home and practiced medicine and entered into politics while the younger one stayed overseas, preparing to reconnect with his big brother. Until . . .

At this point in the story, the song is interrupted because the death of the big brother had occurred. I might have stopped the story with this version of history because, as all children know, there are questions that are best not pursued, promises about stories that you shouldn't count on or insist on knowing. I even suspect that children know, intuitively, that their role, in these kinds of circumstances, is to distract the adults from the unbearable weight of the loss and to give rise to, between the scattered pieces of their broken parents' hearts, new trees, palm trees, papaya trees, a greener forest. A coffin vanishes to the bottom of the ocean. Explanations never come about, the story is never told, and, to top it all off, parents pass on in turn taking with them whatever meaning could be attributed to what they had lived through in the past. What else can you do but write to re-create the secrets and taboos?

Because memory can create revolutions: it spins around us in a spiral, right up until we stop and take notice and finally begin to make sense of it, grasp its gyrating meaning. The spiral whispered to me, by its persistent rotation, that tragedy had invited itself into my family story, like burning hot, bitter cold pepper. It had turned the destiny of two brothers upside down, plunging the one into complete darkness and the other into the fullness of light. It was no longer possible to remain in this comfort zone in which I had taken refuge for so many years, trotting out the pretty story I had been told. The trajectories of both my father and my uncle were reflected in my personal dual geography.

In the depth of this story, in the depth of the water, there is a recurrent preliminary question that makes it so that I belong to this land without really belonging to it or without completely belonging to it, an inquiry that invites me to pursue my other borders and places me in a peculiar state. *Where do you come from? Where are you originally from?* I have been asked this question all my life. Sometimes it was asked unexpectedly. Other times, I could almost anticipate it coming. Since I was born—a whole life!—people have been asking me: *Your name, where is your name from?* A sweet name, yes, which means "the tides," the regular and plural movement of the waters that, from one continent to another, create the connection between my places of origin.

French origins, Parisian, but also Cameroonian because I'm always sent back to this space, even while it is six thousand kilometers away from here, and also because, for eighteen years, I have held in my hands a residence permit that means, "You were born here, but you are not from here." I want to show my loyalty to my second homeland, and so I navigate somewhere in that direction, toward this imaginary place that connects with an enormous arm of the sea. I feel great there. I float, I wait, I drift on my back while I look at the stars that are no doubt projecting the same brightness from one continent to another.

In the depth, at the bottom of the water of this text, there is a man who has disappeared into obscurity but reconnected to another, propelled into the light, and both men are holding each other's hands. The first man is my uncle Marcel; the second, my father Francis.

In the depth, at the bottom of the water of this text, there is a question mark. At first it is plump and courteous then it straightens up, charges straight ahead and imperiously poses the questions: Why did I grow up in this country? I know very well, my parents met each other here. But why did they choose to live far away from their country and their people? As a matter of fact, did they choose? Do we ever choose the place where we will spend the greater part of our lives? Or do we merely let ourselves be carried by waves that deposit each of us where he or she must find his or her way from sand to solid ground, on which we build a life?

As a child, I was always hearing talk about *going back*. Returning *to the house*. In the Douala language, *mboa* means both "the house" and "the country," a country rid of its administrative scales, taking on different shades of affection.

My parents lived, I believe, happily, and my father, like Ulysses, took a long journey, which took him from one shore of the Atlantic to numerous other coasts. But his return, this famous return to *mboa*, never did take place. It transformed into a myth and hung, suspended onto the firmament of those ultimate ambitions, for eternity. My parents had landed by water, there where they thought they would be taking a respite in the middle of their journey. That landing became precisely where they would moor and leave the algae to attach itself to the anchor, the salt to erode away their certitudes, while the return boat vanished into the distant horizon.

At least that was what I believed for a long time. Until I was driven to learn more, which came about in my later years. I began to inquire further back in time, before the story of my family. And there my pirogue glides into the silence of the night. I plunge the paddle into the water in a rhythmic movement. The waves wrinkle the reflections of the moon but what does it matter: the only thing that matters are the rays of light that give meaning to my crossing. Gently, propelled by my determination, I advance and try to piece together the thread of a story silenced for far too long . . . I wash up ashore on the beach. I walk on the sand where there are traces of footsteps: My uncle? My father? In the distance, if I prick up my ears, I can hear a melody.

I have to dig, rummage through the sand of the lagoon, take in the smell of the land, inquire without really fully understanding what I am looking for in the tall grass, go back to the estuary of the river to find the shadow of an instrument floating amid the waves, a flute made from papaya leaves with notes that fade away far too quickly, or a stethoscope, sucked up by an underground whirlwind, try to understand how men of their caliber could disappear one bright morning into the deep waters of memory, when their names ought to be chiseled into the marble of monuments attributed to the dead in their country.

Set the record straight. Thumb my nose up at the injustice of it all. Put an end to the silence that holds people back from being proud of who they are. Honor the memory, so that, in turn, I too can raise my head up and say:

– You see, these here were my people. Aren't they worthy of recognition, belonging as they did to some of humanity's most beautiful creations? You're unaware of it but they had names, they were "Big Somebodies," as they like to say nowadays in the African streets, and they valiantly confronted, head on, the questions raised by their times.

And I would have had to wait for a long time—perhaps to be ready—to really look into this part of my family history of which I knew practically nothing. I am walking. I've left the beach. I am standing beneath the canopy of the equatorial forest. And my uncle is here too, planted among the trees. His name was Marcel and Eyidi, his African first name. This second first name has the allure of a euonym and means "forest" in Douala. One day in 1966, his star shot up far beyond the canopy.

And here I am, standing beneath these trees, looking to illuminate a bit of the sky of leaves, to put the words and names on my Jeanne d'Arc and my very own Vercingétorix. It's a vertiginous feeling to reclaim this memory from which I had been dispossessed as a little girl, my parents having sought to protect me from a suffering that they didn't wish to bequeath to me as a legacy. They succeeded. Yet you better believe I have a responsibility to stand

here, standing guard before this screen, and take note that these people—
they came, they saw, and their victory is made apparent in these documented
words so many years later, to commemorate them.

I would come to understand, looking back, why my father aimed for the
moon with the neck of his guitar and how my uncle lost his way, in his desperate longing, hoping to save his sick country from the avatars of colonialism.

−7−

My parents sent money orders to Douala. That Saturday evening in Paris, they organized a wake and numerous people streamed into the apartment, starting from mid-afternoon until late into the night. I stood in the entranceway at times when the door opened, and I would watch some women abruptly change their demeanor. Eyes that would be dry a moment ago suddenly flooded with tears, and they would collapse while crying into my father's arms, who I could sense was completely annoyed by the theatrics of sadness. *Ayoooo! Mba ndé, hééé . . . Ay! Woe is me!* cried these near professional mourners. Our sizeable living room teemed with adults dressed in their Sunday best. We had to borrow chairs from the next-door neighbors. Conversations, initially hushed, became increasingly loud. Bowls of peanuts got passed around along with fried plantains, cans of beer, meat brochettes, and fruit. Some people spoke about the dearly departed. Otherwise, sadness soon gave way to the pleasure of getting together to talk about what was going on now and indeed in the home country. People even got carried away in laughter before regaining control of their composure. Eventually everyone started trickling out, closing out the evening farewells with a final sorrowful expression. During those long hours, Francis's facial expression remained tense.

That Sunday evening, someone called to share how the funeral ceremony was carried out. Laconic, my father listened but did not shed a tear, and soon retired to his bedroom. The next morning, his silence weighed heavily as he got ready to head to work. The weight of his silence would persist for weeks. We did our best to stay out of his way, making sure when we were around to make the least possible noise, and went to bed without making a scene when our mother asked us to do so. In response to our worrying stares, she would simply say:

– Your father can't get past it. *A'a senga ndutu*, he is suffering.

We had some very odd weeks at home. Perhaps it was only a few days, to be honest, but to us it felt like weeks. During the summer, an unexpected jolt would come and shake up the ambient lethargy. The owner of our apartment announced that his daughter was getting married and his wedding gift to her was going to be a home. He needed to have the apartment back. That evening when Francis came home from work, he found his wife quite anxious.

– I'm telling you, *igni*. That's exactly how he put it to me, assuring me that Paris is filled with empty apartments and that we'd have no problem finding a place to live.
– In any event, we do need a bigger place, Francis responded reassuringly. With five kids, we need more space. Listen, we're going to look around and we'll find something, and in any case we don't have a choice. But I promise you, if we don't find something, no worries, we'll go back home. Empty-handed if we have to, but that's what we'll do. We should have done that ages ago. Perhaps destiny is giving us a nudge to forge full steam ahead.

So just like that, he was ready to seize upon the stroke of fate to put an end to our stay in Europe. Let life make the decision for him, so to speak. And too bad if the return home didn't trumpet a triumph, because, in any event, the one person who meant the most to him was gone . . . *If we don't find something, no worries, we'll go back home.* Was that how the decision was made? Was that how our return transformed into a myth, an eternal return whose date was never fixed and would be endlessly postponed? Wasn't it really because it was too dangerous to go back? Marcel's friends had called to give some news, explain his death—if one can imagine there was something more to explain—but also to say, in veiled terms, because everyone was also mindful of phone tapping, that the family name carried the scent of state treason and that having that name was simply not a *good* thing. It was best to wait.

Was this how my father wound up, once more, waiting for the life he imagined, as it passed him like a train going through a station at full speed, without stopping, as he stood on the platform? He finally chose to take a special train, his very own space shuttle, headed for an entirely different destination than the one that had initially been planned.

Francis visited many apartments and remained completely laid-back during the whole process. Looking for an apartment was a real ordeal, but he was prepared to confront the owners' expressions, at times surprised to see him and trying to conceal their distrust or disappointment. He had gotten rid of his Cameroonian accent over time and could thus create an illusion by phone and at least get the chance to schedule a visit before showing up in his reassuringly smart suit with his UNESCO pay slips tucked under his arm. Often the apartment *had just been rented*, but what did he care, he felt above it all. He would deflect with a flight-attendant smile and return the sender's disdain, if necessary—have it ricochet. Like the chutzpah Sidney Poitier portrayed in the film *In the Heat of the Night*. Meanwhile, our mother packed up our lives into boxes without knowing whether the boxes would be on a plane to the home country or wind up in a new Parisian living room. And during that carefree summer, we galloped around from one room to the other, playing hide-and-seek games amid all the objects and scattered furniture: the Vendean doll dressed in the typical folkloric attire from the region, the miniature chalet from the Alps, wooden napkin rings each carved with our first names, the wax tablecloth in red and white gingham from the kitchen, the kora brought back from a trip to Mali, the Moroccan ottoman pouf, the *alghaita*, the oboe from Chad with a nasal tang. In the final days, at the very last minute, Francis and Madé found what they were looking for: a five-room apartment on a small, quiet street in the thirteenth arrondissement. Francis was overjoyed.

– We don't have the option to buy it so it's still not really ours, but at least,
since we are renting from a real estate company, the owner can't just evict us
at the slightest whim. It's ours for seven years.

A lease! We moved to 18, rue du Champ de l'Alouette, fourth floor on the left getting out of the elevator. "On the right, if you walk up the stairs," Marcel Jr. said by phone with the seriousness of a butler. The luxury building had just been built, and we were among the first tenants. Before the furniture arrived, our father took us to see the premises. He parked the car at the entrance and turned toward us and gave us a lecture in a serious tone. Besides my youngest brother, swaddled in my mother's arms, we were all seated in a row on the backseat of the white Ford Taunus.

– Children, I want you to take note, your school is less than five minutes by
foot from here and the public library is not too far away either. You won't
need to make a lot of effort to go study. And believe me, I know what

I'm talking about. It was entirely different for me. When I was a boy, I had to walk for a long time to get to school. So, I'm counting on you to do your best at school. It's important to realize how lucky you are.

I tried to understand the deep meaning of this particular injunction, but I was only five years old and, like most children, I couldn't possibly imagine a life worse than mine. I believed that parents were lucky to have so much power: to give us orders, give us an earful when they wished, and punish us as they saw fit. The condition of the child was, from my point of view, often the difficult one to live. I did try all the same to imagine what my father must have experienced on the way to school in his time. *You should realize how lucky you are!* I frowned. What kind of stupid country obliges children to walk a long distance to get to school? I just didn't get it. I had a hard time trying to imagine this experience and comparing my fate to that of my father's, I struggled to understand what he was trying to get at. Especially because he had told us on more than one occasion that instead of going to school, he had deliberately chosen to skip school—an option he made absolutely clear we did not have . . . So when he started up the car again, he noticed my expression in the rearview mirror.

– You're frowning, huh? That's good. I can see that you're thinking.

He gave me a smile of complicity that, while discreet, didn't escape any of us. It had been a long time since we had seen a smile coming from the corners of his lips. That summer of 1966 the sun had disappeared into a huge black hole, and I had just caught a glimpse of the promise of a less somber season. I heaved a sigh of relief. *Of course I will put my best foot forward, I will work as hard as I can, you can count on me, papa. You can count on us.* If that was what it would take to have clear blue skies, we would do anything to please our father.

Mid-September, I entered the preschool on rue Paul-Gervais for the first time. Right from the start, I was completely won over by the grounds. The austere appearance of the building appealed to me. I loved how silence reigned once the bell rang out to mark the end of playtime. I enjoyed the fact that we had tasks to complete, following a planned schedule: gather on the school banks; roll call; choir singing; listening to a story, discussion session; gymnastics; toilet runs; washing hands; lunchtime . . . All of it was documented in a personalized preschool notebook that brought together the traces of our activities and gave me the impression, when I flipped through it, of being a subject that one might have talked about on televised news. A grown-up, as it were.

I loved being the child with a schoolbag, who slipped on her pinafore to go and live a parallel life between walls to which my parents had no access. Which is why I liked keeping secret the details of our school activities. I liked hiding the work I created with great brush strokes on sheets of white paper that covered the walls of the classroom. I wouldn't say a word about what we painted, molded, or cooked. I only opened up to a few well-chosen confidantes—my dolls and my teddy bears—and I took particular pleasure in raising, ever so slightly, the veil for my parents. After all, was I made privy to the conversations they murmured to each other in their room at night?

In truth, I lived each moment in the present with such intensity that even the lunch menu was forgotten once it was snack time in the afternoon. (But I love pretending that I do remember.) *You might have said that . . . We carried on as if . . . It would be . . .* I saw myself cheerfully skipping along to school, happy to get to Ms. Lucas's class, who was my teacher at that time. Thanks to her, I learned to sing my heart out to ritornellos and old French songs; and I painted, absent of any mastery of my movement. *Cadet Rousselle a trois maisons.* Life was beautiful at school. Work felt like play and when we would go out to the playground, every day there was a new intrigue to delight in. My classmates and I tried to unravel the mystery of the rustling of Ms. Torchon's skirt, the lunch lady with an imposing behind. We lived in fear of what she might do with the dishcloth on her shoulder. I went from fear to love when, at first sight, my heart started to beat for Christophe Laisné, in my eyes the most handsome student in the class. I would spend hours during break time moping around. Would he notice me? Who could I confide in?

Before the Christmas holidays, my parents were invited to meet my teacher. To my great surprise, the message written and signed in red in my report card immediately stirred up concern. My parents took this meeting rather seriously, as if it were a confrontation with the administration. The week prior to the meeting was spent going back and forth in conjectures:

– Did you do something wrong? What happened? my father asked me.
– I better not have any reason to be ashamed of you! my mother mumbled, on edge. What will people think of us?

So much so that in the end I began to wonder myself. What were they going to accuse me of? Did Ms. Lucas or, even worse, Ms. Torchon have reason to reproach me? Had someone figured out, watching the way my eyes ran all over my secret crush, that I had feelings for him? On the evening of the scheduled meeting, my parents waited in the school entrance, looking quite uptight. They were clearly imagining they were going to have to justify themselves. But for what? Nothing was ever really a given in this country when you were visibly foreigners. In anticipation of the meeting, my mother had slipped on her Sunday attire and twirled up a rather sophisticated chignon. Terrified, I attended the meeting, standing stiff in the classroom a few steps away from the adults. The teacher opened a large folder of drawings and showed my paintings as she kindly asserted:

> – Your child feels at home here. She's doing quite well. Look at this! And furthermore, she is great with her classmates. Her behavior is irreproachable. She is a really smart girl.

Taken aback by the compliments, my parents relaxed and looked closely at my work before giving me a tender warm gaze.

> – We're proud of you! Back home, you don't get to meet with the teachers like that for no reason, they admitted to me on the way home. We weren't really worried . . .

As for me, I felt like it had been a close call. "Smart!" Now there's a word that gave me some relief and, like a talisman, had the power to reassure my parents. But it also made me aware of what was at stake, the magnitude of which I was barely beginning to fully grasp. Don't be fooled little girl, school is far from being a mere playground, a place for creativity and games and pleasures: you're also going to school to represent your people brilliantly and therefore your behavior must be exemplary to avoid the risk of shame. Symbolically, you are continuing the destiny of former beneficiaries of *l'école des Blancs*, who have spent their whole lives proving that they are worthy of the faith that had been placed in them.

What do you do when you become aware that school is extremely important in your family and you are holding the wisdom card in your hand? Tails, you make every possible effort to meet the expectations that the word implies, and you settle into the position that makes everyone happy—parents, teachers, friends, and family. Heads, you keep clear of the beacons and you take on an even more daring path and let the little girl, eager for freedom, run free. But already this country was starting to mold me, holding me to behave well;

I was realizing that no matter where I went, I might draw attention, become the object of gazes, amicable, tender, curious, kind, distant, or condescending. In the game of prince and princesses, I knew I was never going to get the role of Snow White. So there I was, off to conquer a space that was already circumscribed by parental demands and expectations, with the desire to please them so that I would be loved. I also hoped to reassure those I loved by offering a proud vision of a bright future.

As I walked back home feeling triumphant, holding my parents' hands, I was ready more than ever before to play the role they envisioned for me. A role that proved, moreover, to being a generator of far-reaching smiles . . . My father seemed to be gradually coming out from under the paralysis in which mourning had plunged him. My school results, along with those of my brothers and sister, lightened him up and reassured him. He may have been living far from his home country but at least he had managed to pass on the rule his brother had taught to him: work hard, succeed, shine. This was the only way forward; there was no other option. Prepared to play by the rules, I was to going to put my whole heart and soul into cheering up my dear father, who was still heartbroken. Who knows, perhaps I could become the good fairy who, with a wave of beautiful drawings and Cadet Rousselle, would be able to spritz a perfume of insouciance right to his aching heart. And take away the pain.

Two years went by and I was now hopping and skipping all the way to school. The journey was short, but I would reinvent new routes in my mind, transforming a dark strip of asphalt into a countryside pathway, which I inspected each day. I would be very offended when dog droppings marred the habitual cleanliness. In the evenings, I would use a stone, or a branch from the nearest square, to move the ignominy out of my way with a disgusted pout. Then I would invoke the gods of the sky to make it rain and carry away the unspeakable, foul-smelling spots. In every single respect, I wanted to exemplify my perfection.

On the way to school, my younger brother, Patrick, was never in good spirits. Our mother would hold his hand firmly the entire journey and, when necessary, apply a few little taps on his buttocks whenever he tried to make a run for it and head back home. Childhood memories are like dreams, strewn together with exaggerations. I also see my brother take off into the air like a balloon: a single tap elevates him, and before you know it, off he goes soon disappearing into the rays of azure-colored sunlight. While on my way to school each morning I see my path adorned with flowers and my ears are reverberating with instruments from an imaginary brass band, my brother, on the other hand, is screaming, holding the entire world hostage to his anger. To no avail. School is super important, Patrick, can't you see that? It's the only real way: it's the one of effort and personal measure. No one can really avoid it.

> – We probably won't have much else to leave you, our parents explained, if not the ability to make a life for yourselves on your own: by working hard. Don't ever forget that.

I've been hearing these words ever since I was very young. All five of us would hear these words so often that they ended up taking on the value of Gospel. There is no other choice but to pass through this way, to go to school, to head to the nearest library, study, succeed. Be as brilliant as you can be.

And in this way, you will be loved?

The summer leading up to first grade, my mother taught me to read. I had no desire for my parents to stop reading stories to me and to have to start doing so myself. So I began to hate the little black marks that were being scribbled all over the pages. All I wanted to do was play with my dolls, go outside to the square and join my brothers playing games of hide-and-seek and manhunt for hours on end. Thousands of things appealed to me for sure, but reading was not one of them. Unfortunately my mother was determined to get the mystery of the alphabet into my head, and naturally I had to submit to her will: were I to behave otherwise, I would have been cooked. Every day she had me sit on a low stool and repeat after her. For better or for worse, I ventured into the labyrinth of the words of *Mamadou et Bineta*, a textbook about two children living in an improbable African country.

Did my mother really think the context was enough to interest me or was it more that the book appealed to her because it was a reminder of her first years in school? Two years prior, my older brother had had to submit to the same "grin and bear it" exercise with the very same textbook, and I would remember my sister also undergoing a similar process the following year.

Tears streamed down my cheeks as I tried my hardest to grasp, in vain, the meaning of the words. The images meant nothing to me either. I didn't understand any of it and kept asking myself, when my attention wandered off the page, why my mother, usually so kind, had transformed into the Hound of Hades, determined not to let me get past the threshold, insofar as I had not succeeded in clearly associating the letters *A* and *B*. Every afternoon I was being tortured, achieving miserable results, unable to relax, my mind blocked by a resistance that was all the more mysterious because it was unintentional. And each time my mother was more insistent to slog it out further. The start of the new school year was approaching, and I still didn't know how to read. Every so often my older siblings would slip into the room where I was learning, under the pretext of picking up a toy, and try to whisper a word or give me a hint after quickly glancing at the page. My mother would clearly notice these maneuvers, become angry, and the session would inevitably end in tears.

Shopping for the new school year was a great distraction for all of us from the general tension. Our mother would take us to the stores close to place Denfert Rochereau. That year, I would not only inherit my sister's clothes, which were still wearable, but I would also be fully equipped from head to toe to highlight my entrance into elementary school. At La Toile d'Avion, on avenue du Général-Leclerc, we deliberated for some time over shirts with raglan sleeves, Peter Pan collars, smocked dresses, bias-cut skirts, jumpers, and thin polo-neck sweaters in Tergal, wool, jersey, polyamide, nylon, Rhovyl, and fine-ribbed corduroy . . . The sales girls talked up the virtues of each piece, capable of lasting for several seasons.

On the first day of the school year, I finally discovered elementary school. Intimidated, I sat beside a classmate who bragged about having more school supplies than me. "I have glue, do you have any? And colored pencils, you too?" I tried really hard to pull off a disdainful pout, but I didn't get very far with it. Was I really going to have to spend my days in this room with tables arranged in tight rows before a podium and a big blackboard? Where were the jars of paint and the wide sheets of paper I used to express myself so freely in preschool? The teacher took the roll call and wrote the date on the board, which I immediately hastened to try to say out loud. The simple gesture of raising my hand nevertheless made me nervous. Shortly afterward, the school principal entered the classroom and we all got up from our seats, as if we were one person. A private discussion ensued and a chin was pointed in my direction. Finally, the principal pointed at me and ordered me to gather my belongings.

– Young lady, you know how to read, you're skipping a grade.

I looked at the blackboard and realized that the words written there meant something to me: "Monday 14 September. It's back to school." Likewise, I was suddenly able to decipher on the big geography map hanging on the wall, the words, Auvergne, Loire, Seine, Paris Basin . . . I had finally achieved, without realizing it, the mission imparted to me by my mother. I could read. Last evening, I still hadn't been able to do so. All of a sudden, the words were as clear as my mother's goal. Being able to read was useful after all: to outshine my fellow classmates and, at the same time, make my parents proud of my progress. I gathered my belongings and left my seat, head held high, in front of my classmate sitting next to me, who was taken aback. It was my turn to show off.

With the beginning of elementary school, a new epoch began for me in which the enchanted veil of childhood was torn away each day a little more to bring into view a reality whose contours were increasingly defined. Every little detail about life seemed to come out of nowhere and stick brutally to my retinas and lead to yet another interpretation. Symbolically, I had let go of my mother's hand and my map of the world was getting bigger. The universe was no longer confined to our apartment and to school but expanded to the streets, to buildings, and to the neighborhood shops. Each object, each fact, each person crossed in my childhood began to take on a place and make sense in a puzzle that increasingly revealed a complex reality.

As soon as a visitor came to the house, I would perch on the barstool in the living room, with my imaginary spectacles on, my microscope adjusted, and begin to take notice of thousands of little details that I hadn't spotted before: the darkness on the upper lip of Auntie Grace, the one whose first name I couldn't conceive of writing without including the double *ss* to underscore the width of her size; the messy head of hair of a guest whose scruffy artist attire left a lot to be desired, according to my mother at least; the nail polish color of a woman who smoked using a cigarette holder . . .

I set up a second observation station behind the window in the dining room. At the end of the day, once I had completed my homework, I got into the habit of staying hidden there for a good stretch of time, tucked by the net curtain and the double curtains, on the lookout for any movement in the streets and the comings and goings in the buildings facing us. I had a keen interest in the people in the neighborhood: the twin girls on the third floor, the boy who went out every evening on a baguette run. And when an unexpected event did take place, the surprise of it got me all shaking with excitement.

One day a majestic catafalque passed through the entrance to a building. Excited by this novelty, I lay in wait for the curtains to this new theatrical scene. Who died? That was the least of it for me. What I hoped to have the chance to see was the coffin leaving, accompanied by people dressed in dark attire or wearing armbands to mark their affliction. That evening at dinner, I took advantage of the opportunity to shine by asking my parents to explain to me the meaning of the different colors. Ignorant of my ambitions as a detective, they congratulated me on my curiosity: they considered anything that could further enhance our French knowledge and culture a godsend. I learned that red roses signified passion, and no one other than my father should offer them to my mother. I also learned that yellow clothing, whose extramarital meaning escaped me, were suggestive, in slang terms that were never to be spoken beneath our roof.

On exceptional days, I was lucky enough to see our streets taken over by the troops of the National Guard. I would call out to my brothers and sister, completely excited, to have them come and see the riders in their red and blue uniforms and the impressive croups of the horses and their flaring nostrils. The show was over in no time, and as the sound of the clip-clopping hooves diminished into the distance, we commented as we made disgusted faces at the want for good manners of these animals, who despite all their great panache, could not help but mark their passage by leaving horse manure in the streets. From my lookout point, by squinting my eyes and leaning forward through the window—when no one was looking, because technically I was not allowed to open the window—I could almost see each end of the street. However, very often my gaze was fixed on the building facing us, on the housing project where families of modest means, as the adults liked to say, resided.

During these autumn and winter nights, when the apartment interiors were lit up and stairwells evoked luminous spinal columns, I tried to imagine the lives of others. What were they doing? What did the inside of their homes look like? Did they eat at the same time as we did and similar meals? Did they also get packages from the provinces—as we did from Africa, thanks to someone's journey there—packages of pulses or grains you couldn't find in Paris, ingredients that had been affectionately put together by the women in the family, from far away, so that the women *from here* could prepare their meals as they did *over there*?

From one question to another and from one detail to the next, I would get lost in these obsessive prospects. Did they have, as we do in our living room, a velvet brown, four-seat sofa next to a black, imitation-leather, swivel arm-chair? Did they place their guests' glasses of whiskey on stacked coffee tables? Did they own ashtrays like ours, whose buttons in the middle pulled the butts down by twirling it downward?

In their bedrooms, did my classmates do their homework sitting at desks, fitted with architecture-styled reading lamps, then go to sleep in bunk beds? Were their bedroom walls covered in the same Vénilia washable wallpaper as ours? In our home, the wallpaper for the girls' room was dominated by a moss-green color. Thousands of tiny flowers seemed to compete for their place. The walls of the boys' room looked like wooden-ribbed planks. In the girls' room, posters of classical dancers covered the walls. In the boys' room, there was Jacques Anquetil, Eddy Merckx, King Pelé, a map of the stages of the Tour de France, and posters of animals carefully removed from the center spread of the *Télé 7 Jours* weekly magazine.

The foyer to our apartment was covered with orange, brown, and yellow wallpaper with a pattern of rounded rectangles that could play tricks on your eyes. In the living room, my parents had put together louvered metal shelves that were placed against the wall and progressively filled with books and doz-ens of records my father kept accumulating.

What did other people eat at home? What did they talk about at the table? Did the young children have the right to speak? Did they have to do as we did at home, which is to say, let the adults speak first and only open their mouths to answer a question?

It would be a long time before I would have the least idea of what happened on the opposite side of the street. In those days, classmates hardly invited each other over and when, by chance, it did occur, it was organized between the mothers first. We would spend one or two long weeks waiting impatiently for the days to go by before a child's birthday party would finally take place. Then it became a really big deal because, first of all, what do you wear? How do you dress to show your respect to the host family without looking like you are all done up in your Sunday best? Personally, the fact that I didn't have to wear a pinafore as I did for school during the week was enough to make it an exceptional outing.

My mother would drive me to the given address, and during the journey she would repeat the rules of proper conduct I ought to display. When you greet someone lower your eyes, hold yourself up with your back straight. Smile, as a matter of good manners. Do not take a second serving of any dish, no matter how tempting the cake is, and refuse by saying "no thank you" neither too quietly nor too loudly so that I could be heard articulating clearly. Help to clear the table. Play without getting all worked up. Don't make a scene when they would come to pick me up. Don't get involved in any disputes and most certainly do not get into a fight. Answer to adults politely. Avoid asking them questions. Avoid having to go to the restroom and, if I did, make sure the toilet was clean after I was finished. Ask to wash my hands afterward if there wasn't a sink in the toilet . . .

The to-do list of social etiquette was interminable, yet I knew them all by heart; and if it turned out I hadn't heard one or two of them, I could take a guess because I had completely integrated the golden rules of how we ought to conduct ourselves in *this country*. Because it was about *this country* where, as the guests we were, we owed it to ourselves to behave well at all times.

Our parents did a lot of entertaining. Between the ever-expanding Cameroonian family of uncles, aunties, close and distant cousins, and the work colleagues from UNESCO, there was also the endless comings and goings of a good number of relations and acquaintances. Just as my mother had seen it done when she was growing up, she was always ready to invite that person to join us, who had spent the entire afternoon chatting and was still around when dinnertime came.

Our dining room was now filled with a number of bourgeois objects, symbols of wealth even: a long, wooden china cabinet; porcelain dishes; cutlery; tablecloths; and even placemats. In the top part of the china cabinet, behind the sliding glass doors, there was a collection of glasses that my sister and I were responsible for keeping crystal clear every Saturday morning. These glasses were brought out according to the occasion, the type of drink, and the importance of the dinner guests. It was also essential to be able to arrange them on a drinks trolley without running the risk of shamefully discovering that a spot of water had marred a glass that ought to be sparkling.

Thanks to the small, square Marabout Flash collection, our mother regularly decoded the rules of the art of entertaining and French *savoir-vivre*. For the "important occasions," when you have to, for example, "entertain your husband's boss," she placed "the little plates in the big ones," as well as double or triple series of cutlery, for the fish, the meat, and the cheese. Of course, she would prepare "an exotic meal," but also include some French dishes so as not to make guests feel uncomfortable, especially those who were less inclined to culinary explorations. Glasses multiplied alongside the plates, and I was requisitioned to fold the table napkins according to the rules of art learned at school in home economics. Certain details sent me into an abyss of queries. What in the world could "VSOP" possibly mean on the Courvoisier cognac bottles?

More and more, the adult world gave me the impression of a circuitous mountain route on the edge of a precipice due to the hypercorrection, in every aspect, in the way we expressed ourselves and in how we carried ourselves. For our parents as well as for us, who were supposed to demonstrate how well brought up we were, each event became the occasion to show that we had understood and integrated all the different social norms. The constant nervousness, this caution mixed in with potential criticism, the need to be vigilant at all times to make sure you did everything well—in other words, perfection—day in day out of the image we gave of ourselves and, by way of our own representation, that of all Africans . . .

At the same time, we were also meant to be fully schooled and ready to apply a number of the principles of the society of our origins. Speaking the Douala language was the first of these. But if the daily practice of a language proved viable among the seven speakers we were, learning the everyday Douala customs and practices proved more difficult, living in Paris and managing our Douala greenhouse. This became clear in the form of injunctions whose meanings would completely escape us children and take us by surprise at times. One Sunday, for example, while dining with guests, Francis carved up the chicken then served each person a portion, accompanied by rice and fried plantains. I bit enthusiastically into the crispy skin and the fleshy leg before breaking the bone and sucking the marrow with relish as, apparently, my grandmother used to do.

– Who wants the gizzard? My father asked, sweeping the table in a circular glance.

I held up my plate eagerly, but he pushed it back and declared in an irrefutable manner:

– *Kem*, no, Madame Kidi. Not you, he said in Douala.

Seeing my crestfallen expression, he added:

– Back home, girls don't eat the gizzard. They don't have the right.

At first I was silent, offended, and let time allow this new law to make its way into my thinking. Then I made a feeble attempt to argue, evoking equality between men and women while my older brother, jeering, swept up a portion of the giblets and my father took the rest. Why should the women forego the pleasure of eating chicken gizzards? My father got annoyed and reminded me of my place as a child.

– *O si mènè pon nyolo bu!* You've got quite a nerve!
– That's how it is, back home, my mother kindly concluded. It's not up for discussion.

I wound up having to keep a lid on it but not without giving her the evil eye. How can you embrace injustice and accept the unacceptable? And that was how the home country took up its very own seat at our table, far away and damned elsewhere, but whose reality was fixed such that it was never called into question. Today, I understand that by respecting the practices of their youth, my parents were trying their best to teach us a way of being as well as making clear to themselves—or to their guests—that they were staying loyal to their origins, full members of the family of the *bana'a mboa*, the children of the home country, despite the distance, as we constituted a branch on the genealogical tree. It was about preserving an intangible asset, not losing this other place that was gathered deep within, and by way of your offspring, being able to perpetuate it as if, at any given moment, you should be able to go back home and immediately integrate into the society you left behind, and that this imagined return could be facilitated by this immortalization of the "African education."

For us, as children, the art of growing up consisted in shifting between the *mboa* and the *mbènguè* borders, "home" and "Europe." We had to learn and/ or guess the different details and subtleties between them. In raising us, our parents went about doing what they thought they were doing over there, according to principles that had been applied during their childhood: a certain severity, a great moral fortitude that translated into maxims, spoken at the first opportunity—We must not . . . One should not . . . Whomever does this, will have that . . . A young lady carries herself like this . . . In our home, a brave boy doesn't cry . . .

To this panoply of wisdom were added those gleaned from the French tradition, which appealed to them because they shored up a similar stance.

Raising children was like the art of gardening: provide water to the sapling but also be sure to prune it; set it upright and in case it needed help, use a stake to support it so that it didn't just grow every which way. You had to watch out, for any signs of laziness. Every morning our father greeted us with a resounding voice:

– Rise and shine little lambs! The early bird catches the worm . . .

Those expressions were to be understood literally. God help whoever had decided to prolong their night in the arms of Morpheus. Sleep-ins did not exist in our home: we had to quell our inclination for a lazy day hanging around in one room or another in pajamas and nightgowns. That kind of fantasy was an exception, reserved for the morning after parties, like Christmas Eve. Exceptions aside, every day we had to get up and get everything done that was expected of us, from personal hygiene to the shared chores.

Our mother had no intention of being dominated by her little troop, and each of us had to complete, according to our age, the chores that were assigned to us. That was how, with age, more and more responsibilities kept piling on my shoulders. Growing up proved less pleasant for my sister and me: we had to devote our time to preparing meals while my brothers had lighter tasks or, better yet, were left to go off and play.

Before so much injustice, I quickly developed a salient feminist consciousness, which was reinforced at the least occasion of an ambient fatalism. I squarely took on and refuted one by one the ready-made formulas my brothers would trot out at will: a young lady does this; a young lady must do that; you have to suffer to be beautiful . . . Fortunately, equality was usually reestablished when our mother gathered us all for the biannual major cleaning of the kitchen or bathrooms, from top to bottom. The idea of a whole day devoted to emptying the kitchen of everything, then washing and making every single corner of the walls and cupboards shine, annoyed us in the strongest possible terms, but we submitted to it without ever daring to complain.

Numerous other chores punctuated our lives: making our beds and tucking in the covers correctly, sweeping our rooms and the other rooms in the apartment, vacuuming the carpets, scrubbing the toilets, the bathtub, removing the dust with a sponge, cloth, and feather duster, disinfecting the kitchen floor with a damp cloth soaked in bleach, setting and clearing the table, washing, rinsing, drying, and putting away the dishes. We were doing chores to the point where I suspected my parents of having brought us into this world just so that we would carry them out. Nothing was more unbearable than that moment when I would be completely relaxing and an adult voice would travel across the apartment ordering us to *come here, right now!*

These interruptions were like a Machiavellian cavalry, planned precisely in the moment when, in the middle of a board game, I was about to move a pawn or put my card down on the table. And I had to have the wherewithal to hold back my sighs of exasperation so as not to be seen as a brazen child . . . There was, however, one duty I completed with pleasure: doing the shopping. On those days, I stepped out enthusiastically, proud of my responsibility and happy for my freedom. The simple idea of going out to buy bread or a few slices of ham expanded my world, gave me the feeling that I was out to conquer the world. In my pinafore or in home clothes—pajamas, nightgown, and a pair of slippers—I would dash into the staircase and gallop right to the bakery, A. Jeanne, or to the creamery, Boulanger et fils, at the other end of the street. I would arrive, out of breath, and slide into the line behind a woman whose hair rollers were peeking out from beneath her scarf. Once I got to the register, intimidated and overwhelmed because of the responsibility I had been given, I would give my order in a tiny, husky voice before holding up my wallet to the shopkeeper.

–Two baguettes, not too crispy, please.

But more than all the daily household rules, work constituted the real blueprint of our family Republic. It was the ultimate criterion, the norm, the singular standard by which we were all measured. As our father would often repeat:

> – There will be no inheritance when we are no longer around, nothing of consequence. No one is rich in our family and it's not over there, in *mboa*, that you can hope to ever discover you have a rich uncle in America. But there will be what you know how to do with your hands and your minds, by working. Solely by working. Trust me.

We had heard these words so many times since preschool that they began to take on a new meaning within the first years of elementary school, when the way I saw the world began to change. It seemed, moreover, to be the same for my siblings, because each of us was determined to play the game, position ourselves, each one better than the other, on the starting line, with the objective of bringing home the best school grades and making our parents' eyes shine bright with pride. It was as though we each intuitively hoped that good grades would keep tragedies at bay . . .

Going forward, an extraordinary competition developed in the heart of our little Republic. At the table, riddles and witty jokes would burst forth.

– What begins with an *i* and ends with a *d*? my little brother launched one day with a facetious smile.

And when each one of us grew tired from racking our brains and had finally given up finding the answer, he exclaimed triumphantly:

– Yaoundé! The capital of Cameroon!

In the race for parental approval, our maternal tongue, Douala, added salt and pepper to the competition. Because while we spoke French outside of the home, it was Douala that dominated the moment we crossed the threshold to our apartment. Our fluency was such that we also used Douala outside the home when we wanted to share among ourselves in taunting complete strangers in the street or in public transportation.

Hoping, pining, and sometimes, only sometimes, playing, enjoying, making the most of it all—and breathing expansively. During my entire childhood, I felt I was walking on a tightrope between all the different expectations: school and its demands, family and its demands, the home country and the weight of its demands, despite everything, beyond what was rational, and regardless of the distance. In the same way that we spoke French, and thanks to this language we were immersed in French culture, similarly, we spoke another language and became members of this other place where, as it were, we never grew up. To not disappoint, to reassure, to please, and to smile. I knew how to do all of it, as a consensual girl, concerned as I was with being "proper." Convinced that I was going to win the prize for the most delightful child in the family, I held on more than ever to my studies and doubled my efforts so that I would get noticed in class.

I did everything I could to eclipse the brilliant trails my older siblings had left before me with teachers. I kept on working to please my parents, each time with my secret and absolute dream of succeeding at definitively getting rid of my brothers and sisters so that I would become the only daughter, the only child in the family. In the evenings, once our hive had quieted down, at times I would look at my mother and ponder. I was not always sure that I was dealing with the same person, when I compared the severity of what she was, at times, capable and the gentleness of her arms when I would finally wiggle my way in for a privileged moment of tenderness. Sometimes I would imagine myself going up the steps of city hall in a white dress beside my father, not without having dismissed by a simple brush of the hand those who would criticize such an impossible union, and with the blink of a golden eye, disappearing with him into the great blue.

Progressively, Francis began to cheer up. On Saturdays, we would look out for his smile, when we needed him to place his signature on our report cards. Our school grades became the magical formula to transform his mood, and before you knew it there was great excitement in the home.

My younger brother Patrick finally accepted preschool, especially once he realized there was much to be gained by it. He also succeeded in upstaging all of us for several weeks. This new love for school was, however, not to indicate a sign of maturity: he had quite simply discovered a love for pastries! At the end of each school week, he came home with a new cake recipe he wanted to re-create. He and our mother would close themselves up in the kitchen for a good while after which he would emerge with his forehead and cheeks powdered in flour, his head held high and wearing a triumphant smile. The wonderful aroma of the baked cake would take over the entire apartment. But we would have to patiently wait for several hours before being able to taste it at dinnertime. We would each go back and forth by the kitchen, whistling in a casual manner. We could never chance a glimpse of this most coveted object, which would have been placed as high as possible on a shelf or atop the refrigerator by our mother, far beyond our reach. Once we finally did taste the cake it was always very good, which only intensified our jealousy. I wanted it to burn, just once. My exasperation finally went off the charts when my brother was asked to bake some cakes for the Sunday midday meal, where it wasn't unlikely we would have guests. My father did not fail to seize on the occasion:

– We have a very talented little fellow in the household who has prepared the desert . . . Isn't that so Baker Boy?

And I just wanted to yank at the tablecloth and have the entire table setting come crashing down with the most spectacular noise. Better still, strangle my brother and be rid of him for good, thus putting an end to watching him batting his eyelashes and carrying on with his false modesty. Didn't Papa realize that we girls spent hours with our mother preparing meals while the boys were only asked occasionally to quickly run an errand or set the table? Didn't he know that I could also make cakes and that he could very well call me "Baker Girl"? All said and done, baking was not such an exceptional skill!

Summer would finally interrupt these long weeks of stardom. However, my rage would resume with the new school year once I realized my brother had found a new way to extend his status as the little darling of the family. From the very first day he entered elementary school, he would choose the most noble cause, one that would interest and mobilize our parents' efforts above all others. He was determined to compete with a certain Maria Rueda Diaz who aspired to be the first in the class on a weekly basis. I never actually met Maria Rueda Diaz and I knew nothing about her besides her name, which was repeated in conversations on weekends.

– Who is at the top of the class this week? My father would ask before opening my brother's excellent report card.

And at times, my brother would answer in an embarrassed tone:

– Maria Rueda Diaz.

When that did happen, I would happily join in with my brothers and sister to mock him cruelly for being in second place. Who does he think he is imagining he's going to stay at the top of the podium all year long? Girls can also be great students and, like Maria—just like myself—they are very much capable of bringing boys down a notch.

At other times, overcome by a kind of pity mixed in with fraternal solidarity, I couldn't help but feel sorry for my brother and try to console him. Who does she think she is, this Maria Rueda Diaz? Did he want me to go and let her know exactly what I'm made of after school? I could trip her up and no one would be the wiser. That way she would need to go to the hospital where they would need to keep her for a while because they would be all out of plaster. Once they were able to get their hands on some plaster it would turn out to be sub-quality, and her bruises would swell and become purple, which would give her headaches. And finally her mother, troubled by all the misfortune, would stop sending her to that school and recruit a private tutor for her daughter . . . I hoped my brother would appreciate my indulgence, learn a lesson from the situation, and realize that there was a price to pay for wanting to be the star when you were the youngest one in the family: you were pitting yourself up against a brilliant, versatile, and resourceful competition, and could never be sure which way the scale was going to tip.

As for our parents, we were indeed all afraid to risk seeing paternal eyebrows frown and our mother's disappointed pout. *We probably won't have much else to leave you, if not for the ability to make a life for yourselves on your own: by working hard. Don't ever forget that* . . . In any event, between that Spanish student and my brother, her Cameroonian opponent, these two foreign students took up the gauntlet and accepted the challenge to succeed in the free, secular, French republican school system . . .

I began to live each moment of every day in competition with my brothers and sisters. During the week, the day began like a sprint, marked out with hurdles. You had to be the first one up in the morning to be able to get to the bathroom. We were all participating readily in this discipline because we all knew that the last one in had to clean the sink and the bath after everyone else had used them. My mother would gently soap me up with a glove then lovingly rinse me off. I cherished these moments of intimate complicity, believing in some kind of special love, one that was stronger for me than for any of her other children. I would finally be shattered on the day she decided I was old enough to start giving myself a bath on my own. The natural order of things, the prescription of this world, would become apparent through the matter of personal hygiene. My mother had put up a wall between us that I experienced as an injury. I tried to make an appeal, demand a reevaluation of the sentence. Nothing. My brothers and sister giggled. Why such disfavor?

In the autumn, I did everything I could to capture my parents' attention. I even dreamed of eliminating my brothers and sister. I envied my friends who were only girls their new clothing, not passed down from anyone else, and their beds without an upper level. I wanted to practice the activities to which they were privileged, such as taking classical dance classes and becoming a ballerina. The ballet students in the television series, *L'Âge heureux*, led a life on call that appealed to me. I watched them perform splits and bolting diagonals and leaps. I pleaded with my mother to sign me up for a dance class. I wanted to walk with my feet outward, "en dehors," and when it was time to prepare for performances I would spend hours in front of the mirror putting on eye makeup. At home, I would give demonstrations of my talent, entering into rooms leaping and leaving on the tips of my toes, rounded arms above my head. The year-end performance gathered all the parents from our group into a small theater. The whole family came to see me. I saw each of them, through a hole in the red curtain. My heart was pounding. I felt I was going to finally know fame when I would appear on the stage in my Sylphid costume. My fame was to gradually vanish when, right in the middle of my soloist variation, I suddenly forgot my movements. The entire group had to take a break three minutes in advance of the final tableau, during which time Tchaikovsky's music continued to play over the loudspeakers. We stayed on the stage, hesitating to leave, giving each other sideways glances, panic-stricken and mortified. The choreography I otherwise knew by heart had completely abandoned me.

Fortunately, the public—my family, first among them—filled that moment of uncertainty with enthusiastic applause. I bit the bullet and smiled. I still dreamed of dancing *Swan Lake* and *The Nutcracker*. Romantic music was no longer a mystery to me. In my dreams at night, I was Maya Plisteskaya. I had become "the dancer in the family," with whom no one would try to compete and who would therefore have fame and prestige. Besides, I already had proof of my success: seeing me dance, my parents were pleased and proud of me . . .

Back home from school one afternoon, I found a piano in our living room. We were now obliged to play this fabulous instrument, which our parents undoubtedly thought would further complete our profile as well-rounded children. I wasn't quite sure what to think of this latest development. How and when would I be able to finally admit that my musical dream was to play the transverse flute? I had already anticipated that it would be difficult to say it out loud and that my parents would insist on our good fortune to have in our possession such a beautiful, prestigious, and, of course, pricey instrument, and also the pain I would cause them in refusing such a wonderful opportunity. I was uncomfortable about the whole thing. In time, my brothers came back from school and ran in to see the new attraction. Had they known about it? My younger brother was immediately fascinated and itched to sit down and give it a go. But our mother forbade us to touch the instrument. We would have to wait for our father to come home. That evening, a small ceremony was organized. Our father solemnly lectured us.

> – This extraordinary instrument is for you, he concluded, looking at us all joyfully. You are all going to learn to play.

He slowly lifted the lid, unveiling the long range of black-and-white keys. My younger brother immediately rushed up to it. Without even taking the time to sit down, he freely ran his fingers on the keyboard. With no reservation or fear, he instinctively created the music he enjoyed playing with all of his fingers, refining the speed and sounds. We were all captivated and in awe. Francis discreetly went and got a tape recorder to record the performance. I began to feel a slight sting of jealousy. Then I set aside my reticence and decided I, too, would learn to play, and it went without saying, I would be better than him.

Before you knew it, we were lined up at Ms. Grégoire's home at the top of boulevard Blanqui, the music teacher that friends had recommended. Instead of letting us play, she made us hold our backs upright, read the music, and hold our fingers curved toward the keyboard. We discovered classical music by experiencing it first in our bodies. It wasn't about playing. The verb belonged to that group of words that didn't have the same meaning for us as it did for adults. Soon, we were astonishing Ms. Grégoire with our ease in contrapuntal playing. We had, she said, "a musical ear." She was clearly unaware that Bach and Handel were recurrent features of our family repertoire.

I loved everything more than those terrible sessions where the melodies only took form after having resisted me for a long time. In the process, I learned that consistency led to gratification but also that the lightheartedness of improvisation would gradually disappear the more lessons you had. I slipped into this new corset and the worst moment for me was when, intimidated and trembling, I had to perform in public for our parents' guests.

Piano lessons continued for weeks upon weeks. Slowly, our hands began to relax and we acquired a suppleness and speed in our fingers that made our little tribe an attraction. When the final performance of the year came around in June, we were given particular attention, which yielded an admiration tainted with annoyance by the parents of Ms. Grégoire's other students. The following school year, my sister and I began to study a new musical piece with a cheerful rhythm. Our fingers leaped from one octave to the other, and sometimes we would sit together on the bench to execute it even faster, each playing with a single hand. Our father became interested in the composer of the work, but once he discovered the title he immediately ordered us to stop playing.

– It is out of the question that you play a piece with a title like this under my roof.

The piece was titled *Le Petit Nègre*, and while it had been composed by the great Debussy, it was out of the question for us to play it. Our parents' engagement would manifest itself just like that, right before our eyes as children, by refusals, acts of invisible rebelliousness that would come to gradually modify the color of the world for me. While *Astérix et Obelix* became a part of our library, *Tintin au Congo* would never have a home on our shelves. Over time, I came to understand that, thanks to the keys of education and culture, it was our responsibility to open up the doors to a world where we were not expected and to understand both what was going on behind the scenes and what was at stake. It was not that obvious when, reading Tintin, you took yourself precisely for the hero and not one of the caricatured indigenous people in the comic book . . . We were conforming to a family project whose contours were being defined on a daily basis, and which our parents were themselves constantly circumscribing with each step they took. We were building our very own little independent Republic, a one-of-a-kind space protected from the boundaries of real life, which addressed the news of the events of May 1968—the assassination of Martin Luther King Jr. and the Biafra famine. Yet childhood and our parents protected us from that real life. We invented our own codes. We were at once Parisians, urban dwellers, Cameroonians, Africans, foreigners, friends, and neighbors both from across the hallway and in our neighborhood streets . . .

−8−

On weekends, in the wide, white family Taunus, we would escape the city to visit friends in the countryside. As soon as we got beyond the Paris city ring road, the drive took on the feeling of a real adventure. We fought over the window seats to be the first to see a cow! A horse! Geese! At times, we would shriek with horror and pinch our noses at the smell of the manure as we went by. Once we arrived at the family friends' home, the big farm dogs would come rushing and terrify us. We despised these dogs but the grown-ups encouraged us to pet them, to let them greet us by licking our hands or, even worse, our faces, and get to know us. You had to pretend to be tolerant, cheerful, and even affect a feeling of satisfaction while you were really feeling nothing short of disgust. Politeness, above all.

Once or twice, we took even longer drives. Nostalgic for the sea, our parents would suddenly decide from one day to the next to take us to Normandy. That would bring on full excitement. We prepared shorts and trainers. We rushed to buy bread, ham, and slices of dried sausage with garlic at the local deli. We went down to the cellar and brought up the icebox, the table, and foldable red-cloth metal stools. At the crack of dawn, we were already on the road. Up front, our parents chatted away, while in the back seat, lulled by the humming of the engine, we fell right back to sleep, our heads on each other's shoulders. Later we would play card games. Eventually we would leave the highway and randomly take some smaller roads in search of a place where we might pull over and have lunch. Papa laughed as he talked about peoples' surprise, coming upon our little group at the turn on the road:

– They'll tell their friends: I was coming back home and suddenly, just like
that, I saw some Black people. A whole bunch of Black people sitting on red
stools, picnicking! Can you imagine?

We would open up the table and carefully arrange the provisions, the
plates and glasses, and table napkins. As we peeled our eggs or bit into our
sandwiches, we kept on the lookout for whatever might be crawling under our
feet that could possibly disturb our dining arrangement. We preferred to
stand rather than risk little creatures. Only my younger brother tried to
snatch the elytra of beetles and catch earthworms with the tip of a short stick
that he would balance under our disgusted noses. His encyclopedic curiosity never failed to intrigue our parents, who often used him as an example.
Before getting back into the car, our father counted and recounted his cargo.

– There are just so many of you I have to be sure no one is missing, he would
say maliciously. As a matter of fact, I'm only going to count heads because
arms and legs would certainly make me dizzy!

At the seaside in Dieppe, the huge pebbles made it hard for us to rush out
toward the waves. The water was cold, the sky was pale, the air fresh, and the
town not so welcoming. We tried to hide our disappointment with forced
smiles. In the end, we improvised some games: throwing a huge pebble, drawing in the sand. We eventually caught up with our parents, seated, tucked
away from the wind on some huge rocks. The cold was overwhelming.

– Button up your cardigans and wrap your coats around your legs! our
mother instructed us, concerned as she was for our bare legs in shorts.

In no time a wind-whipped drizzle definitively dislodged us, and we were
soon all sitting, bunched together, shaking inside a brasserie, sipping on hot
chocolate and hot lemon juice waiting for the sky to clear up. The seaside
owed us a rain check.

The following summer our wish would be granted.

In the month of March, I brought home a message from the school doctor following a medical examination. "Visible signs of Vitamin D deficiency."
Each of my brothers and sister came home with the same prophetic news.

– What does that mean? What else did he say? Did other kids get the same
message? Madé was immediately anxious.

We each took turns describing the medical visit. We had to strip down to our underpants and undershirt. The nurse came to get us. They took our pulse and looked into the back of our throat while pressing on our tongue with the help of a spatula. The doctor had us sit and then cough, while he listened to the inner workings of our chest with his stethoscope. After discussing it with Francis and what it was going to cost her, our mother decided to deal with the matter head on by going to meet the school doctor who had accused her, it was clear, of being a bad mother. Discreet and shy, she always suspected that at some point she would be reproached for something or another. At least she would make it clear to the president of the tribunal that once a week she gave us each a spoonful of cod liver oil.

> – You come from a warm climate. Your children need more sun and iodine
> to grow in good health. Can you take them on vacation?

Madé was both surprised and upset. She looked at the pediatrician unsure of how to answer. Was he accusing her of not having made children sufficiently tough to be able to deal with living in this country? *Up until now, friends, neighbors, teachers found them "adorable, "polite," "always smiling." Furthermore, they were first in their respective classes, and you are now telling me that seeing their legs slightly bowed means they are in need of sun?* The doctor would never hear these thoughts our mother kept to herself.

> – Please understand Madame, he continued, I am not suggesting anything
> serious, it's quite simply physiological. In order for your children to grow and
> have strong bones, they need more sun. Perhaps, you will be heading back to
> *your home country* for the next long vacation period?

Unfortunately, vacation in Cameroon was not foreseeable in 1968. Another year would have to go by to allow the authorities time to forget about uncle Marcel. Going back would be risky. The word was that things were still quite difficult back home, that some were falling ill and dying after having had a simple aperitif at a reception. In addition to the police force, numerous civilians had joined in and were playing class monitors on behalf of the authorities of the regime. No, this was not the time to meet up again, neither with the family nor with the perfumes of the land. And even if it hurt, the idea of having to wait to approach the sepulchre, the house, the section of a wall, where someone might point out and say: "He came here and he was leaning there . . . You know, this is where he is resting, peace be with him going onward," they would need to kill time before doing so.

It was decided: we would head to the South, to Sète. Our parents were going to organize themselves like everyone else in this country and become real vacationers. Vacation! A word that sounded absolutely French . . .

A few months later we were back on the highway, along with the long cohort of summer vacationers aiming to get to the South as quickly as possible, among whom were those who didn't hesitate to step on the gas or dangerously cut somebody off. These were the days when people drove fast, hair blowing in the wind. You charged ahead, you weaved in and out, you accelerated.

– Step on it Papa! Go! Don't let them overtake us!

For us children, traveling by car was a real adventure. Our excitement was such that, from the moment we got up at dawn until we arrived at the seaside, we practically never closed our eyes. It was Saturday, August 3, 1968. On the radio, the lively voices of the presenters were commenting the event. "Ever since this morning, the August vacationers are on the roads of our beautiful country. Once again this year, thousands of French people are going to be taking advantage of the paid vacation system . . ." The farther away we got from the Ile-de-France region, our mother would turn the radio frequency in search of the news and music stations. Sitting in the backseat, we enthusiastically hummed along to some of the popular tunes. *Elle m'a dit d'aller siffler là-haut, sur la colline! De l'attendre avec un petit bouquet d'églantines.* Joe Dassin was in love while Françoise Hardy was asking *Comment te dire adieu.* The Beatles celebrated *Lady Madonna.* Julien Leclerc was high on his horse. In the car, we were forbidden to love *La Maritza,* Sylvie Vartan's song. How can an adult still be singing with the sulky voice of a little girl who plays with dolls with no shame? That did not hold me back from lip-synching, as we did in those days, *Comme un garçon,* my favorite song at the time.

We would all meet up in a single file at the same crowded tollbooths, then at the same rest stops, overloaded cars and caravans everywhere, everyone, like us, in search of the blue waves of the Mediterranean Sea. All around, people looked at us from their car windows, sometimes on the sly, and they would smile and give us a thumbs-up. We were a real surprise, however, when we stopped and got out of the car to stretch our legs. I would get out, protected by this invisible shield and respond to the stifled comments with words in Douala that I launched casually: *Ombwa tè ba nu'unan! O'a pula duta l'am?*

Look at that one! You want my picture? Oh, the exquisite pleasure of being able to shrug your shoulders in the face of ignorance! Keep on with your mutterings, carry on in your rhapsodies! You really haven't seen much of the world? You've never traveled? I tried my hardest to believe in that other place where everything was so much better because that place stuck to me like a shadow. I therefore owed it to myself to defend and glorify it in spirit, rid of all its defects, and to make of it the place of a happy and absolute humanity, the most exemplary space of knowledge and sophistication. Even if, naturally, my knowledge of this other place was partial, so limited that I often had good reason to make it all up . . .

On this journey, I reconnected with my brothers and sister, of whom I was otherwise so often jealous, and we formed an indestructible tribe. I became once again a member of this thick, reassuring, fraternal fabric, to which my existence attests and constitutes one of its indispensable threads.

Back in the car after a coffee break, we struck up songs in four-part-harmony. Our big brother took on the role of choirmaster, mimicking our school music teacher with his harmonium, his eyes twitching as we learned to sing poems and traditional French tunes: *Déclin du jour, derniers rayons, les nids dormant dans l'ombre/Un trait de flamme à l'horizon, barrant le ciel plus sombre/L'esquif léger attend au port, allons rêver bien loin du bord (bis)/ La rame frappe à temps égaux sur l'onde calme et lisse/La barque glisse sur les flots, au gré de nos caprices/Ô paix du soir si douce au cœur, repos du corps, parfait bonheur . . .*

That was a long day. After some riddles and general knowledge questions my father asked: "What is the capital of Iran? Of Columbia? Of West Germany? Of the Soviet Union? Of Cameroon? Who knows what a *ptarmigan* is? Who can spell *ornithorhynchus*?" We let the sound of the engine lull us. Silent, somewhat cramped, we dozed off until our mother suddenly launched, pointing her finger:

– Look children, the sea!

Almost immediately our excitement shot up. We rolled down the car windows to better take in the blue expanse and inhale the famous "sea breeze" that was meant to do wonders for us. Unfortunately, we had a hard time taking it all in as we were still a good distance from the coast. The last few miles felt like the longest. Finally, we arrived before the entrance gate to a complex.

Once we went past the gate, we advanced toward the welcome area, into a pine forest, where bungalows were spread out. Several families occupied identical ones within this vast enclosed space. In the reception office to "Village Vacances Familles," we were provided with bedding and instructions concerning various information, such as meal times and the curfew after which time vacationers were expected to be quiet. My parents went out and took a stroll, taking in the fresh pine scent, the lavender plants, listening to the chirping of the cicadas, and recalling a distant summer in Menton. Their secret!

To kick off the vacation, Papa took us out to a restaurant in Sète. We sat by the port and shared plates of sardine and bouillabaisse. My sister choked on something and nearly suffocated. When she finally vomited, she brought up the bone responsible for it along with her lunch. Disgusted, I pushed my plate away. My parents immediately shouted out:

> – Eat! Look at this child who's never gone hungry a day in her life! Don't you realize that in the very moment we are speaking, in Biafra, children are actually dying of hunger?

I had to pick up my fork because in our home we were not allowed to leave anything on the plate. I tried my best but I couldn't see how filling my stomach was going to help those poor starving children . . .

As I write, I now recall that an old lady also came by that evening dressed in a white blouse, a Provençal pattern skirt, and a shawl crossed in front of her chest. Supported by a cane, she advanced slowly toward us. Dumbfounded, she then stopped, took a look at us coming out of the car, and finally gave out:

> – Personally, I like foreigners!

She was the Lady of the Wood and lived further up on the hill, where she raised peacocks. Two or three specimens would, at times, escape over the walls of our property.

We improvised what we did each day of the vacation. We enjoyed the summer cheerfulness of the markets in the South, the warm fougasse bread bought at the bakeries in the villages, the lilting melodious Midi accent, and the warmth of the shopkeepers. Here *vacation* took on its true meaning: People looked surprised to see us, but didn't seem bothered. Everywhere we went, the looks we got were friendly and our nerves, worn from our parents' menacing decrees, were gradually liberated from the endless duty of perfection. Until we got to the seaside, where our family drew attention, more so because of our modesty than because of the color of our skin. Our mother had sewn colorfully striped terry-cloth beach bags, pulled together at the neck with an elastic band. To remove our wet swimsuits all while remaining dignified and discreet, we found ourselves in all sorts of contortions and nearly strangled ourselves with the elastic band tight around our necks. I also had the surprise of discovering my parents almost naked, in swimsuits. Our mother even dared to wear a bikini, in fashion at the time, whose details, I seem to recall, were a blue and red print in a botanical motif with a gold fastener in the back of the top piece and a ring, also in gold, between the two triangles in the front. Madé didn't know how to swim; she splashed around in the water like a child, mindful of swallowing a mouthful or getting her hair wet, which was protected in a bright pink waffle-textured swim cap. At night, once we got in from hours spent at the seaside, covered in salt and sand stuck to our feet, it was a race to be the first to get in the shower, leaving the last person with the task of cleaning up. Some days, the vacation center would organize activities for the residents. We managed to get away from our parents to learn to play chess and checkers with other kids, and participate in bag races and badminton tournaments. The adults would play volleyball and I came to realize that my mother was quite good at it. Some evenings, my father would borrow a guitar and charm the whole gathering with a song in Douala.

– Do you also know how to speak Black like your father? a fellow playmate naively asked.

As the days went by, my copper-toned skin got even more tanned in the sun, and I began to relax and feel more at ease. I felt like I was growing up. No one knew it yet but later on, I was going to become a ballerina, a pianist, and an international civil servant. All at the same time. Because I would dare. Yes, and why not? Papa told us to dare to be and do what we wanted. As we finished our dinner in the gentle night air one evening and were quietly listening to the crickets chirping, our father suddenly addressed us. In a solemn voice, he said:

– A few months ago, some people killed someone very important, a pastor named Martin Luther King Jr. He was a pastor, like my father, but in the United States. He and I were born in the same year. He fought by daring. By daring to say the laws in his country needed to change so that they would be the same for Black and White people. So that Black people would be respected. He dared to say it and he died for it. So, you too dare. We can do bold, courageous things, without having to fight with our fists, precisely like King did. Dare. Don't die, but dare! Dare to do what you want.

Before heading back to Paris three weeks later, we visited winemakers' cellars and cooperatives in the area. Under the pretext of an educational outing, our parents refined their knowledge of French wines. Because, little by little, they were adapting to this country and, because of us, putting down roots. They began to appreciate French habits and customs. Is it the country that adopts you or you who adopts the country when one day you decide that a meal needs to be accompanied by a good bottle of wine and that a great party is celebrated with champagne bubbles?

One morning, we went on a hike and after two hours arrived at a scenic viewpoint from where we could admire the landscape, shading our eyes with our hands. Francis slipped a fifty centimes coin into a telescope and while we were all pushing past each other to take a look into the optical instrument, he turned toward Madé and mischievously declared:

– If one of us dies, I will go live in Nice.

When, at the end of the vacation, the journey home is a smooth ride, and later in September you share a bottle with friends and the sunlit memory of that summer makes you teary-eyed, isn't that a sign that this country has become more deeply a part of you than you could have ever imagined? That it's the air you breathe, present in the social etiquette and the culinary tradition, and that melodious accent and hospitality of the South. You buy postcards to send a "thinking-of-you" moment to your friends back in Paris. You love it. It no longer corresponds to the images you had as children, when the severity of primary school teachers or the brutality of the administration never allowed you to imagine anything but a severe and policed world. The White man who frightened you and before whom you bowed has now disappeared in favor of the neighbor with whom you have a good relationship, the postman, who talks to you about the village from which he originates, a friend you invite to have crepes or a quiche lorraine—a woman's recipe—and with whom you share the mystery of the language, the genesis of the French culture, made of borrowings, conquests, and integration.

With this vacation, our first French-paid vacation, a new perspective opened up, like a sliver of blue ready to extend into the gray sky. For my parents, there was something here in France they could not find back home. In this country, you could come and go with your own car, you could readily have access to a doctor whenever you needed one, send your children to study less than five minutes from home. You could even, during your vacation away from Paris and the phone calls from back home, make your own choices without having to think about everybody else, forget for a little while the community and act alone and selfishly, satisfy the desires of those close to you.

A kind of appeasement permeated our little tribe as our parents found themselves living more serenely in France, and without realizing it, they began to truly love this country. But the pleasure of being here, present in the moment that is happening, fully being yourself, in the right place, so to speak, did they ever dare to acknowledge it? Did they ever share that satisfaction with each other with a clear conscience? Did they ever allow themselves to do so, knowing as they did that they were on a mission for the others—that family, that community—so far away, yet still so demanding? Wasn't that the kind of secret that was shared in the darkness of a cozy bedroom between husband and wife?

Thinking of them, among the images of poorly developed photographs that come to mind, two divergent pictures stand out. In the first, a smiling family with a Parisian street as the backdrop, parents in love and affectionate, surrounded by five children. In the second picture, some children and adults—uncles, aunts, cousins, nephews—are standing together in front of palm trees and banana trees. In their eyes you can read they are awaiting a return. They ask the lucky ones who have earned scholarships to study far away to come back, covered in success, and guarantee those who stayed behind the certainty of beautiful tomorrows.

If my parents did gradually become happy in their new life, it undoubtedly took a very long time before they would fully articulate it, so as to maintain a certain kind of loyalty with respect to their community. As if a personal exigency made it difficult to take note of the mutual adoption that was nevertheless at work. The endless demands they placed on themselves and on us betrayed their fear of letting themselves go and enjoying a little too much of life, their fear of forgetting whose hopes had accompanied them all the way to Europe. They probably considered that their degrees, then my father's "excellent situation," his promotions, our school results, our success with the piano, constituted so many tokens, destined to prove their loyalty. *We are far away, but we are always with you and don't ever forget that if we shine, it is to you that a part of our success is due.* But tokens are not enough when it comes to discharging oneself of the debt of never going back home. This eternal never going back. Our vacation in the South that year had clearly allowed them to relax and enjoy the deliciously acidic taste (likened to those boiled candies from Pezenas) of absolute freedom.

When did my parents truly decide to settle down in France? Did they ever make the decision? Did they, one day, come to feel that going back was becoming a myth that would always remain a dream? A three-room cloud above the equatorial forest? Did they imagine, before experiencing it, that they would make of us the children from *here*, more accustomed to the world in which they had grown up than to the land and culture of their origins? Did they ever say to each other, "That's that, it's time to turn the page, we won't be going back, we will never go back"? The question of returning remained present for many years, like a background on which photos came to be glued, highlighting family events. And as they waited to bring it back to the fore-front, under the burning hot spotlights, we simply continued to live.

−9−

That vacation would lead to many more, and the following year it was even more symbolic. After dinner one evening, Francis and Madé announced that we would be going to spend the greater part of the summer in Cameroon. The prospect was exciting. Although our country, the ultimate reference that was brought up every day in our lives, similar to my brothers and sister, I had no conscious recollection of the last journey there and with good reason: I had been a baby at the time. The solemn tone and the repeated warnings from our parents, however, quickly tempered our enthusiasm.

> – We'll be staying in an apartment in Douala, in a building in the center of town, close to your Auntie Gogo, your mother's sister. Many people will surely be coming by to visit with us, they explained. We'll have to be mindful of those who claim to be "family." We expect you to behave well when we are the guests. Don't trust all the smiles that come your way because some of them will be hypocritical . . .

At that time, I didn't understand why we would be afraid of our native land. Our uncle Marcel's shadow was perhaps still there and tainted with mistrust, a reality filled with imaginings. But I wasn't able, at the time, to understand these things. For me, the news was so important that I seized on the moment to get my classmates' attention at school. The next day, I could read the admiration on their faces when I told them that my vacation was going to be taking me on a long-distance journey by plane. I impressed them and won even greater distinction once I described what my arrival in this African country, far away and unspoiled, would be like, where every step, every sigh, every breath would require courage and forethought. Glad to find myself progressively as the center of attention, I rolled out my story, adding little anecdotal touches here and there.

There I am, surrounded by cheetahs and lions, in the middle of the forest. I manage to escape by the skin of my teeth by diving into the river's current, infested with crocodiles, and there again, after having survived the usual fatal bites, I regain footing on loose soil, covered with red ants . . . For someone who had only seen a real lion at the zoo in Vincennes, I was completely taken in by my own story, embellishing the real and wielding the suspense like a true expert. It was that much easier to make it all up given that my classmates and I all grew up sharing the same imaginary. Much like Tintin in the Congolese forest, I was both explorer and reporter, capable of confronting the most dangerous situations and facing every challenge thrown at me. I was letting myself get carried away by the flow of my own story until I suddenly caught a glance of my sister on the sideline of the circle of my admirers. I had completely forgotten that, though we were in different classes, we were attending the same school and therefore had the same breaks. Her ironical smile made my beautiful fantastical fable wobble.

My father's words came back to me. We'll be living in the city and not in huts in the heart of the forest. I would not be alone, rather surrounded by my family. Rethinking my parents' warnings, I tried to reject the truth in its entirety, by shrugging it off, but the charm had already been broken. The lion, instead of tearing me apart with his jaws and claws, suddenly disappeared into the distance. The python loosened its rings around me that were cutting off my breathing. Some of my classmates' disparaging remarks made me uncomfortable, and, in the end, I lost my momentum. I tried to dismiss them with a retort full of pity and contempt.

– No, it's not like that anymore! Everybody knows that! No one walks around completely naked in Africa. That was before, hundreds of years ago. Nowadays, people over there dress just like we do.

But the strength of my speech had suffered from a few seconds of discomfort that left me agape. I had lost my groove. My classmates shook their heads slowly. Strangely enough, their skepticism struck me right in the heart. Within the exotic décor I had so enthusiastically tried to set up, they all imagined women and men walking around half-naked, their waists, in the best-case scenario, belted with raffia. There I was presenting myself as this bold, brave explorer, and, in their eyes, I was nothing more than a little savage, half-naked,

lost in the jungle! My sister and I exchanged glances, disappointed and pro-
foundly mortified that we had been compared to those kinds of savages. Back
at home that evening, neither one of us spoke about the Technicolor film of
my life in the bush. We both realized that the shooting had come to an end
once we had understood that in the eyes of our classmates we could never play
the role of the hero.

– Back home, our mother explained, they think we are always on vacation,
living the "European good life." They don't know that your father works hard
to provide for all of us and that it is a part of the UNESCO contract to offer
the opportunity, every two years, to return to one's own country at minimal
expense. Everybody thinks we're rolling in it. Everyone is looking to benefit
from us.

A real desire and a sense of obligation and guilt would have my mother, during the weeks prior to the journey, spending her days going back and forth to
the shops, looking out for sales and crossing off the names from a long list. *My
sister, Aunt Edna . . . Check. Cousin Sami and his wife. Clara, Rosa, Maa Djé,
her sisters Musima, Léonara and all the others, also done.* In addition to our
luggage, she dedicated an entire suitcase to the gifts that each person would
come to pick up, *as though it was normal to do so,* she said, resentful in advance,
*sometimes even going as far as turning up their lips, without ever saying thank
you, no, it was all due to them, after all we're the ones living in the City of Light.*

A few days later, our body parts sore from the vaccinations against yellow
fever, meningitis, and cholera, dressed in our Sunday best, we finally climbed
up the jet bridge into a huge DC-9. As we stepped out of the airplane, we were
greeted by the shock of the sticky heat, the chaos at the airport, and then the
dozens of eyes watching our arrival because everybody had come to wait,
airport style, and, finally, the shrieks of joy, the warm reunions, heart against
heart. My brothers, sister, and I stood a bit apart, stiff, before all these people
we didn't know. They nevertheless interrogated each one of us:

– Do you remember me? Yes? Who am I then, tell me, who am I?

Unable to answer, sheepish, we kept quiet, slightly scared.

– Come on, try and remember! some insisted. I held you in my arms, my
very own arms that you see right here, I cradled you, I sang to you, gave you
the bottle, comforted you right here on my hip, when you were only a tiny
little baby . . .

Our parents threw us persistent gazes. *Go on answer! Don't embarrass us and don't upset anyone. Don't say you don't know the person who is speaking to you . . .* But we just stood there, awestruck, shifting our weight from one leg to the other, looking lost.

You could read the disappointment on their faces. With a nod from our mother, we began to make confusing excuses. It's a miracle! The shrieks burst forth from everywhere:

– *Ba bana ba ma topo Douala!* The children actually speak Douala!

Disappointment metamorphosed into cheerful smiles: we had spoken in *our* language. How was it possible that we spoke it so well and yet we lived so far away from *our* country? We left the airport between two hedges of admirers, proud to know children so remarkably intelligent. Our parents smiled: thanks to us, the proof of their loyalty to their land and to the memory of their ancestors remained intact. As for me, I realized that if over there, back in France, I was meant to, at times, don the role of the foreigner, in the eyes of everyone here, I was already wearing the luminous costume of the perfect little White person. Vacation could now begin.

Exiting the airport, daytime quickly gave way to nighttime without warning, spreading unexpected darkness everywhere and contrasting with all the lights in Paris. We left in a convoy, honking horns all the way into the city right up until we arrived at our grandmother's home, because the apartment where we were supposed to stay had not worked out.

– Brother-in-law, you know the *local realities*, explained an aunt to our father.

My mother's sisters squeezed together into one room. We, children, piled into another, lying head to toe on a single mattress, the girls on one side and the boys on the other. Our parents occupied the adjacent room, separated from ours by a thick wall. My mind was not at ease. Would I be heard in the case of an attack by a wild animal? The whole night, I was practically on the lookout, my eyes wide open in the dark. In the end, the experience proved to be quite the opposite of what I feared. The roaring of the wild animals became characteristic humming. My adversaries aimed for my hands, my neck, my ears, and my face: I constituted an apparently ideal target for mosquitoes. They were determined to absolutely celebrate my arrival with an unbridled saraband. I can still recall how much I was in tears the next morning, holding up my hands, swollen from the bites, to my affectionate, loving grandmother, so that she could coat them with an ointment. Although the following night the household would pull out all the stops with the mosquito coil and the mosquito net, I suffered so much in the first days that I decided to seriously detest this country that had welcomed me so poorly, especially as I was only a child.

The following days would give me more reasons to feed my aversion when I quickly came to realize that vacation here would have nothing to do with the happy days spent with my family swimming in the sea and discovering the villages of the South of France. We didn't visit the country; we were the ones who were visited. The ballet of visitors began, as had been anticipated, beginning on the very first morning after our arrival. White-haired elders, adults, children, whole families—the family turned out to be gargantuan. Some people, coming by foot from quite a distance, would knock at the door to our grounds in the early morning hours. I came to realize that our presence marked a veritable event and that each family member, however distant, was duty-bound to travel the distance to come and visit for a long while with the family from Paris. *Who will dare to say I didn't come to see you?*

Like my brothers and sister, I had to also take my turn to politely embrace dozens of perfect strangers. Amid this family merry-go-round, compared to the uninterrupted flow of relatives coming from the most remote villages, the nocturnal hordes of mosquitoes were but a slight bother. Without ever having deemed it necessary to explain it to me, I was also expected to know what my relation was to each and every person. Quite naturally I failed at trying to understand who was who, all the more so that the numerous nicknames complicated the treasure hunt. Auntie Gogo, the closest sister to our mother, well, her first name was Henriette, according to a logic that went right over my head. I would incidentally learn that she acquired her nickname from her very own exclamations as a child—*gaulle, gaulle*—when, many years ago, the great General de Gaulle had set foot in our country. When I insisted on trying to unravel all of this, the explanation I was given left me speechless:

> – Maa Djé is the sister of the second wife of the aunt of your paternal grandfather, the son of your uncle Sam, the one who was raised by your mother's cousin. So now you understand why you have to call her auntie. She's family.

From the moment they arrived, visitors would clarify where they sat on the genealogical tree or the friendship that went way back between two now defunct ancestors that connected them to our parents. My grandmother and my aunts approved and greeted at length. Everyone checked in on how the health of every member of the family was coming along, doing their utmost not to neglect a single name. The visitors were then invited to take a seat. Sometimes the wait could turn out to be quite long because our parents weren't always home. Most of the time, when I would wake in the morning I would learn they had already gone out. In those days, no one thought of explaining to children the goings-on of the adults' world, and the constant disappearances would send me into a deep, latent anxiety, which would stay with me right up until the moment they returned. I was completely unaware that my parents were themselves subject to the same ritual and therefore had to go and pay their respects to elders and esteemed members of the family so as to avoid, on the day of their departure at the crack of dawn, being taxed with bad manners. *Who's going to say that they didn't even catch a glimpse of us before we were gone?*

In the dining room and the living room, chairs were lined up next to each other. If there was a chair missing, my brother was sent to borrow one from a neighbor. The girls, we were assigned the task of taking care of the drinks— soda, beer, ginger juice, coconut milk. And we also helped to prepare quite a sizeable buffet should the wait extend right up until it was time to eat. *Who's going to say they were poorly greeted?*

The mornings dragged on for hours as we sat waiting. My grandmother and aunts did their best to keep the conversation going, but we soon ran out of things to talk about and silences settled in with sliding slippers and the clearing of the throat. Once my parents would finally make their appearance, a brouhaha of welcoming good wishes greeted them. I would wait for my mother to appear and head toward her with extended arms, all ready to ab-solve her when she would take me into her embrace. But the guests would always come between us and begin all over again with their greetings and charade of politeness. I would wipe away my tears, looking on at my parents as I tried to quiet my raging sighs. Releasing a swarm of nocturnal mosqui-toes into their room, in the form of a punishment expedition, would never suffice to temper my anger. My bitterness was intensified by an immense feel-ing of betrayal. How could my mother ignore me as she did to give herself over to such mundane protocol? What did I really mean to her then? I already foresaw my destiny as an orphan, tragically abandoned by her family without mercy, and I would keep on sulking right up until the last guests decided to go. I would make my way toward my mother and throw myself into her arms, finally letting my whole body unravel in tears.

– Ndjé bodi? Ndjé pè yé? What is it? she asked, surprised.

How could I possibly find the words to explain that while this trip to Cameroon had allowed me to discover a family considerably larger in size than our nuclear tribe, it was also keeping me from my own family?

– Émbè nyolo! My father whispered with a frown. Come on, show some courage now . . .

He who was otherwise so affectionate back in Paris, why didn't he understand what my tears meant? Couldn't he tell just from looking at me how much I missed him every single day we were here?

At the end of the first ten days, the pace of the visits finally began to slow down, and I was so pleased at the prospect of returning to a much more intimate family circle. However, my parents continued to leave the house for hours at a time. So be it. Head held high, I planned to oppose their absence with a sustained indifference. In time, we would come to learn, much to our misfortune, that parental authority extended to all the adults in the household. Girls as well as boys were expected to respond diligently and with a smile to all solicitations, however diverse the source. Moreover, Uncle Robert—called "Uncle Mustache," yet another unfamiliar relative—had shown up from Yaoundé and settled into Auntie Gogo's room without as much as a sound.

– He's your aunt's fiancé! They deigned to explain to us. The wedding will take place at the end of the month. We'll all have to go over there!

Uncle Mustache proved particularly remarkable in the art of interrupting us in the middle of a game. Pure luck or deliberate torture, he submitted me above all the others to his will, giving his orders with a smile.

– Nu muna é ndé o wèni? Where is that child? *Wanéa mba madiba . . . Owea mba nin mboti . . .* Bring me some water. Wash this piece of clothing for me . . .

One morning he decreed me responsible for polishing his shoes, not without presenting this chore as though it were a privilege. In a quick pleading glance, I tried to get my mother to see the injustice. But with an intense knit in the brow, she refused to intervene on my behalf before conspicuously turning away. Disappointed by her attitude, I wanted to have the courage to turn my back on her for three weeks, without caving in right until the end of the vacation. Perhaps then she might understand how much she was hurting me. Clearly, neither she nor anyone else had the least idea what I was feeling.

According to an unjust law, all young girls *here* had to respectfully devote themselves to serving the community. My sister and I were both subject to this ordinance, whereas my brothers managed to escape from permanent house arrest. I envied them being able to go out and play soccer by the fire station. No matter how much I tried to tell them that I could easily come and join the team, just like I did in Paris on the lawn on avenue de Breteuil, they just turned away and avoided answering me. And yet it was not so long ago that my position as a striker was not even up for discussion and my kicks on the shin were more than valued for what they were. As far as my brothers were concerned, they now saw my place as no longer on the field, but rather, in the home with the aunts. Soccer became the exclusive domain of the boys. Carry yourself well, smile, and obey. Keep your wits about you. I hated this country that was suffocating me, separating me from my immediate family, this country that was constantly asking me, just like in France, to behave well and demonstrate my good upbringing. My docility and affable smiles confirmed to everyone how much I deserved the admiration they had shown me ever since my arrival at the airport. *Francis and Madé's children are so well behaved. They are polite, they are smart, they are helpful, and, even more, they speak our language, even though they live so far away over there!*

At one point, the situation just became unbearable, and I couldn't take it anymore. I managed to sneak out of the complex and made my way all the way to the back of the courtyard. I hid behind the huge cisterns used to collect rainwater, my heart beating fast. Eventually I regained my breath, amazed at having escaped adult supervision. No one had followed me. No authoritarian voice could come and track me down here. Was I finally going to have a minute to myself? From the courtyard, the house suddenly seemed to me so much smaller and somewhat sad, with its gray cement walls and tin roofing, hidden in part by the trunk of a mango tree and the leaves of a banana tree. At that point, I didn't even have a clue as to what the city really looked like. Perhaps it was simply made up of brown and gray houses, competing for space among the plants and the trees. As was the case in Paris, I only knew the neighborhood by way of the surrounding homes, the street vendor, who, in late afternoon, set up her corn fritters stall at the corner of the street, and the shopkeeper from whom, escorted by my older brother, I once bought matches and salt. Looking on at the gray walls, I got lost in thought, wondering how I was going to go about replacing the story of my life in the bush with the wild animals once I got back home. Suddenly someone tapped me on the shoulder. When I turned around, I saw two young girls barely taller than me.

– We're your cousins Fanfan and Cricri, they declared. We came and greeted you on the first day, do you remember? Sometimes, we see you in Grandmother's house, but you seem so busy! Come play with us.

I discovered another courtyard adjoining ours that opened up behind the cisterns. My cousins lived in a house all the way in the back, a refuge for me at that hour. They pulled me under the awning and rolled out a mat on the ground where we all sat down to get to know each other better, as young girls, because I recalled neither their visit nor their faces. At thirty degrees in the shade, the ice quickly melted. They admired my ability to express myself *in patois*, which also gave them a good laugh. Unlike the people from *there*, I pronounced all the syllables and used very few contractions, which gave me a more literary tone, almost aristocratic. As for me, I had the impression, while listening to my cousins, that I was discovering a new French language whose phrasing called to mind a song. What we had in common as children, however, had nothing to do with linguistics. Above all else, we loved to play and make up stories, imagining, by turns, schemes, secrets, misunderstandings, and conflicts, like young girls the world over. I did my best to tell them about France, the black-and-white cows with long eyelashes, the dogs yelping and jumping up and down, the olive trees, the Mediterranean Sea, and Paris, my square, Le Gall, my school on rue Corvisart, the shopkeepers on our street, the butcher whose family name was Boulanger . . .

In time, I got into the habit of disappearing to this little corner of the courtyard as soon as I felt the need to get away from family obligations. My cousins taught me a new version of playing teatime, the *dibo ndoko*, realized with the remains from food that we would cook on a real firepit. Given that I was not allowed to so much as touch a match, running my hands over the flames was a genuine thrill.

Finally, from the steps of my cousins' home—because I wouldn't dare to push my runaway stints so far as to venture into the streets—I would watch, as in Paris, the movements of the neighborhood. It rained nonstop, but that didn't discourage people going about their daily activities. Day and night, water filled the sewers and charged into the gullies, so much so that I wondered, in the event of a fire, if the firemen would be able to work. Some children took advantage of the opportunity to go out and bathe, laughing beneath the raindrops. Annoyed to see them playing and singing as they would leap around in pools of water, I would shrug my shoulders, sniff, and throw them scornful looks, never really sure whether I was criticizing their nudity or actually envying their carefree spirit.

I knew deep down precisely what I hated about this flagrant spectacle: it gave me a glimpse beyond, through the doors, to a free world that I was so hungry for, one in which my parents could take a break from their demanding roles as work inspectors and let themselves go romping around in the water or enjoy a glass of rosé with some squid prepared Sétoise style. I longed for that summer feeling when I could have them entirely to myself. I knew this was selfish, but I wanted them all to myself, no siblings, just all for me, and if I closed my eyes, I dreamed of them granting my every wish, however whimsical. I got the feeling that I would never stop despising this country, *my country*, where constraints upon constraints challenged my craving for attention.

A few days later, the entire household was rustling with excitement at the prospect of the marriage of Auntie Gogo and Uncle Mustache. We, the nieces and nephews, were to be bridesmaids and groomsmen, dressed identically, cut in pink fabric for the girls, and gray and white for the boys. A key role would be assigned to us: to hold the bride's veil to prevent it from dragging on the ground and becoming dirty. A tailor, recruited for the occasion, came and set up his Singer machine and began to take each person's measurements. While I had imagined that the unplanned orders and the constraints of the daily visits were all over and done with, I found myself, once again, subject to the will of yet another adult, unknown to me to top it off, who submitted me to frequent dress fittings. I would come out each time riling, my arms and legs scratched by the needles. Only the prospect of soon being able to wear a dress with a Peter Pan collar, smocking, and puffed sleeves, adorned at the waist with a velvet ribbon, made me put up with the situation. Perhaps I might be able to bring back this unique piece for my wardrobe in Paris? I would be able to triumphantly show it off to my classmates . . .

More than ever, the vacation in the home country became synonymous with constraints, and I was not far from definitively loathing each and every aspect of our stay when, by way of a parental decision, whose suddenness always surprised us, we found ourselves packing our suitcases and moving on to Yaoundé. We would spend the last three weeks of our vacation there. Our parents had rented a house, whose modern elegance we would come to discover after dark, following a long drive in a huge Peugeot 404. My grandmother joined us on the journey. Not only had I barely seen my parents during our entire stay in Douala, but my grandmother was also out most days either attending some bereavement ceremony or participating in activities connected to the religious or feminist organizations to which she belonged. Sometimes I managed to just about catch hold of a piece of her *kaba* as she went by, just the time to say hello. I would have loved to slip my entire body beneath the many pleats of her dress, which was reassuringly sizeable, and live beneath it, forever. Before leaving, she would lovingly examine my hands and comment on the progressive healing of my mosquito bites before making some joke in Douala that I almost never understood.

When I woke up on my first morning in Yaoundé, I found her sitting with her back to me on a chair, outside the kitchen, near the French doors. She had already laid out the bowls and plates, the stainless-steel cutlery, chocolate powder, and a box of sweetened condensed milk. Hearing her light sniffing, I knew she was having her tobacco, as I would sometimes see other women of her age do. The hissing of the boiling water in the kettle muffled my greeting as I approached her, yet she turned and immediately gave me a playful smile. *Muna muto o busi ndé nèni?* Little girl, how are you? Bright colors enlivened my retinas: the miraculous blue of the sky, the deep green of the plants, and the reddish-brown of the soil. All those miles we had traveled the day before seemed to have distanced us from the rain. The air was dryer than in Douala and the temperature more pleasant. We lived in Bastos, one of the residential neighborhoods in the city. I pulled up a chair, sat by my grandmother, and enjoyed the shared silence in that moment. I yawned and stretched, as if with these movements my body would expand and occupy the space in which I was finally going to be able to be more creative and fill up to my liking. My intuition told me that this property would open up a new terrain of exploration for my newly acquired emancipation. The real vacation I so desperately wanted was finally within reach—it was finally going to happen.

Once I had had my bowl of hot cocoa, I slipped into my light sandals and took off to explore our new settings. My brothers and sister soon joined me. They were equally surprised by our newfound freedom. We spent the morning running around and hiding from each other in the garden, happy to be able to once more enjoy the pleasure of playing together. Once we went back into the kitchen to get a fresh glass of water, our younger brother drew our attention to the frightened arrangement of cockroaches, clumped together behind the refrigerator.

> – They can't do anything to us, he explained, sure of himself, because they're the ones who are afraid of us.

Nevertheless, I had a hard time accepting the presence of these little creatures. Back in France, when they got to be barely the size of these ones, I would scream out, frightened by the very sight of one of them. And I was just as afraid of the fickle nature of the little domestic geckos that would either kick off with a frenetic sporty traction after long periods of standing still or bolt as though they were expected at a meeting. Back outdoors, we listened to our brother, who, in the manner of a little know-it-all, waxed on about the flora and fauna, information he had learned thanks to his collection of posters from *Télé 7 Jours*. We went along with him, admiring as entomologists, half curious and half afraid, the intrepid determination of ants, amazed by their extraordinary size, watching their movements as street cleaners responsible for swiftly picking up the slightest spoils to add to their reserves. We would no sooner go back to being the city dwellers we really were, frightened by the sight of the slightest gnat.

The hour of vengeance would call when, aware of our power, we knowingly chose to join with the forces of darkness to punish the insects for being alive, for abounding and making our skin crawl, despite the intense heat. Overcome by a sudden exhilaration to dominate, we began to systematically crush the specimen beneath our heels. This first pogrom made us hungry for more. We launched into systematic destruction, throwing stones at the anthill, whose exits we insisted on blocking by introducing obstacles of all kinds. The ice-cold water brought from the kitchen helped to drown all those who tried to escape.

What kind of macabre feeling had pushed us to behave this way? What kind of cruel tendencies had surfaced from within our little beings? We were certainly taking big risks, besieged as we were by the insects of our miniature jungle. It was obvious and easy to understand. Although our younger brother screamed at the top of his lungs to warn us, and try to get us to change our minds, we carried out the operation to its finale after discovering a huge orange caterpillar dotted with black spots. Our hatred spread mercilessly. The objective beauty of the caterpillar made it strange and too horrific in our eyes to allow it to go on living. We were relentless in our pursuit of the helpless critter and submitted it to every conceivable form of torture: beating it with a stick, hurling rocks at it, and dousing it with water . . . We explored all means to make it suffer and relished watching its instinctive attempts to get away, right until the moment it succumbed, remaining coiled in on itself for long enough that there was no doubt it was finally dead. Of course this did not stop us from pursuing yet another final useless gesture: setting it on fire after having planted matches, in the way banderillas are used in bullfighting, into its skin.

We were overcome by a silent shame once the dismal ceremony was over. Revolted, our younger brother was speechless and looked at us in disgust. While a foul smell of charred flesh consumed the air, leaving us with an acrid and guilty recollection of our crime in our throats, we realized that even though it was always easier to feel safety in numbers, this wouldn't make it any easier to erase the memory of the shameful acts we had together committed. Victory had come easy, but it was completely unspeakable and we would do well never to repeat it to a soul.

Miraculously, our parents were home at lunchtime. My mother came toward me, stretched out her arms, and embraced me. I immediately forgave all her infidelities of the past weeks and crushed my whole body against her, reading in her gesture the promise of a new era. In the afternoon, my sister and I joined her in a taxi to the city center. Before we headed out, Madé gave our outfits a proper inspection. I finally understood the meaning of all the Sunday outfits she had slipped into our suitcases. We had to play our role as impeccable young Cameroonian-Parisians, should we have occasion to come across acquaintances in the city.

We got into the car, not a hair out of place, dressed in white cotton T-shirts and Tergal pleated skirts, ankle socks, and closed-toe shoes, raincoats in hand—completely superfluous paraphernalia in the tropical heat. God forbid someone dared to complain about it being too hot! Under the shopping arcades of avenue Kennedy, we entered into a fabric supplier's shop, then into the spanking-new temple of the department store, Printania—an exhilarating space of luxury of which I would be sure to speak to my friends once back at school. Near the exit, writhing on the sidewalk, lepers reached out their infected hands. Startled, I jumped backward. I was a perfect little girl, immaculately dressed and my hair styled in four braids that formed a chignon. *Muna bwam*, a little girl from a good family. No leper, no paralyzed person should ever dare to come within an inch of me.

The three weeks we spent in Yaoundé would prove to be the happiest time of our vacation. In part, because our garden would soon become the home of an inhabitant with four legs, a goat that we, the children, would baptize Biquette from the first moment we saw her. As usual, no one explained why she was suddenly there in our garden, tied to a post. We immediately took a liking to Biquette, on whom we doted all our attention, seeking, perhaps unconsciously, to erase the memory of our very recent past as torturers. We made every possible effort to have her like us, brushing her black-and-white hair, taming her with our smiles and tenderness. But a goat is neither a lecherous cat nor a faithful dog. Biquette, therefore, resisted our desires of adoption even while she had rekindled, merely by her presence, our interest in playing in the garden rather than indoors.

A few days later, when we returned to Douala for Auntie Gogo's wedding to be followed by our return flight, we would discover with disgust and indignation the fate that had been reserved for our dear Biquette. Her remains lay in dishes, cut into pieces, covered in a brown sauce. We refused to eat our goat, and tears expressed our sadness. How could grown-ups be so cruel?

Several things happened during the last days of our vacation that wound up reconciling me with Cameroon. In Yaoundé, we made a few visits. When we arrived at our hosts' homes, about fifteen or so different dishes greeted us, displayed on a long table covered with a traditional tablecloth with the effigy of the president. It was a given that we would taste each dish. And that was how my country, which I had otherwise determined to wholeheartedly detest up until this point, gradually won me over. By way of my taste buds. Despite the looks my parents tried to relay by the expression in their huge eyes, I could not control my self-indulgence and greed before the *ndolé, ekoki, miondos, missolè, béqwem, wuba na ngond'a, sénguéti, ngondo, mbéa toè*, and other flavorful, delicious dishes. The expectations were, in fact, contradictory: our parents demanded that we display good manners, but our hosts hoped we would disregard all the rules and honor all the dishes laid out, by tasting each and every one of them. I took refuge in this sort of educational no-man's-land and gobbled up as much as I could. I found myself on the verge of indigestion at the end of each meal, my belly as bloated as a soccer ball.

Late afternoon, my parents would announce that we would be heading back. I would sit quietly, rubbing my aching tummy discreetly because I knew someone would soon exclaim:

– Leaving already? But no, listen, didn't you just get here? What can we offer you? What about another drink?

A second round of the visit would kick off wherein the adults went right back into lengthy discussions, leading with their recollections of France. *When we were students over there, in Paris, and we experienced the first cold weather, my God, how we suffered. We had the wind, the rain, and the snow!* The challenges of the climate were followed by contradictory evocations of the minor humiliations and the great admiration, and the mistrust and the unwavering friendships. A tender nostalgia shrouded the memories of those days, when liberty and youth rhymed and no one had yet really reached the age of responsibility. Certain details took on greater significance: was this boutique, that person, the advert on the building wall, were they all still there? *They had painted Cinzano and "Du beau, du bon, Dubonnet." I used to see it every morning on my way back from the university. Was it still there? And the woman at the haberdashery, who always seemed to be in a bad mood? Each time we came into her shop to buy some thread or buttons, she would look at us as though she thought we were going to steal something. And then afterward, she would offer us a button or a piece of thread. Was she still there?*

Every street and every avenue that had been roamed, the shops they'd been to, it needed to all remain intact so that the photo had no dents or creases. That way they could continue to cherish the city they had once known, letting go of the less-pleasant memories, as we all tend to do, of those snow-covered winters or the icy raindrops that fell directly from the gutter deliberately down the back of the neck.

Finally, the most serious subjects were raised, those that had my parents, as I could understand it at least, considering the prospect of eventually coming back. It was no small matter that we came to spend the end of our vacation in Yaoundé. The administration, the ministers, and the national radio were based there. My parents took advantage of those three weeks to make some contacts, meet people in various positions, and ask themselves, as you would at the end of a long meal, about the best way to go about things. The same questions and reactions kept coming up, like a refrain in the mouths of each and every one. *You want to come back home? Why do you want to come back? I hope you are thinking of coming back and building here. Come back, we need you here. Don't come back: you are more help to us over there. At least we know we can count on you in case of trouble . . . You have more money. You're the richest one among us, right?*

Many of the friends with whom we visited had returned back home to live, abandoning their past as Parisian students to put on the suit and tie of a public official or leader.

Some envied my parents, who had stayed *over there*, the distance having absolved them—at least that was what they thought—from the burden of the responsibilities placed on them by the community. *We don't have the time to strut about like you, at the wheel of a beautiful American car, driving around our family!* they would say maliciously. They would love to be given a second chance to show these White men, prove to them as they imagined my father spent his time doing, that *the Black man, he too, can succeed.* They would love to say, as they imagined Francis was able to, with conceit: "I live in Paris, I am an international civil servant. Let me introduce you to my wife and my five children." That would be a class act. They were eaten with up jealousy.

Others were patting themselves on the back, proud to be holding high-level positions. Of course they would never mention that quite often they were so bored in their jobs that they had begun to do what everybody else was doing: go to the office in the morning to deposit their files and briefcase, then disappear in to town to take care of their personal concerns, abandoning to their secretaries a line of people waiting, sometimes for hours, for their eventual return.

There was nothing better than the job of a civil servant: you did as you wished, and at the end of the month, you got a paycheck. *We too, we live pretty well here. Look around! Here is my wife (and my second wife), my children (ten, eleven, twelve), my house (much bigger than your little apartments), my car (that my houseboy washes every day), my garden in which the houseboy tends to each and every plant and essence, my office (my "second office"), the plantation I bought back in the village, the house I'm having built for my parents. And all of it, under the sun, what do you think! You can also come home. We can surely find a position for you somewhere. The national radio, isn't that interesting for you? You are a qualified journalist. Nothing stops you from becoming managing director, after all? We can already see you. We'd call you "our CEO"! Among those of us who were over there, some have become ministers . . . This is the moment, if ever there was one, to take advantage, to corrupt, to set things up, at our discretion . . . Come, join us, come and play in the*

big game of grandstanding with all its advantages, for those who know how to
fend for themselves . . .

What kind of compromise was hidden behind these itineraries? What
kind of seedy arrangements had been made with the authorities in place?
What kind of personal maneuverings? What kind of ethical compromises?
The great ideas launched only yesterday on the back benches of the cafés by
the Sorbonne, could they really hold up against the lure of power and the
financial advantages that created blind spots in the rearview mirror of
memory? Farewell ideals! The major reforms for the benefit of the people—
overboard.

No one would dare to have the indecency to bring those up to them. No
one had the right to take the moral high ground when they didn't live here,
right here, experiencing the famous *local realities*.

Among all their fellow classmates, was there even one who continued to
hold fast to their ideas of yesterday? Was that even possible? And did they
even want to? Francis probably couldn't answer that question. It was clearly
impossible to sincerely ask about the finer points in order to know *the real*
deal. Because it was obvious, *the country had gotten tougher. You didn't really*
know who was who. Who worked for the authorities and who was merely just
trying to get by, keeping a low profile to avoid putting their family at risk.

The 1970s were on the horizon, and they promised to be joyful, succulent,
and lucrative for the educated and well-trained elite, who knew how to take advantage of the times. They were rubbing their hands together in anticipation.
Why would anyone turn down that kind of loot? Who would be that crazy?
Flowing champagne starting at breakfast; whiskey aplenty starting at 4 p.m.;
and parties among dignitaries and babes in bell-bottoms with Colgate smiles
and Afros. James Brown was Black and proud, and Sidney Poitier had been married for some time to the daughter of Katherine Hepburn and Spencer Tracy.

Europeans were still there, continuing to take their part of the treasures
of war or as a cooperating country. Certain of them maintained that nothing
better existed beyond their civilization: Victor Hugo, Chateaubriand, the Age
of Enlightenment, and classical music. They were unwilling to let go of their
arrogance. At least they were no longer the only ones giving orders. Some of
their blond women were now to be found on the arms of rich Black men, with
chests puffed up with pride.

A handful of people presided at the head of a republic that was about to
see its day. You had to take advantage of the insane manna that had been

highly improbable a few years ago; quickly slip through the revolving door of these golden years; snatch up the gold, the diamonds, the teak, the sap from the rubber trees; and drain the sea of the shrimp and the canopy of its most unique species. Streets had to be built, not for the benefit of everyone, but so that you could go directly from the capital to your hamlet. Build a basilica almost as vast as that of the pope. Become more royalist than the king, the emperor.

Opportunities were readily available to those who had forgotten their principles and swapped out ethics for profit, enjoyment, and riches. It was just really all too tempting. No one wanted to look like the imbecile, the village idiot, incapable of living in the present because they were afraid for tomorrow. Tomorrow? Who knew what tomorrow would bring? Tomorrow, just like yesterday, would no doubt leave the ignorant masses by the side of the road, left holding the short end of the stick, as the saying went . . . Those who hadn't seen it coming and therefore had not been clever enough to position themselves. The mousetrap of colonialism had loosened up, structural adjustments had not yet been established, but cronyism was in full swing. In the meantime, let us shimmy and sway, live, enjoy, breathe, sweat out the drink under the sun, such were the ways of those in the know. Nope, clearly the future was still a ways away.

I can never know if my parents would have better resisted the persistent wave of desire for the material comforts that everyone was so insistent about wanting to display or see—all the visible signs of wealth and success. The life some would establish the moment they returned to their native land made clear a victory at the finishing line.

My father was clearly hesitating about jumping in. Viewed from the top of the diving board, the prospects were appealing, but the waters, somewhat troubled, hardly allowed you to measure the distance to the bottom. Jump? Dabble like the others? Say farewell to the days of great ideals and shamelessly forge ahead toward that phase when the pleasures would have been reaped? It was not exactly Francis's style. He had grown up following the discipline of a Protestant education where everything was earned by working for it, where only effort could lead to reward and allow for a victorious outcome. He could not fully grasp the overall laxity and was feeling more so contempt for it all. He was far too anchored in those indelible demands his elder brother had insisted on. He believed that those who had had the good fortune to go away and study and discover other parts of the world had a responsibility, upon return to their home country, to change their very own. Or at least try to do so.

But how could you make that happen? By throwing your hat in the political arena? His brother had taken that risk, and it swallowed him up. The family, worn out by so many difficulties, was still working through the pain and heartache, suggesting that what they had already been through had been more than enough. In fact, Francis couldn't find one person willing to talk about Marcel. As for us, the children, we did our best not to bring up the unpronounceable first name of an uncle, lurking in the thick clouds of taboos. Was his tomb located in Douala, in Yaoundé? Had someone taken Francis and Madé to kneel, hand in hand, in a place that was dedicated to him? Did such a place actually exist elsewhere than in the hearts of those who still kept thinking of that valiant soul that conspirators had destroyed?

There was no doubt Marcel would have been the best person to advise Francis, because he had shared with his brother the experience of having left and lived elsewhere. Like him, he had been exposed to other ways of living and doing things, had expanded his world, and could, thanks to that experience, offer the benefit of this openness to his own people. As brother and peer, he would have understood what Francis was feeling and continued to show him the way. Reluctantly, Marcel had had to let go of his brother's hand, and Francis was now left feeling distraught.

More than ever before, my father's heart sunk. *Émbè nyolo.* Courage. Yes, but what to do? There was no longer anyone around to advise him. The family wanted to forget the difficult times and preferred to bury the memory of his older brother in an abyss of silence. He couldn't find a single soul to take up the torch and stand up for what Marcel had defended in the past.

Certain people in the family went as far as to warn Francis. *Don't go and do like our brother. He suffered enough and made us suffer along with him. Because having the same name had not been a sinecure, you can believe us. When we told you to stay far away over there and not move, it wasn't for naught. The people in the government kept an eye on us for a long time. And it's still going on. Try to get a job somewhere in the Highest-of-the-Highest and you'll find out that they will not let you climb the ladder. They will ask you: "Francis, whose son? Whose brother?" and all of a sudden, they'll tell you they're "going to see" and will never see a thing. Tell us where all those great ideals took your brother? To his grave, no further. A doctor! If that wasn't merciless! He said he was fighting so that we could all have a better life, but all, who was that? We are his family, and now the mere mention of our name makes people shudder. They're afraid there'll be other hotheads like him who want to change things. So you, just don't make the same mistakes. Stay away from politics. Don't even talk about politics. Be happy to live and let that be that! Live as best a life as you can. And help us to live a bit better with the money you earn over there in the* mbènguè *of the White man. But let us say it again: don't go near any of it, the great ideals or the politics. Those who have, have. And those who don't, don't. This is how the world is made; we can't change it.*

Despite everything, Francis tried to put a foot in the door. He tried as best he could to approach former classmates from the university days. He wanted to live here, close to his own people, because his degrees would mean a lot more here. He wanted them to have the benefit of his experience. As the saying goes, you are never as good as when you are *home*.

But time had passed and people had changed. Many of the till-death-do-we-part friendships had naturally come undone. Francis got going all the same. Made contacts, met people. He even participated with a former classmate in creating an advertising message that he recorded for national radio broadcasting. *Hello friends, Hello Guinness.* During our stay, we heard his voice, full of conviction, several times on the radio. Win-win scenario, he told himself; I do a favor, and when the time comes, they'll be ready to return the favor.

Needless to say, bowing and scraping was not something with which Francis had much experience. It had never crossed his mind that a lot of small talk was required when you asked for something, that those in a position to help you needed additional motivation. Before anything, requests called for smooth talking, you needed to grease a few palms, do a few favors, actions and gestures that would, in turn, make folks indebted. The gangrene appeared gradually in all those who held so much as a sliver of power and then progressed rapidly among those at the top. In this regard, Francis proved to be less than skilled and his family mocked him. *If he imagined that all he had to do was spend two months of vacation back home to land himself a job, by merely taking a slight detour in a corridor, then he was really naïve.*

I imagine, however, that leaving aside his lack of skill or his naiveté, call it whatever you like, something else kept him from daring to stay. Indeed, time was going by, the departure date was drawing near, but if he wanted to, he could have settled down right away, *definitively,* and let the rest unfold. He was educated, after all, experienced, and there weren't so many with his profile. In theory, there was a place for him in his country. *The nation needs you* could be heard everywhere and the word "unemployment" didn't carry any meaning at that time. All he needed to do was simply make up his mind.

Stay. Madé would accept. Registering for schools, moving, quitting UNES-CO, all of that could follow because few things took on a logical order in life. If he decided to do so, yes, undoubtedly, everything would fall into place.

But the vacation had reserved an unpleasant surprise for him that was gnawing at him and making him think twice. The very young student who had left behind his people so many years ago, carrying the encouragement and the strength of a family full of faith in him, was now regarded as a leader in everyone's eyes. Because he had *become somebody* in Europe. Because, in the absence of his older brother, he was the only one who really understood the business affairs and the world of the White men. Those from whom he had hoped to receive comfort at the family reunion had placed him on a throne and were waiting for him to carry himself like a king. In the process, he had discovered loosening soil beneath his feet and arms stretched out toward him in hope. He was the only one among them who earned a decent living.

He had realized this since the very first day when a cohort had come out to greet him. A part of him was angry with himself for hating to see the convergence of all these people—cousins, uncles, aunts, nephews, supposed godchildren—who had introduced themselves first by claiming a bloodline and had subsequently ended up asking for financial help before heading back home. At the beginning, he had shown himself to be generous: no matter what you end up doing in life, a religious upbringing always manages to catch up with you. Kindness, donations, gifts, sharing, his father had fed him on all of these in the past. Then as time went on, he had learned to tighten his boot-straps, but he had swayed in trying to find a balance between helping others and being selfish. In the event of a *definitive* return home, he would have little choice but to contribute. As a leader. No one could imagine he would dream of doing things differently.

Like a noose around his neck, the picture of his own family plunged him into anxiety. The never-ending admiration they all had for him, the certainty that, thanks to him, they would never ever really want for anything. Behind it all, he could also read a bit of jealousy among them. Those who thought, *Why does he have such an easy life? Why him and not me?* He would have loved for them to recognize all the efforts he had had to make to get to the position he was actually in. *Europe didn't make it easy for anyone, if you only knew!* He would have wanted them to know it had been far from easy in the beginning. Nothing, in fact, had been easy. And if he had managed to get over every hurdle with his head held high, gathering up one by one in his travel bag the experiences that had made him the man he was today, everything had demanded determination. Even now, he had to confront difficulties on a daily basis to defend and hold on to his position.

He discovered the painful solitude that comes with being a leader, a king, in spite of himself, adorned in a crown of dazzling expectations by his family.

This vacation compelled him to look back and closely examine what he had left behind. And he discovered, regretfully, that nothing or not much had really changed. His great ideas for the world and for his country would not change anything, based on what he could see, with regard to the neighborhoods he had known. In the streets as much as by the waters toward the estuary, you still came across barefoot children with distended bellies waiting for something to eat. He had an elusive flashback to himself in the days gone by with his mates, poaching and scraping. Everybody was doing what they could to live fast before leaving this earth. There was hardly much more to do. Who could change the destiny of these children? *Whereas you can, for instance, change ours*, his family insisted.

How do you go from the child who is counting on others to the parent carrying the weight of the world on your shoulders? Bitterly. Returning home without the support of the family but in order to support the family would mean starting over from scratch. Having been the only members of their respective families to have had the benefit of an education, a woman and five children, on an adventure, in their land of origins. Obliged to start all over again: housing, job, and all the hoops he would need to jump through in the context of the *local realities*. Without any help, *because, of all us, you are the only one who has succeeded*. Without any beacons, *because you can't be counting on us to help you out, after all. You are the international civil servant, you have authority*. And on your shoulders rests the weight of a whole community.

Francis felt terribly misunderstood. How much time did he spend wavering? On the one hand, Paris and the picture of happiness like in a photo, pretty, a little family, an apartment in a prestigious neighborhood of the city, sincere friendships, American car, vacations in Provence, a respectable financial situation . . . On the other hand, nothing but difficulties. And amid it all, solitude. Not absolute solitude—his wife was with him, his children, his friends, his colleagues—but the kind of solitude reserved for those whom you can count on to lead, the solitude of the captain steering the helm who can't necessarily hope to have the support of anyone. That weighed heavily. Francis was overloaded. Something was rumbling deep within him, a murmur, which he was unable to pinpoint—sadness or unexpressed anger? When all was said and done, the vacation back home had saddened him. His heart hadn't hardened; it was breaking into pieces.

The questions kept coming one after the other: what can I do to help them and still manage to live my life with my own little family without feeling completely selfish? How do I resolve the equation: I am one of yours but I don't live here? Thanks to you, I managed to get out, and I owe that to you, but ... Then what? An unfathomable debt, which paralyzed him.

So before leaving, he made a decision. He would not go back to Paris with his hands empty. The family enjoined him to buy a plot of land on which to build. You have to invest in order to have at least real ground under your feet, something that will be yours. Moreover, a man of your age can't come all the way here, make this long journey, and find yourself staying at your sister-in-law's or your mother-in-law's place. You need to have your own house. It is more dignified for you. You have to show that you are also somebody here, even if you live over there. Buy the land, build on it, we'll take care of the rest. We'll make sure no one takes over your place. And when you come back on your next vacation, you'll be proud to cross the threshold of your own house, isn't that right?

He entertained the idea. Now that was a smart way to take action. There was really no need to think about it. He entrusted his affairs to a brother and an older sister, the one who was keeping somewhere in her home that strange inheritance that had come from deep waters and faraway countries: his guitar, like a family secret. He promised to buy a plot of land and send them some money orders as soon as they identified the best location on his behalf. They promised they would get the house built and keep him apprised of the progress being made. He left feeling that he had once again put his legs as a man back in good working order, acted like a responsible adult. Certainly, Marcel would have done the same. Marcel would most surely have given him the same advice. It was time for him to grow up, let go of his older brother's hand, and make his own decisions. They were a family. They formed a circle on which he could count.

We embarked on our return flight, and a few hours later, we were back in our comfortable building on rue du Champ de l'Alouette, with our neighbors, our friends, the local baker lady, A. Jeanne, the impeccable chrome of the white Ford Taunus in the garage, and the office-with-secretary at UNESCO. We had returned. And the project of going back home for good was postponed. At least we would have a roof of our very own to accommodate us during our next stay.

−10−

– Hello, you have a call from Cameroon. Will you accept the charges?

I remember those calls. The discussions, the arguments, the negotiations, the worries, the doubts, and the questioning. Imagining the space, the neighborhood. The photographs sent by post that never made it. The urgent calls. *I'm telling you it's a bargain. You have to make up your mind.* Paying to finalize the proceedings with the notary public's office. Then beginning the construction. The expenses, the made-up charges, the work stoppages. The rain, which destroyed, corroded, and damaged everything. Starting up the construction site again. The reports and updates by phone. The overwhelming doubt followed by renewed hope was enough for our father to announce one evening at dinner, with a judicious smile:

– Children, next year when we go to Cameroon, we'll be living in our own house.

Then doubt once more, that feeling of advancing blindly on uncertain ground, discovering as you went along the way the obstacles as they presented themselves. Money that had just been set aside would quickly disappear. And finally one day, confronted with the dread of a possible betrayal.

As usual in those days, what happened among the grown-ups was never shared with the children, even though nothing really escaped us in the different stages of the project. After weeks of excitement, our parents went through a grave period of despondency during which time the collect calls were few and far between.

– Children, in life, Francis declared one evening at the dinner table, you'll have to learn to know who you can really count on. It's very important, you'll see: you can't trust everybody. And the first person you need to be able to count on is yourself.

He shook his head slowly with a pained expression on his face.

Strangely enough those enigmatic words resonated first in my body, in my traitor of a body that I hardly recognized after the vacation. I had come back home otherwise reconciled with Cameroon, this dear country, I had finally left with regret. *Mboa'a su* means finally feeling good "at home" and corresponded well with the flavors on my palate and the joyful beating of my heart. The moment I was on the return flight, I had begun to imagine how I was going to narrate in details my adventures in the bush. I would use the experience I had had with Biquette to depict myself as a tamer of gazelles, then I would report in particular the story of my combat with a boa constrictor, whose infinitesimal proportions and yellow-orange coloring before cremation most people knew nothing about.

However, once back home, I was all befuddled. A new person was appearing before me during that brief period prior to resuming school. So even while my environment was familiar to me—here at least there were neither giant ants nor geckos—my toys no longer interested me. I got rid of my dolls and their wardrobes, for which I had sewn some pieces with my grandmother who had taught me how to thread a needle. It now took me only three steps to cross the living-dining room. I kept banging my head into the walls and into angles in the apartment hallway. My trousers and shirts were too short, my shoes too small, and, right in front of the bathroom mirror, I came face to face with a pair of protruding domed discs on my chest. I gazed disapprovingly at this new body, which seemed entirely foreign to me. I had grown.

If the package I was supposed to wrap myself in was changing shape, without having alerted me, then my father was wrong: the first person on whom I could count was clearly not myself.

My mind was getting away from me even more than my bodily parts. My erratic, temperamental reactions would surprise me. I fought with my sister to change the order of who slept where in our bunk bed, and once I got exactly what I wanted, I was still unsatisfied. I became quite critical about all the rules of family life. I got into secret conversations and shady discussions with my brothers and sister as if I were in a council of war. I wanted some new rules promulgated, such as the right not to have to clear the table some nights or to clean the bathtub after oneself. I wanted them to stop asking me if my hands were clean before I sat to eat: I was prepared to take full responsibility for my sicknesses if I chose to keep exposing myself to bacteria. I found it unbearable that the boys got to go do the shopping with our father at the UNESCO commissary while us girls had to stay home and help our mother in the kitchen. Questioning the division of chores merely spurred my brothers on to mock me and criticize, in turn, my budding feminist consciousness without understanding the seriousness of my grievances. I sulked, wrapped myself up in my own haughtiness, disregarded my brothers out of hand, and did my utmost to despise them. I didn't know what to do with this indomitable feeling I had inside of me, which would be sure to rear up on its hooves were it not so tightly harnessed.

My entrance into sixth grade coincided with these ongoing annoyances. I was lucky to happily have a reason for personal pride on the first day of the school year. Each teacher asked us to complete information sheets, and I had the pleasure of writing several times during the day the word *musicologist* on the sheets I turned in. I noticed this word aroused a glimmer of admiring curiosity, and I was only too ready to answer their questions on the topic, all while doing my best to appear modest, by keeping my head and my gaze turned downward. I had a hard time concealing my pride when I explained:

– My father is the doctor for all the people who make music all over the world: they all have to consult with him.

As a matter of fact, my father had been promoted at UNESCO: he was no longer a part of the public information department. Going forward, he would become the director, responsible for overseeing all the programs having to do with music in the world. Over the past weekend we had celebrated the news with a cake and flutes of champagne. I was even given permission to take a sip from a flute. The school year had begun in grand style, and I was already benefiting from a halo of prestige, thanks to my father.

At the end of that first school day, when our class was getting ready to go through the junior high school gates, I noticed a street sweeper carrying away the dead leaves on the other side of the street. I was overcome by a horrible feeling when two of my new classmates turned toward me and asked:

– Is that your dad?

I choked, swallowed, strangely paralyzed by a mix of shame and anger toward the unknown street sweeper. Why did he have to show up and make me fall from my newly acquired pedestal right at the school gate? The students disbanded as they kept on laughing. I walked home alone slowly, deep in thought. I was angry with my father for having such a dark complexion that he could be confused with a street sweeper. I was also angry with my mother for being so polite and always having perfect manners. The nature of my hair intrigued my classmates, and that immediately affected me. I envied theirs, apparently easier to manage than mine. I no longer wanted to spend my Sunday mornings getting braids. I wanted to wear my hair long as well, so that at the slightest movement I could feel it on my neck. I was to inflict yet another form of torture on myself when my mother, war weary, held up a hair-straightening iron to me. I was striving as best I could toward the woman I would become one day. We were still the only Africans in our building and our neighborhood. Would I always be different? Would I ever be allowed to blend into the society to which I was born and where I grew up?

I was at that age where everything weighed heavily on me. My body was changing and becoming an increasingly exasperating nuisance. I was angry at it for all of a sudden drawing the attention of men, for provoking whistles from the construction workers. My brothers' comments about the size of my posterior upset me even if I tried not to show my feelings. From one day to the next, my parents stopped looking at me as a child. I was forced to comply with expectations that I didn't even understand: the image that they had made up of what a young lady ought to be like in *o mboa*, in the home country. Because it was really all about that for my siblings and I: as we continued to grow and make this land and this country, where we were born, our own, our parents strived to make us also belong to their country of origin, that mythologized Eden. They wanted us to be ready for when that day would come for us to seamlessly make the return journey to the promised land.

Luckily I had some calm nights when my deep waters stopped boiling. Usually those were the nights when the habitual rules of life within our family were interrupted by an announcement from our father:

– Tonight, my little lambs, we're going to do Paris by night.

For me, the formula was magical: "do Paris by night," meant going out when we should be going to bed. Travel across Paris together by car, like tourists. An absolute privilege. After getting us all into the car, Francis would sit before the wheel with our mother to his right, always impeccably dressed, in a pencil skirt, high heel pumps, and a distinguished composure . . . On those nights, in my eyes, she was once again a princess. In the back seat, we would be fighting to get a seat by the window. Obviously, there were only two lucky ones—the older ones—who managed to get these prestigious observation sites. For the other three, which included me, all we could do was twist our necks to get a glance of the monuments in their entirety. That scene would repeat itself over and over again, and each time I would become ever more infuriated and end up making such a fuss that I would eventually bring myself to tears.

Fortunately, minutes later, I would be feeling elated: I loved these night excursions. I was convinced that my classmates were forbidden to go out at night, and, each time, I was so excited in anticipation of being able to tell them every little detail—real and imagined—about my Parisian crossings. From the back seat of the Ford Taunus, I would stick out my chest and raise my chin as high as possible, certain I would impress anyone who might be likely to take notice of me. As a treat, at each of these outings, my father never failed to go by the Pont Alexandre III. It was "my bridge," a gift he had given to me and neither my brothers nor sister would have the nerve to challenge me about its ownership. I would look out for this moment, which was an absolute triumph for me: we were shooting a film and I was the lead actress.

– Look, Madame Kidi, we are on your bridge, my father would declare.

Yes, it was my bridge, my exclusive property, and the city was ours. With all due respect to President Félix Faure and Tsar Nicolas. I tried to learn by heart the names of the tourist sites, the important buildings, and some of the many monuments. La Chambre des Députés, Place de la Concorde, the Petit and Grand Palais, Place de L'Etoile, Trocadéro, Les Invalides . . . But also, Musée Rodin, les chevaux de Marly, Place du Tertre, Montmartre. It all made me feel like I was in a dream.

I cannot begin to imagine, in all fairness, how my father must have been feeling, what it must have meant to him, the fact that he was driving his own family, in his own car, through one of the most prestigious cities in the Western world. The bare feet and distended belly of his childhood were far behind in the distance from where he was on those nights. His studies had been his lucky break. He shifted the gear and was joyfully accelerating to the maximum on a new path. The roaring engine signaled that a trophy had been won following a difficult uphill battle against destiny.

Our eyes were wide open, and as we were slowly heading back to our neighborhood, we each savored the pleasure of that moment, an enchanting parenthesis in which there were neither parents nor children, simply protagonists in the same dream.

–11–

Francis woke up with a start.

In the same way a sculptor works with his clay, he'd always thought he was in charge of shaping his own future. He began to realize that nothing was really happening because his were not the only hands in the clay. Family, in the most expansive sense of the term, always had a hand in his life, meddling, stirring things up, and turning everything upside down. He decided to step back from all of it.

Going forward, he would be standing alone at the pier, on the other side of the shore, where there was not one boat in sight that could suggest a possible return journey. Indeed they could always express their appreciation of him, but they would be doing so from a good distance, insofar as he continued sending the money orders to take care of those who couldn't afford to get a given treatment at the hospital and to pay the *school fees* for the nephews and distant cousins he had never met. No one was waiting for him back there; they needed him to stay right where he was. No one had warned him that at the end of the straight and narrow path, there was nothing to be had. Not a port. Not a harbor. He found himself in a *no-man's-land*, as empty as a wind-swept jetty, closed off in the dead-end corridor of a top security wing. Understanding his mistakes, he began to see that his future was not heading in the direction he wanted. Francis tensed in his jaw. Roadblocks and hurdles often indicate the direction one really wants to take deep down inside. He kept dreaming of *going back* home. He, too, wanted to participate in building his country, be there and make a real contribution.

His longing to return was, however, caught in a corridor between two closed doors. Behind him was the door to a country in which changes would take place but without him being able to participate. The door before him, however, was not double locked, but it was heavy and difficult to open. It was the door to a country that, after two wars, still failed to recognize the faces of those that had come to its aid. This country was still not ready to open wide its doors and let him in. The access was certainly there but no one was going to invite him in to take a seat. He could always show up with all his degrees and knowledge, but he would always be an African, in other words, *a Black man*. And if an international organization was prepared to hire him, he had better go for it because nothing guaranteed that he could have an opportunity at this level anytime in the near future at his disposal.

So there he was, caught between two doors with five children to feed and a wife at home. He would have to carry the load, and the load was heavy. An overwhelming sadness flooded him. He had a hard time keeping a smile on his face. On Sundays, he forced himself to take his family out to the city gardens, where the children played together, imitating their favorite film super heroes with capes and swords. When nighttime came they would be hunkered down indoors like the Chevalier Lagardère, surrounded by enemies in the moats of the Château de Caylus. What would become of these children, born far from their place of origin? Would they get a better welcome than he had had? Less harsh? Would at least one door be open to them? Or would they find themselves, much like their father, trapped by their ambitions in a society that had a hard time accepting that they existed? The walls were closing in on him, his head was touching the ceiling and he could barely breathe. Life had become so complicated and yet it had seemed so easy. A wife, five children, and a great job—an idyllic picture in a photo album.

In those days, no one spoke of nervous breakdowns. No one even knew what it meant. Only lunatics suffered from sicknesses of the soul, everybody else—"normal" people—quieted their malaise by quelling it as best they could. In our home, my father held it together by doing what he had always been taught to do: working like a madman. He essentially numbed himself by working like a maniac and enveloped this magical formula within the coarse fabric of severity. He was so hard on himself that he propagated a similar demeanor in everyone around him, insisting that we, his children, advance at his pace. In time, there would be no respite, no breaks were allowed: for him, the only way out of the situation imposed on us, the only way for us to live and have a dignified future in a country that was not our native home, was to work hard and succeed in school—high grades and advanced degrees that we would accumulate, that was the vade mecum that would place us above the riff-raff.

His exacting standards would have a lasting impact on our childhood of golden skies, in that we were suddenly shaken up and made to stand at attention. Our otherwise tender father became hotheaded, such that we were increasingly afraid of him and constantly apprehensive of his outbursts. His silence would give way to periods of irritability that we just couldn't understand. The Saturday ritual of signing our weekly school report would quickly turn into a tribunal. He was ready to point out the slightest misstep. He would read into every little comment made by the teachers, immediately reformulating the slightest remark into a question:

> – *Can do better*. What does that mean, *Can do better*? Why aren't you among the students whose teachers say quite simply: *Very good or perfect*? Surely there are students in that category. Why aren't you among them?

At some point our mother gave up playing her role as go-between, and the adolescent irritation, combined with the demands of our father's regime, would eventually lead to a permanent split between our father and some of us.

By some divine intervention, the return journey to Cameroon would be miraculously postponed to a much later date: UNESCO needed Francis to go on a journey to Africa for a month or possibly longer. At the time, he was unaware that this mission would mark his renaissance. He was tasked with carrying out an inventory of all the music on the continent. When he took off, with his suitcase in one hand and typewriter in the other, he was convinced that he was going to be spending his days traveling and his nights writing reports.

We were, on the other hand, relieved to finally breathe again, freed at least for a while from the paternal iron fist. The angles of the apartment suddenly seemed to soften and the rooms showed some disorder, which our mother decided to tacitly accept as a natural shift in setting.

While we were in Paris enjoying a secret recreational and salutary period, Francis, out in the field, was reconnecting with parts of himself that in the last years had been silenced, buried of necessity, to learn and fulfill his professional responsibilities. On that journey, he was a part of a team with a

German colleague and a French technician. As the head of mission, he had to explain to the city authorities the purpose of his visit and what he hoped to gain from the explorations. While the team's chauffeur skillfully maneuvered the best routes and pursued leads, Francis would, at moments, realize the superior tone he was using and feel ashamed.

When he first arrived, he was also embarrassed to form with his colleagues a stiff-looking group of men in immaculate shirts buttoned with cufflinks. The villagers who welcomed them so warmly, did they see him in the same way they saw the White men who accompanied him? His German partner always assumed Francis knew best how to behave in these circumstances. Although Francis had never had the opportunity to go this far into the heart of these countries, he felt obliged to do his best and to ensure that he knew better than anyone else the depth of the enclave. *Me too, I am African.* There was always that persistent shadow of the burden of a double duty to know and understand as much, if not more, than the others. Before the rural authorities, chiefs, and delegates, he would feign a mastery of the local codes and etiquette.

While he was taking on these situations, the rhythm and customs of another world order was gradually blindsiding his Western posture. He attended celebrations during which his team were overjoyed to discover traditions that amazed and expanded their curiosity. "Forget who you were when you came here, and choose to become who you really are," the masks seemed to murmur. He would admit to no one that he was himself going from one discovery to another, yet his impassioned curiosity was only fooling him. More recently paralyzed in a silent mourning, he was being revitalized through the grace, the beauty, the variety, and originality of the music he was hearing and the performances he saw. Folklore? The word choice was poor to encompass the scope of what he was witnessing, these ways of being and living that he had been neglecting or had forgotten.

He would need to find the words to express in his reports the unparalleled significance of art for these people. *His people.* Because he felt and knew it to be true; he belonged to these communities. His senses, his skin, his heart were telling him so, and his whole body had reclaimed the instinctive impulse that traversed the most secret corners of *his continent*. He had somehow lost his admiration for Africa and didn't know how to reconnect with it. Worse, he feared he might have to start all over from scratch to overcome the disappointments of the aftermath of independence. Yet Africa was here, right before his eyes, in the warm light of the end of the day and the red and yellow banners of light emitting from the blaze, when the percussionists warmed the skin of their instruments and called out the dancers, who emerged from their huts adorned in raffia and ankle bells. Africa was here, sincere, open to listening, waiting to be better understood by those sons who had left to sharpen their intelligence on other continents, so that these proud descendants would fully grasp its importance and impose it on the highest step of the world stage. Francis's heart began to beat to the rhythm of the drums. He was hungry for that new part of himself that was coming alive, experiencing a rebirth, the part that had been hidden, forced into silence during all these years and was now brewing deep within. More than an emotion, it was like a veritable electroshock that was undoing his inner makeup. His beliefs, his knowledge, his training, it was all being put into play with the impact of a well-placed uppercut. *They hadn't taken that away from us. They had not been able to undo, break, annihilate that.*

Our father was no longer the same man when he came back to Paris. His face, so often tinged with sadness, appeared lighthearted when we saw him in the doorway. Besides the gifts he had already anticipated bringing back for us, there was a second bag filled with all sorts of musical instruments. At the beginning, he placed them wherever he could on shelves and on the walls of the apartment.

But the idea of turning these instruments into mere decorative objects would not last very long. In the evenings after work, he would blow into the mouthpiece or tap on the sound box. He would fill the water drum with water and turn the grains of the rain stick. These unexpected companions of our father made him increasingly happier and proved to have mysterious powers themselves as they kept luring him to explore them.

Each time Francis took one of the instruments into his hands, he pushed farther and farther away all the sorrow that had had a grip on him and forced him into silence for so long. As he reconnected to a world that had been closed off to him since the days of his early childhood, Francis's familiar mask of severity began to erode: he rediscovered the pleasure of playing. It was like a knock-out punch, the kind that makes you see a thousand stars and causes you to lose all notion of time and space, a delectable loss of balance that, in the end, makes you lose your grip on everything. Moving full speed ahead, Francis's fingers on the keyboard typed up the edifying report that he hoped the whole world would read: *On the African continent there is an inventiveness that is to be found nowhere else in the world. There is an idea of the musical note and a research of sound that has led people to create instruments—call them "machines" if you wish—that aim to produce original sounds. And Ladies and Gentlemen, this is happening on the continent from which I originate, precisely among my people. And let me tell you, Ladies and Gentleman, I am proud. This creativity; this science of the irrational; this aversion for what you call good taste; this preference for originality, for the unexpected, for the uncommon; it is being conveyed right before our eyes with the music and conception that all these African people, my people, are expressing about the world, the sands of time, plants, and animals.*

Francis was inhabited by these enlightened convictions. There was a sort of strained bitterness toward all those who refused to have him experience his full humanity each time images of the dark side and savagery were evoked with regard to his person. The pages of his report fell from the typewriter one by one, accumulating on the floor into a thick pile that my mother gathered up, numbered, and read. Those pages took the form of a book that revealed the rigor of the essayist and the enthusiasm of the intellectual who became aware of the fundamental significance of his assertions. He was the first African to document these statements. Weeks went by during which our father was so busy, and we were just so happy to have a breather. Then the book was ready to be submitted.

A second divine impulse then drove Francis to pick up his guitar and make it vibrate. When was the last time he had played his instrument? He took the guitar out of the case, tuned it for quite some time, and began to play. He had lost quite a lot of the agility he used to have when he had imagined becoming the next Andrés Segovia. Despite his initial awkwardness, the instrument resonated from the very first chord. Francis decided to pick up where he had left off, relearn some classical works and take on some new ones, such as Handel and Bach, to become second to none as he had always done with everything. He had come up against a wall that had basically collapsed on him and almost crushed him. While in the past he had almost given in, with a lighter heart he was now ready to jump into life feet first.

A few weeks later, with my ear glued to his bedroom door, I could hear him ranting and raving at himself, angry that he had forgotten how to play well. My father would stop and start over again and again. He was looking for just the right note. A piece of music for the guitar was in the making and I stood there, right behind that door, waiting impatiently for this musical treat, excited, wanting to be the first to have the honor of hearing it. My father was walking on the singular path of creators that leads to the greatest discoveries. By working hard to bring forth from within his depths the melody that penetrated his entire body, he had taken up the challenge and was now standing tall, proud, upright in his stirrups, ready to give it his all for the new opus of his life.

I was moved so deeply that tears rolled down my cheeks. At times, music can make you afraid, create a strange kind of fear that nevertheless draws you in and makes you want to experience it again and again, as in a sacred experience. I entered his room, feeling I had finally landed on solid ground after having traversed a turbulent river in a pirogue. Francis was looking for something he could neither describe much less name. He was certain of one thing: the mystery was in the guitar and he was exploring every single possibility. He unlocked the body of the guitar, unsure of what he might find. He allowed himself to be inhabited by a note, a feeling. Freedom was here, hidden within the infinite whirling vibrations, in these sounds that resonated and persisted. Francis had no idea from whence the notes originated that he kept repeating, over and over again until he finally committed them to paper as musical scores. The music theory from his childhood, his personal Bible, finally made sense, so many years later. There were long periods of trances. He let himself slip into them and taking my hand brought me along with him. I closed my eyes, forgetting where I was, and glided into a strange and bountiful torpor.

Then the music stopped, the inspiration vanished; my father and I looked at each other. His finger on his lips, he pronounced the pact that bound us to secrecy:

– What you've just heard stays between the two of us.

I was in seventh heaven. When he wasn't composing melodies that came to him by way of mysterious inspiration, he persevered single-mindedly on classical compositions. He had this vague feeling that if he wanted his personal works that were so particular to be understood, he had to intersperse his repertoire with pieces that were recognizable to those accustomed to guitar performances from the Western world. He needed to master the instrument and reveal himself to himself at the same time, learn to know his limits, understand patience, and work through the moments of exasperation.

One fine morning Francis declared:

– Children, we are going to do something big together: we are going to create
a choir. Junior, you are the eldest so you can sing bass with me. Girls, you
will be the sopranos. And little ones, you will sing the mezzo-soprano. Now,
listen to this. What do you think?

Bona basu, our people, was what the song said, but we were absolutely incapable of discerning what it could mean symbolically. Madé joined in and
accompanied our youthful voices. Our little Republic grew more close-knit,
gathered around the sound hole of the guitar. Inspired by the prospects of this
new personal gamble, in the following weeks our father launched into composing a repertoire and creating melodies that we graciously sang.

Little by little during the course of that year, a miracle took place beneath
our roof. The world flipped backward, the poles intersected and the stars
aligned and swapped places. Screws and nuts loosened. Our voices rose up
the way flowers spring forth in the undergrowth. It had been a matter of till-
ing the soil. The snow had melted and imbibed the soil at the first sign of sunlight. Sunday morning at about 9 o'clock, the house was filled with celestial
sounds: the choruses and oboes of the cantatas and Brandenburg Concer-
tos by Johann Sebastian Bach became our hymns over several months. We
subsequently went on to the sensual complicity of Ella Fitzgerald and Louis
Armstrong in *Porgy and Bess*. I sang unapologetically at the top of my lungs
with these musical monuments, articulating the lyrics as though I were singing with my own friends. Thanks to this renewed oxygen, the atmosphere was
lighter all around. The family puzzle took on a whole new form. Music took
center stage and illuminated everything around it.

One by one, the instruments brought back from Africa—and eventually
from all over the world—would refuse or otherwise give themselves over to
our father's fingers. He would soon add his voice to the sounds of these instruments, and the language of his childhood would most often manifest itself in his musical compositions.

*E titi bu so biala ba muengé mwam o bon bunya . . . Biala ba muengé mwe
na na ma pula no longo . . . Nyol'a ngo . . .* (It's pointless to look up the lyrics
to my song today . . . The lyrics to the song I'm ready to sing . . . For you . . .)

In our family, otherwise so heavily policed, disorder made a grand
entrance into our home that year. Our father gave in to a kind of craziness.
Say it, play it, and take pleasure in it—Francis wanted it all at the same time.

He knew and felt this was the direction he needed to take. To respond to this irresistible calling, day by day he split himself in two. In the mornings, he would leave the apartment dressed in his gray suit, white shirt, and the requisite tie around his neck. During weekday evenings and on weekends, he reclaimed his freedom and slipped into a pair of jeans and his African tunics. *Ebuba e m'ongwanè mba*, the tunic helps me, he would say appreciatively. He reconnected with his long-forgotten bohemian life, those days when he was a student journalist, spending his time in the Parisian underground scene pretending to be a musician from Cuba. This time around, however, the stakes were considerably higher, vital even: to be oneself, to finally become oneself. Driven by an explosive intuition, he knew he had to pursue this exploration as far as he could go.

When summer vacation came around that year, we would head to the South of France but with our mother alone. The journey would take a full day. At the rest stops on the highway, families took out their provisions and ate lunch while Radio Monte-Carlo played in the background. *What is that pretty African woman doing with five children? And the kids are so greedy! Apparently she is the one driving . . . Where is her husband?* some must have asked.

> – Children, ignore the looks, Madé suggested, not in the least bothered. Don't give it a second thought. It's normal that people are curious about you, you know. You are each so beautiful, each and every one of you!
> – We should be showing a little swagger then, decreed my oldest brother.

At the end of the day, after endless winding roads in the mountain between Toulon and the village of Beausset, we came upon our house, situated between two cypress trees with a sprawl of vineyards in front and wheat fields gently sloping all the way back to the highway in the distance. Our mother divided up the rooms, found the armoires filled with lavender-perfumed sheets, and we unpacked our belongings and made our beds before dinner. That first evening, the smallest creaking sounds in the house caused us to jump and the sight of all the cobwebs made us shudder. In the light of the next morning, however, we began to feel more at home in the house. We went out and bought provisions in town and found the local post office so that we could call and reassure our father back in Paris that we had arrived safe and sound.

We rediscovered the pleasures of swimming in the sea, soccer and volleyball matches, and badminton, as well as the wonderful flavors of fruit and vegetables of the Provençal summer. Meanwhile, our father was transforming the living room into a recording studio where tapes kept turning and cables meandered between the feet of the microphone. He was recalling his ambitions as a young man, the promises he had made to himself that summer at Lake Michigan, where he had heard for the very first time the master of the Spanish guitar whose performance had made such a mark on him. It was now his turn to enter into musical paradise. Francis played and enjoyed himself. He played and played and got completely carried away.

One morning he woke up, remembered us, hopped on a train and found us all lined up, silently waiting for him on the platform at the train station in Toulon. He kissed our mother, smiled at us, then did a head count and threw a mischievous wink our way. My older siblings took his luggage. I took his guitar. Upon leaving the train station, he got into the driver's seat of the Taunus, and Madé directed him all the way to the house where we were staying. He visited the house, nodded in a sign of approval, and lingered on the terrace admiring the breadth of the view and the sunlight embracing the wheat fields.

– My friend Jacotte, she was not exaggerating at all. It's magnificent here, he remarked. And I am so happy to see that you have all settled in so nicely.

Then he removed a device from his suitcase and held it up to our eyes, which were filled with surprise.

– Children, this here is a Super 8 camera. I am going to be filming you.

In addition to the guitar and the camera, he also brought his typewriter, his recorder, his melodica, a sanza, and an African keyboard. Over ten days, the sounds would emanate continuously from our parents' bedroom and cascade down the hills surrounding the house. At the end of the vacation, he put away his jeans and sandals to "head up" to Paris. Life had just taken on a more flavorful turn, and we were all so excited.

–12–

When I began the new school year, I felt as though I was split into two different people. Like my father and his suits, each morning I slipped into the uniform of the good student and headed out, with absolutely no enthusiasm for school. I was in ninth grade and loathed my encounters with equations and percentages in math class. Back home in the evenings, when I heard my father turn the key in the lock, I would put on my other face and dash to welcome him home.

– Madame Kidi, *é mala ndé nèni?* Madame Kidi, how are you?

I waited for him to come out of the bathroom dressed in his *ebuba*, sewn from an African wax print. He would pick up his guitar, which was within reach on the bed, and begin playing. In no time, we came together, caught up in the same rhythm and were elevated, soaring, above everything. Feeling the sounds with my eyes closed, my head rocked back and forth. I felt like I understood my father better than anyone and that he perceived me far beyond words. I came into a sphere I had never before experienced, a universe tucked behind all other worlds, hidden from the eyes by six fine strings strung on a varnished wooden box in the shape of a woman. We sailed away, abandoned the notion of time by the grace of notes becoming melodies. I believed I would always be that one person with whom a dialogue would never need words, that woman above all other women, the muse, who inspired and also admired the fervor he brought to the creative process.

Tonight Francis was getting dressed to perform his very first recital. He put on a shirt with a starched collar, and my mother helped him to button up his cuff links, a G clef for each sleeve. She secured the bowtie around his neck and helped him to tighten up the belt in his back with staples. He put on his harness, as would a noble Spaniard, his back arched ready to showcase himself. He cut an imposing figure. She looked at him and recognized the man she had given her hand to in marriage so many years ago. The contours of his face, which had been blurred by her wedding veil on that day, came closer to her to kiss her, and she saw a man who had become even more handsome with time. There would never be another man in her life. He fulfilled her in every possible way.

He was shaking. Not from fear but from the joy that he was going to share this moment with all the people whose voices could be heard as far back as in his dressing room. That must be what stage fright was like: trembling at the idea that you are about to give of yourself. The organizers were rubbing their hands together: the house was full; concertgoers had been turned away. They were themselves surprised by the turnout given that no one had ever heard about the artist invited to perform. But classical guitar was quite the rave those days so that must have explained the crowd that night, in addition to the fact that the recital was taking place at the American Cultural Center on rue du Dragon in Saint-Germain-des-Prés, *the* place to discover new artists. Francis slipped on his jacket. He had broken in the sleeves earlier in the day and would be feeling less restricted by the stiffness of the fabric once he began to play.

Play. A word he never thought would ever apply to him; a word only authorized for children. From this day forward, it was going to be his word; he was going to be enjoying himself, playing. Playing. Playing professionally. And enjoy being able to impart to the audience the vertiginous sensation of no longer belonging to one's self, suspending one's presence, all while the music, this invisible force, soared imperceptibly straight to the heart. At a quick pace, he entered the stage and the spotlight followed him. The audience was so taken by surprise to see a Black man in a black tuxedo with a guitar in his hand that they forgot to applaud his entrance. The poster had indicated his name and announced, "Works for guitar." You could hear the squeaking of his shoes and then the stool creaking once he took his seat. The silence made everyone attentive. He felt and knew that what would happen that night would forever shape the future. The fingers of his left hand approached the neck of the guitar while his right hand turned toward the center of the instrument. He began to play.

In no time the bass sounds hammered out a cadence that resonated like a calling to everyone present. *Come. Gather round, someone is about to take the floor!* A high-pitched note in the trebles was heard, as in a speech filled with directives. *Have you seen the world? Do you know it? Let me tell you, it is immense, it is virtually infinite, and in this immense world men are multitudinous . . . Do you know that people, everywhere, however different in their appearance, all seek in the depth of their beings answers to the same questions?* Narrated by the guitar, the long litany about the world and about life filled the stage, swelled and extended as far back as the farthest rows in the room; and it overwhelmed the senses of all the people present, capturing their hearts and seizing on their whole inner wiring. Never—and when I say never I mean *never*—ever before had they experienced a similar shock to their being. The music spoke in a language that no one knew but that together everyone understood. Francis kept on playing and the piece—titled *Black Tears*—would go on for twenty minutes without interruption. And during all that time, I doubt a single person moved, coughed, or even blinked. The sounds circulated, filling the room and creating a collective trance. I can't, of course, be certain of exactly what took place that night and whether, in reality, things happened as I have described them. Of all that was unfolding while the art genie transferred his energy into his interpreter, who in turn transferred the divine elixir of the music that was flowing out note by note. Listening in a trance. Senses stunned. Unraveled by a feeling of euphoria. Surrendering, happy to have experienced this unusual journey.

When the artist stopped playing, on a final chord whose notes took off into the arches, no one dared to move. No one, not even Francis, who wondered whether or not the silence itself was not a sign of deception. He raised his tense, inquiring face slightly. Six long seconds passed before the first applause erupted in the first row. Suddenly there was a sort of surge, the cork had popped out of the bottle and the whole house finally exploded in exhilaration. Francis hesitated for a minute, smiled, stood up with his guitar in hand, shook his head, then bowed before leaving the stage with a sprightly step.

His life had just made a leap toward the stars. Beyond his wife and children, his music could actually make people's hearts flutter! Until that moment, he himself had not been able to judge the quality of his work. He had allowed himself to be led by his intuition and followed blindly without ever knowing in which secret chest the treasure might lay. And there it was, before him and in his ears, in the people smiling with him as though they, too, had been liberated, letting the droplets of sweat drip from the musical encounter they had experienced together. There was no more reason for doubts. There was nowhere else to go looking, no further outcome to fear. His life was opening up right before him, mapped out by the beam emanating from the spotlight. The path was there, behind all those hours he had devoted to practicing his instrument and all the work he had dutifully carried out at UNESCO to favor the greater good of culture and worldwide education.

Once he hung up the phone; sent his secretary home; filed away all the reports; completed the conferences, the speeches, and the recommendations that the State more or less disregarded; once the entire racket was behind him, Francis was finally free to go home and enter his nook situated at the end of the corridor with nothing but his six-string instrument. There he would create the music that made it possible for him to rise and greet each new day.

There was something mystical about his initiative. It was not that candles were lit up and priests gathered to follow a real liturgy. But he knew—he felt it—something had happened to him and was going on inside him ever since he had given his first public recital. Something coming from very far away, from the waters of the Atlantic Ocean, had perpetuated.

His brother Marcel had also been present in the concert hall, not to monitor him but in the audience, carefully paying attention to that "good" note, serene, thrilled to be able to relax for a moment and delight his ears with a performance his eyes could no longer enjoy. Francis had dedicated the performance to his brother: that unique musical bond whose ephemeral quality deserved to be relished. To do well, going forward he would need to innovate. Re-create the magic of the music performed at the concert, keep playing melodies, like the alghaita players do, blowing and playing all at once. Infuse new life.

He knew he had now found a way to tell his story. Finally tell the story of the Africa that as a child he was told to erase, put behind learning about the Gauls in school and Bach at his father's church. Thanks to his guitar, he was finding his way to the house of the fetish priest, the medicine man who used his thumbs to pluck the keys of the magical box—the sanza. In the past, it had been understood as unwise to get too close to his home for no one really knew what he was capable of or the full extent of his powers. Francis now made a point of learning everything he might have learned from the medicine man.

He wanted the whole world to finally know the power of his people's culture. He wanted to be the messenger, the mediator. He could not succeed as he had hoped to do at the institution where he worked. They were speaking about music without really understanding that it was literally impossible to speak about it. *Music has to be lived*, Francis kept telling himself. You've got to take it in, breathe it in and out nonstop.

He was about to make a major decision.

Following that first concert, my father was never the same. What had inhabited his entire being had finally made its way to an enthusiastic audience. He could hardly believe his own ears. What this meant was that it was not only about pursuing this work, but it was also possible to imagine sharing it. That first major success encouraged a persistent faith that drove him to keep on going. This man, who had spent most of his life obeying and adhering to reason, discovered a space that allowed him to let go completely. His heart finally freed itself of the glaze that had covered it up.

The first recital was followed by a second engagement. Then another. And then another. *Might it be possible for you to come to our home and perform? We are a small organization from the village, but we have access to a banquet room. We hear that your concert is a truly unique experience and that we absolutely have to see you perform. Might you be able to . . .?*

On Friday or Saturday evenings, guitar in hand, he got on the train. He was performing. News about his music was traveling by word of mouth. Was he now an artist? He was cautious and kept his activities from his UNESCO colleagues. And, likewise, he kept from the concert organizers and theater owners the fact that during the daytime he was working at an international organization in the seventh arrondissement. He reconnected with the whole scene: the changing rooms, the backstage setting, and the memory of those nights when he used to hang out in the Parisian basements pretending he was an American or Cuban musician. He used to play the maracas and the congas with Manu, my mother's cousin, a saxophone player, who loved to throw me up in the air and hold on to me by the tips of his fingers, laughing the whole time.

Wherever Francis went, his performances were a success. The usual pieces of the masters of classical music were readily discerned, followed by compositions of novel chord progressions and syncopated rhythms that were being discovered for the first time, and which surprised and delighted. Chords that stirred people emotionally.

He decided to submit one of his songs to a production company. In those days, that was how it was done: you sent in a score, a text, or a recorded track. He sent in a tape. Without taking it too seriously, he chose a song he really enjoyed and recorded it in one take. The song had come to him when he recalled the sun on the sea during his walks on the beach in La Rochelle. He had been far away from his native country at the time, but certain strolls would remind him of the mornings in his own neighborhood in Bona Kou'a Mouang, when Douala was not yet a major city. Just looking at the color of the sky and taking in the air and the sounds all around, he felt great, at home in Charente, by the Atlantic Ocean. The song came to him quite naturally; the words just came out without him having to think too much.

Idiba y busi bwam, é sè weï mbidi mbidi, é sè weï mbidi mbidi . . . Ya so na! Di alé djènè mwayé! Morning rises happy, it is so warm the sun, it's so beautiful the sun . . . Come on, let's go, leave the sad face behind. Come with me, let's go see the light!

The tape, arbitrarily deposited in a record company's letterbox, got the attention of a producer. Hey, come here man. Come and listen to this. What do you think? At Pathé Marconi they took things seriously. Many other staff members listened keenly to the recording. The secretary came and wrote the shorthand version of the letter to be sent to the artist.

Dear Sir,
It was our pleasure to listen to the song you sent in to us. We would be pleased to meet with you to discuss . . . Please accept . . . Yours sincerely . . .

Rehearsals in the studio, the recording and pressing of the vinyl, the whole operation remained top secret. The disc took the journey—by boat? By plane?—to Africa. We would receive a call from Cameroon telling us that Papa was playing on the radio. We were having dinner, and I was the first to leap up and pick up the receiver. Unsure, I turned toward my parents.

– Papa, someone says your song is having quite a success.
– What song? my brothers and sister asked in a chorus.

My mother took the receiver from me and finished the conversation.

– *Idiba*, my father answered while I was looking on at him, suspiciously.
Madame Kidi, he added, I think it's time I taught you how to dance.

He got up, placed the record on the player, and lowered the needle. The song began, set in a xylophone arrangement I had never heard before. He came and stood right before me and took my hands.

> – This is how you do it. You take a step like this, to the side, and then you bring your other leg close to the leg in the first position without losing the rhythm. Then you start again on the other side, without losing the rhythm. It's very easy. The more you practice, the more flexible you'll become in your hips. This dance is called the *makossa*.

At first I stood motionless, hurt that I had not been in on the secret about the disc that was made. And there I was thinking I was always among the first to hear all his compositions. In the end, I let myself get carried away by the rhythm, as would the numerous men and women from many different countries who heard the song on the radio in the weeks that followed.

Some weeks later, a manuscript born of my father's imagination would find its way to his native country and dock among the projects at the singular local publishing house. Success rang the doorbell when the postman held out a telegram to my mother, who was immediately worried. The telegram read: *Novel accepted—Stop—Contract sent—Stop—Signed: CLE.*

The Center for Evangelical Literature in Yaoundé was going to publish his work, discreetly overlooking the details of the comedy of manners my father had included. Imagine, somehow, in a Cameroonian village, a woman gives birth to a White baby she swears she conceived with her husband, a Cameroonian just like her! The novel, *Le Fils d'Agatha Moudio*, brought Francis even greater success among his peers.

In time, he began to reflect on how to go forward. He would eventually gather us to inform us of his decision. He was going to be making a great leap: he was resigning, goodbye UNESCO.

We listened to his decision, shaking our heads, failing to grasp the boldness of his choice. We had no idea what was at stake or the courage it took. Visitors—friends, colleagues, family members—came in droves unexpectedly to try to talk sense into our father about his decision. *Have you really thought about it? No, but seriously, are you sure you've given it careful thought? You can't just abandon a job like that. You have a wife and children to feed. Five children! Do you need to be reminded of that? You don't resign from UNESCO. You don't walk away from a prestigious position as an international civil servant. Who knows what kind of work you'll get later on? Who knows if you'll*

even be able to find a job? You don't want to work in an office anymore? You just
want to make music and write books? So you are in fact as crazy as they say
you are. Have you thought of your family over there, back home? Many of them
are counting on you. You know that, right? Come on, cut it out, come down to
earth, be reasonable.

> – Yet another one trying to get me to change my mind, my father said clos-
> ing the door. They all keep saying the same thing: you will no longer have a
> diplomatic passport. How can you give up such a situation? The truth of the
> matter is that they're all just talking about themselves . . .

He resisted the pressure, deeply convinced that this time it was his life that
was at stake. He was not going to ignore what was going on deep within him,
however confusing, the desire to create, to imagine, and to play. He didn't
know where it would lead him. But who knew what tomorrow would bring?
What he knew was that he was suffocating and that to regain his breath, he
was the only one who could open the window on to his freedom. He knew that
his very loving wife had always accepted the way his imagination worked. She
was with him, prepared to take the leap too. She was open to diving into the
craziness because, like Francis, she was also ready for a change. *Let's do what*
we want, at least once in our lives. Do what we want and take advantage of the
fact that we are far away and therefore unreachable. Stop counting on us all the
time. Perhaps it's selfish, but we'd like to live our lives, too, feel what it's like to
live a life that is not wedded to the script of always doing the right thing.

He resigned. He had never done something like that before, but he did it.
Good or bad decision, he would find out in due course. On the road, coming
back from vacation that year, all squeezed into the white Ford, he stopped the
car at a rest stop on the highway and gave us children a wink in the rearview
mirror. A gleam of happiness sparked from the corner of his eyes.

> – Children, something tremendous has happened to me. I am going to
> finally, for the first time in my life, go home and leave my suits just where
> they are in the closet. I will no longer have to wear a tie every morning. I will
> no longer be going to a job where people come to me full of hope and share
> their amazing ideas, after which I have to send them back to their countries
> and especially to their political circumstances. International civil servant, it
> is o-v-e-r, done with. Now, children, keep working hard in school. Do your
> best. I am counting on you. I'm going to do the best I can, too, with my guitar
> and my typewriter. I can't be sure to succeed in my new life as an artist, but

over the last few months some people have believed in my talent. And in life, what greater pursuit is there than to try to work with your talent? We might go through some lean times, but rest assured, children, we are going to have a blast.

I had never heard the expression *lean times* before. It wasn't clear to me what it was supposed to mean, but I didn't dare to ask. I simply noticed the satisfaction beaming from my father's face, a face that until quite recently was almost always surly despite all our efforts to lift his spirits. I discovered a father who sought but one thing: to show the face of the man he had become. In a hushed voice, I tried to express my compassion:

– You know, papa, I can stop going to school if it costs too much.

That autumn marked the advent of a new father, a man who no longer slept, neither by night nor by day, eager to catch, whenever possible, the shooting stars of his dozens of ideas. Francis planted a metallic microphone stand in the middle of the living room and bought himself a professional eight-track tape recorder, whose reels turned continuously. He also invested in an Eminent 310 electronic synthesizer, whose imposing size made us rearrange the layout of the furniture and objects in the room.

Pleased, my father announced:

– Finally we're going to have some fun in this room.

Have fun. He had used the expression when we had come back from vacation, and I came to realize that, for him, this idea was synonymous with working differently, in other words, to create, to invent, to imagine, to breathe, to eat, to sleep, to wake up with musical notes and words to put together and give rhythm to pages. For him, it was all about composition, and the universe all came down to this suggestive power, this emotional enthusiasm that music alone provoked. There was my father, knee-deep in new explorations in which electronic sounds from synthesizers were mixing with the instruments brought back from his African travels. He recorded everything that came to mind. When I would get back from school, he would take me by the hand and lead me to the sofa in the living room. This part of the apartment had been transformed into a recording studio where, using traditional methods, the music took form. I would listen to the melodic details that had recently been added to the work in progress. Weary from all the math and Latin in school, I welcomed this escape. My heart was soothed at the mere thought that I had a role to play in this huge change that got all his senses going and brought our whole family to life in its wake. My father was at the helm, and although he was the captain, he needed an apprentice. I was all ears—listening to and discovering the juxtaposing sounds that were fusing to make new music.

> – Listen to this, Madame Kidi. I composed it this afternoon. What do you think? This, he explained to me, this here chord is like the backdrop to the piece, like a tablecloth on a table, or a mat in a hut, it's the sand: the grains of sand that adorn the Sahel, bordering the desert. They cover over everything, everywhere, and when the wind picks up, they go everywhere, even in your eyes. Unfortunately, the desert moves, you know. It's a disaster for the people living there, who would love to have some rain to make the plants grow, and still it's amazing! The flute you hear above the notes of the guitar, that's the sinuous movement of the serpent. He undulates on the crest of a dune up to the foot of the slope. The boom-boom thump of the drums marks the advancing caravan. Do you get it?

I not only understood but I could actually see what he was talking about. I slipped joyfully into his poetic inventions as easily as into his sonic brain waves. With my eyes closed, I could see the arid landscape. Then, as early as the next day, thanks to a good rain shower, some plants started pushing out their fragile branches from the soil up toward the sky. The day afterward, a caravan of Bedouins appeared and you could hear the braying of the donkey. A donkey braying in a steady rhythm, you had to be a musician to be able to create that sound. A light wind began to pick up grains of sand, obliging the Bedouins to readjust their turbans. Once they arrived to the caravansary, I opened my eyes again. The exhausted travelers dismounted and relieved their animals of their harnesses.

Then I was back in our living room, my eyes open wide, as though waking up from a dream. Before me stood the most improbable instruments: a spoon was clinking against an empty soda bottle and sheets of paper were being crinkled up for the recording. The latter would subsequently disappear because the test run had deemed them unnecessary.

With a nod of the head, my father welcomed my reaction of awe and silence. An album was on its way.

The year proved prosperous, with a flourish of activity. Our living room transformed into a theater stage. As the seasons advanced, a whole different style of guests began to spend time with my parents. A colorful community of filmmakers, musicians, playwrights, dancers, painters, would disregard the meteorological severity to make it to the warm light of our apartment. Their discussions would become heated disputes between people who spoke loudly and smoked continuously. Everyone was passionately defending his or her vision of the world. Ideas were effusive and political views would raise the tone in the room. Conversations would go on until dinnertime, whereby Madé would graciously improvise an informal buffet without much fuss.

People sat on stools, on the arms of the sofa, even on the parquet floors. The men wore bell-bottomed trousers, moccasins with shiny buckles, or crepe-soled suede shoes. The black lines of their sideburns were carefully groomed, going from their ears right to the middle of their cheeks. The women wore Afro hairstyles, false eyelashes, and tricolored eye shadow. Their bare legs were on display in their minidresses and culottes, and jumpsuits hugged their hips and thighs. The contours of their bare breasts were veiled in shirts with psychedelic prints.

I floated around amid all these people, trying to hide my disapproval of some of the outfits I judged to being unkempt. At least my mother knew how to dress in her jersey tunics and her hostess dresses. She had stopped wearing her braids up in the form of a crown and preferred to wear a chignon, from which a hairpin would stick out at times. I emptied the ashtrays, put out plastic cups, the Kleenex, pepper, and the Maggi sauce for those who asked. I pushed along the golden wheels of the trolley in varnished wood that contained all the bottles of alcohol.

– Let me introduce you to Madame Kidi, my father would say pointing directly at me. Do you see how well she plays her role as the young lady of the house?

The conversations would kick back into high gear and sometimes go on all the way until midnight. My father often closed the evening by playing his latest guitar compositions. The conversations would stop and his performance would captivate his listeners right up until the last chords gave way to silence. Applause and criticism would abound.

– No. You? . . . Seriously! Since when have you been playing things like that? Where did you learn that music? You are as learned as the White man! Aren't you ashamed to know their music so well? It's beautiful, but seriously, shouldn't you just leave that stuff to them? Classical music, that's not for us . . . It's not who we are. When we make music, it's a political act.

Classical music? He had always known and heard it in his home and in his father's parish. His friends used to listen to it when they were younger. Had they forgotten?

> – This music is also ours, he would hit back. An instrument like the guitar is not only European. It's been African for a long time now. It goes all the way back to the fifteenth century when the Portuguese came to our shores. I can play whatever I want on it, I can do whatever I want!

But some of them shook their heads:

> – We have to come up with our own stuff! We have to return to our rhythms, our instruments, our music! They have cut off our legs one too many times– it's time for us to stand on our own feet. Let everyone hear our tam-tam drums and balafons. Since the Bandung conference, we can't seem to come together and agree on anything! The anti-imperialist revolution has got to start there . . .

Francis welcomed the criticism with mixed feelings. He was more than ready to follow the guideposts of his predecessors, the Senghors and the Cé-saires. These poets had been bold in acknowledging that their ancestral culture was worthwhile. He was following in their footsteps. In fact, wasn't he in the process of making something happen by taking on this new life in which he was exploring the secret recesses of his soul to unfold his talent? He tried to explain that he had had the opportunity to give recitals, several since then, *yes, yes, I was alone before an audience with an acoustic guitar,* and that what he had played had enraptured the public.

> – They liked it? Of course, you played *their* music for them, fired off a woman with a hissing dismissal. Real progress, that will happen when we manage to get them to hear our music without them saying it's not as good or it's infe-rior to what they know how to do . . . Then and only then will we have won. Our music, we dance to it and we sing to it!

Francis didn't see it that way. During all his work trips in the field, he had seen enough to understand that court music is also African and that it's not unusual, in all the countries on the continent, for people to take the time to sit down patiently and listen to instrumentalists perform and vocalists de-claim. It can last for hours without anyone even considering getting up to dance. He would love to explain it to this woman who was so critical, but he worried she would only see arrogance in the knowledge he wanted to share. *I've seen, I've admired, I've understood that we were far richer than we thought.*

If you only knew! Our rhythms are sophisticated, we have innumerable instru-
ments; our vocal techniques are remarkably diverse! We are making a mistake
ourselves when we reduce our music to tam-tams and balafons. We have classi-
cal music, we do. Over there it goes as far back as the dawn of time. This is what
we need to know, if not learn, and especially invest in anew. For him, music
belongs to the person who plays it, no matter where he or she comes from.

For the time being, he was playing again, his supple fingers freely strumming away so that the evening ended graciously. And it didn't matter! He had
begun to earn a living with his guitar and with his so-called way of playing
White music. He had mixed into the same repertoire pieces by Handel, Bach,
and Villa-Lobos, from Europe and the New World, Germany and Brazil.
Then he added his own compositions, pieces of demanding bravura whose
duration sometimes went on for as long as fifteen minutes.

And to make it symbolically clear as to the direction he had taken, he had
put away his black tuxedo and his frilled shirt from the early days. Classical
musician perhaps, but with a classical African guitar. He decided that in the
future he would be wearing the cerulean-colored *gandoura* he had received in
Chad, when he had been on a work assignment that had opened his eyes and
turned his world inside out. Back then he and his team had been on the road
for quite some time before arriving at a remote village. The stunned silence
of the inhabitants had made him uncomfortable at first: he had not liked the
feeling of showing up this way, as if out of nowhere, to discover total strangers, men and women, like the explorers must have done long before him. Fortunately, they had been given a polite welcome, similar to their experiences
elsewhere on the continent. As early as the next day, they had had the pleasure
of attending a "mask ceremony." The entire village had come to the square.
Women and children clapped their hands while the instrumentalists beat in
time the tautly stretched skin of the drums. A musician whose inflated cheeks
looked like balls blew into an alghaita. The alghaita emitted, in continuous
sinuous coils, loops of a twangy melody. Francis had discovered with great
admiration that the instrumentalist knew how to recover his breath without
interrupting the melody. Among the gifts offered to the travelers when they
were leaving had been a cerulean-colored gandoura, which Francis hoped to
wear as his stage outfit for future concerts.

–13–

Coming back from school one afternoon in March 1975, in what was my fourteenth year, the buds opening up on the chestnut trees in our neighborhood signaled the arrival of spring. A sudden shower had just refreshed the sky and the sidewalks. I was walking triumphantly, excited to announce my superb score of 19 out of 20 on a written assignment. Besides my grade, I was feeling great without really knowing why. Was it because our gleaming, vivid-red building seemed to outshine the others on our street? Or because our strange father had, with the wave of a magic wand, reinfused our family with joy and made each one of us an accomplice, beholden to a project of remarkable creativity? My heart was full of pride for living the double life of a secret agent and a middle school student, a life I kept even from my closest friends, all the while hinting, by way of allusions, at its extraordinary qualities—you had to know how to carefully handle these matters.

I had not even rang the doorbell before the door opened to my home, and I was met by someone holding a finger up to their lips, ordering me not to speak. I tiptoed into the apartment and tried to avoid the numerous cables strewn all over the parquet floor. A projector shone brightly on two people in the middle of an argument. The sound of the humming motor was coming from the padded casing of a camera whose objective, I noticed, was pointing toward the actors. My father was standing behind the lens, so absorbed in the scene that he didn't even acknowledge me. A technician I had never met before was perched overhead, holding a microphone lowered just above the actors. So just like that, I had turned my back on the studio for one day and the living room, the recording studio, was now a film set. A film shooting was well underway. My mother beckoned from the corridor to come and join her. I was about to take refuge in the bedroom when my father's voice stopped me in my tracks.

– Cut! he asserted, self-assured. Hey! Madame Kidi, stay right there, I need you.

I was suddenly the target of the artificial light. My school items were taken away by someone I had never met, and I had to turn around in full view of everyone.

–Walk, right up to here, my father instructed me. Then you stop, you think for a minute, you express that you have an idea, and you resume walking, but this time you pick up the pace and run off.
– And very important, don't look my way! the cameraman reminded me.

Where did all these people come from? What kind of magic had Francis worked to convince them to join him in launching this new commando operation of his imagination? Play, play some more, and then even more, and just like that this was what he was calling a life of relentless hard work, where ideas became discs, books, films, as though all you had to do was to think it to make it happen, and making it happen was the easiest thing in the world. There I was, my body shooting up out of nowhere, weighed down by hang-ups with my heart and mind bloated by questions and problems trying desperately to strike a balance, and there was my father satisfying his longing for freedom in an express form of active adolescence, a new life in which he was welcoming all the crazy ideas born of his imagination. When all was said and done, you only live once, you may as well go all the way, live intensely now and try to get as close to the stars as you can with your dreams! The film was shot, then edited and shown, and at no point did my father's enthusiasm become overrun by fear or doubt. The challenge was most certainly immense, I realize that today, but during that period it was all about hope and joy.

During the 1970s, Africa was being presented in the news in the best possible light and appealed to a lot of young volunteers attracted to these rapidly developing nations. They were taking off to the Ivory Coast, Senegal, Mali, Niger, the Upper Volta, Burkina Faso, Cameroon, Gabon . . . Leaving from Paris, Bordeaux, Nantes, Strasbourg, volunteering for military service, far more motivated by personal reasons than invested in the political concerns of the day. They were considerably more honest about their motives than the businessmen who preceded them and who had had no qualms about bleeding the forests and extracting mineral resources. After having pursued the prospect of Asia or South America, here they were now in Africa. What was the difference? This little unknown dot on the map, these places with outlandish names—Ougadougou, Bobo-Dioulasso, Kankan, Bonkoukou, Timbuktu, Ouahigouya, Limpopo River—made it easy for them to escape martial law. They literally just turned up, explored, marveled, widened their field of vision, welcomed, were welcomed, learned, surprised, were themselves surprised, and some were even won over.

In the long letters many of these new explorers addressed to their families (often no less than eight folded pages, in envelopes stamped *par avion* blazoned with multicolored stamps displaying the flora and fauna, fruits, presidents), cities were profiled with boutiques; banks; cars; hotels where Europeans were basking poolside at the weekend, being served Brittany crepes accompanied with cider and mango-papaya cocktails. They shared descriptions of the modern skyscrapers in Abidjan overlooking the lagoon, or the incredible skating rink at Hotel Ivoire, *and it's not synthetic ice, I assure you, Madame!* An ice-cold smoke screen that made it a lot easier to glide on while the resistance movement kept counting victims in Cameroon or a certain Zairian general lorded over his fellow countrymen with an iron fist and his leopard toque. In the evenings, they attended dance halls, where hips swayed to the rumba rhythm that had left the Cuban shores to reconnect with its Congolese ancestors. Some actually landed right in the heartland, where they learned to live *the African way of life* in fully furnished huts to which serpents did sneak in all the same. In those parts, to have proper drinking water, it needed to be filtered. The women did the cooking on wood fires at night, because there were no electricity torches or petrol lamps to light the homes and scare off the wild animals that might be on the prowl. Storm lamps, however, made it possible for the explorers to write lengthy daily journal entries, in which there was a cocktail of comparative ethnology.

You could see them coming from a mile away, and whose side they were on. There were those who formed part of an inner circle, part of the "club," who, accompanied by their wives, would spend their evenings at the consul's or ambassador's home, all dressed to the nines, attending lavish dinner receptions, served by butlers wearing white gloves, deaf and mute to all the criticism being pronounced against them, their own people, *the natives*, even if one ought not to use that word. But *here we are among ourselves, my dear, go on, no problem* . . . In the village, they took themselves for the Great White Man of Lambaréné, especially in the mornings, when mothers and children formed a line to see a doctor or get a vaccination. In the main, they came out ahead in these experiences of discovering a part of themselves of which they had been unaware up until that day they had made the journey to the African continent.

This was what was called *learning about life* or *gaining experience*, depending on the person. Those places, those people, that incredibly powerful nature, those remarkable spaces, where, at times, they had been so taken aback, awestruck, they had *never felt so happy*, thrilled by such an unparalleled sense of freedom. Some came to appreciate their time there so much so that they became infatuated with a princess of the desert whose skin was as smooth as a baby's bottom, and would dream of marrying her. When it was time to go home, the spell under which they had otherwise been enthralled would suddenly break. The heady smell of the incense of love would dissipate as they gradually came to their senses. They would cry their eyes out, then turn away, leaving behind broken hearts and dishonored families. Others returned home with the young lady with the grace of a gazelle, whose charm often, unfortunately, failed to win over a morally superior family, who would express by their long faces their disappointment at the return of the prodigal son. Some chose this new way of life *for good*, settled down—became devoted teachers, doctors, administrators, soccer coaches, engineers—opened more businesses and threw their weight around, barking orders. Had they remained in their own countries, these new settlers would have been nothing short of your run-of-the-mill loafers. It was true what they said, the sun could make the head spin at times and give way to even greater stupidity, especially for those whom the depravity of their characters had long preceded their migration.

In the 1970s, Africa was scintillating and the images of Biafra children were now in the distant past. For Francis and his peers, explorers of the European world, the time had come to stake it all, talk to people, and attest to their experiences. It was important to show that Africa did in fact have a lot to offer. There was a kind of urgency, a real challenge. Each day was about showing what one was capable of and going far beyond one's limits. The only way to get ahead was to get to work. Working was the only way forward.

–14–

Following the film, Francis wagered on yet another artistic project. Already a center for debate and reflection, the apartment became, for weeks, an exhibition space. Painters came to show their work, and musicians performed their compositions. As the artworks, offered as gifts, kept on multiplying on our walls, certain melodies persisted in Francis's ear. How would he go about reaching a larger public with this music? Mainstream record companies refused to take on what he proposed, suggesting the public was not ready for these faraway sounds. So be it! The best way to respond to these rejections was to break down the barriers with alternative propositions. This being the period of great aspirations, Francis invested the sum he had received upon resigning from UNESCO into setting up a recording company. In addition to the traditional songs and music, it was time for him to introduce the world to the new artists originating from the Ivory Coast, Cameroon, Chad, Angola, Uganda, and the Congo . . . commercial music from Africa.

Within a few months, a plan was laid out for a collection of singles. Taking on the role of artistic director, Francis organized recording sessions then participated in the orchestration and musical arrangements, and finally the mixing. He photographed the artists for the record covers, which he designed with the help of a graphic designer. We, the children, watched from a distance some of the photo shoots in the streets of our neighborhood. While the artists posed for the camera, we commented on their attitudes and physiques— Rachel Tchoungui with her penetrating smile and that gap in her front teeth; Prosper Nkouri; Mario Rui; Willy Le Paape, the singer with a bizarre name, always sporting his dark sunglasses. We laughed our heads off at these so-called stars, whom it would have been impossible to come within an inch of, had they really been stars. It wasn't until many years later—once we were ourselves adults contending with the day-to-day frustrations of life—that we began to understand that that period of intense, effervescent creativity, which had appeared so laughable and seemingly frivolous in our eyes, had been an observation deck, the hallmark of remarkable determination, in short, an exceptional display of courage.

Francis went on from artistic concerns to those of a business manager, worried about the pressing and eventual distribution of the records. To advance the promotion phase, he would send the discs directly to the nightclub managers and radio programmers. Refusing to wait around for affirmative answers from this avenue alone, he kept on going. He got in touch with former colleagues from Sorafom who found networks to diffuse his tracks. This was how, for example, the Bantu-style performance by Rachel Tchoungui of *Romeo and Juliet* came to hit the African radio waves and become a major success. *Romeo na Julietta, ba ta ba dja Verona . . .*

When we returned to Cameroon that year for vacation, many of the songs that had been recorded within the walls of our home were now suddenly blaring from everywhere. Personally, I had not heard a peep from any of the French radios, no more than I had seen any of these artists' performances on the *Sacha Show* or any another Maritie and Gilbert Carpentier show. It was a whole other matter in Douala: these songs were blasting from taxi radios and all the bars. At every turn on the streets, the songs were coming at me in a festive spirit, yelping and jumping like an excited dog. At every family gathering, *Romeo na Julietta, O Bia! Sache bien! Méfie-toi* and *Kinshasa*, the hits of the moment, played and put everyone in the mood to get up and dance.

The visit to Cameroon that year took on a whole new flavor, especially for me: I was the daughter of the man responsible for the music everyone enjoyed. I accompanied him everywhere he wanted me to go and spent time with him, holding his hand, so that I could bask in the light of the gilded success with which he had been crowned. National radio talk show hosts invited him to speak: I would be standing behind the window of the radio booth in the studio. The owner of a film house organized a concert for him, and tickets sold right up until the last minute: I absolutely wanted to be there and thought

I would die from anger when my mother announced that *given the concert will be starting late in the evening, we will be staying in and leaving papa to go alone tonight.*

I would later learn that the concert fell short of my father's aspirations. For the occasion, he had worn a white *gandoura* with gold embroidery and a matching round toque, similar to the one worn by men in northern Cameroon. As luck would have it, this symbolic allusion to the culture in our country had been interpreted as a direct homage to the president of Cameroon, who was originally from the North. After the concert, back in the crowded dressing room, Francis had had to bite his tongue so as not to express how annoyed he was that his chosen attire could have been misread as an allegiance to the current government. *So, just like that, you're now playing for all the president's men? You're now a part of the inner circle?* some mocked him. And to think he had made a deliberate point of turning his back forever on this whole gang of auxiliaries, who were, in his eyes, responsible for his brother's death . . . The so-called friends who came to congratulate him kept on nipping at his pride with critical remarks about *this music that perhaps he should not have performed and how disappointing it had been.*

It should be said that among the audience who had been chanting the lyrics to his songs while patiently waiting for the artist to come to the stage, a good number had been flabbergasted at the first flurry of notes, without words, he would play. Backstage, the manager of the theater had swallowed loud enough for everyone to hear, then pouted in a way that had made it clear he was not happy. Now he understood why this artist had rejected all the musicians he had proposed. It wasn't that Francis was planning to lip-sync with an amazing soundtrack, it was that he was planning to play *this, this music that no one expected, meanwhile the public were all riled up and excited, really pumped up in anticipation of hearing his* Idiba, *his* O Bia, *and a chorus had even been keen to sing* Romeo na Julietta *in light of Rachel Tchoungui's absence. The public was expecting anything but this complicated music. They had come to dance.* The theater was like a huge ball ready to explode that night. The manager worried the crowd might start a stampede or, worse, start breaking the chairs and demanding their money back. The air was thick with tension. Just in time, Francis had begun to play the simple versions to his most successful songs, as though he were strumming a few chords to remind his friends of the melody to a song. Friends calmed down and joined in on the refrains. *Except he was without the orchestra to back him up and that was not good. Finally he closed the show, again with a classical piece.* As it was unheard of to start throwing eggs, everybody agreed that what this man was playing was some really good stuff, really, really good in fact, so people stayed right until the end. But the next morning, the headline in the newspapers read, "Concert in the Film House Abbia: The Singer of *O Bia* Disappoints."

As for me, what I saw the next day was a father who was strangely, relatively calm. Around 11 a.m., he got ready to meet the head of CLE publishing house, which was on its way to becoming *the* literary publishing house for Francophone African literature.

– Good morning, starts the tall, heavyset man as he shook his hand. Gerard Markhoff, a pleasure to meet one of my authors coming in from so far away!

He then leaned toward me and pricked my cheek with his beard with reddish highlights. His daughters were with him, twins who smiled at me right away. Their skin was as milky white as their father's, and their arms and shoulders were covered in freckles. Only their hairstyles made it possible to distinguish between them when you first met them. Hypnotized, like me, by their double smiles, my sister came up to us, and we led them inside the house. The four of us immediately became friends that summer, and while our brothers were playing soccer, us girls, we spent hours sneakily trying to put on makeup with used matchsticks and talked about the boys we were interested in. Unlike us, the Markhoff girls were born in Africa and had been attending Cameroonian schools right from the beginning. Fanta and I envied this undeniable superiority all the more so once we learned that they were being raised without their mother. She had died giving birth to them. We weren't in a position to brag about anything that serious. But they were also envious of the connection we had to the famous musician of the moment. They owned copies of his albums, and so we spent afternoons dancing with them to my father's music. Thanks to these girls, we also discovered the vocal intensity of James Brown, and every afternoon, the four of us would be screaming our heads off singing, *"Stay on the scene! Like a sex machine!"* and wiggling our bodies *just like the Americans did.*

That summer, I realized I had not experienced anything like that over the past two years. We spent a short time in Douala before moving into a rented house in Yaoundé, where, to my great relief, I was able to get away from the demands of the adults' ritual visits. I would later learn that this new life, far from the family nexus, had not been planned at all. The distance hinted at poorly kept adult secrets, which my adolescent antennae allowed me to decrypt. Following the joyful family reunion in Douala, my parents had found themselves caught in a web of family issues that they had been asked to sort out.

Madé had been the first to be called upon to arbitrate. The issue at stake concerned her half-sister Épiphanie, one of the children of her father's second wife. Madé knew practically nothing about this last child because the marriage with this wife, much like the birth of the children, took place after she had left for Europe. She had therefore been totally surprised to learn that she was considered best suited to speak to the young lady. *You live over there*, they said, *you can understand*: Épiphanie is keeping company with a White man. And not only is she keeping company with him, she's infatuated with him and he with her, to the point that the lovebirds want to tie the knot. Can you imagine? The family can't accept such a union. No one in the past has ever dared to go this far with *Europeans*. We can come together to work, even become friends, why not; but to marry, have children, and therefore bring the families together, never! Madé was tasked with bringing Épiphanie back to her senses. For their own sakes, they had to give up on this plan. Moreover, if the marriage were to take place, it wouldn't last very long. What kind of children could she possibly have with a White man? We all know that they have this bizarre color that stands for nothing short of shame and problems. Which country, which world, would be willing to accept their offspring and allow them to live in peace?

Once Madé had a better understanding of the reasoning for this discussion to happen, she suddenly felt exasperated and discouraged. All those years she had been living in France she had learned to appreciate many aspects of the society. She could even count friendships whose solidity she had had occasion to test over and over again. She was sure that they didn't see her first and foremost as an African. She was a friend, who was very dear to them, a person whose skin color was absorbed by the universe's color chart. Mixed couples, as it was termed these days, were formed at times.

When Madé had first arrived in France, she would come across mixed couples on the streets and they would draw her attention. No one was used to seeing a White woman being held at the waist by a Black man any more than him holding her hand in the street. (Because that was the way it had been back then, who knows why; you saw even fewer Black women with White men.) She had been surprised that they dared to flaunt it. She had not been sure whether to consider them arrogant or audacious.

Since those early days, she never paid much attention anymore. Mixed couples were all around her; they were her friends, her acquaintances. She passed young people on the street with their long hair, barefoot, wearing *peace* and *love* chains around their necks. You saw just about everything on the streets of Paris.

Madé reflected on it. Evidently her family couldn't possibly imagine the kinds of changes she had been through and experienced. Had she herself had any idea about what she might experience? She was only now coming to terms with the scope of it all, as the young lady, Épiphanie, advanced in her direction. What kind of torture had they decided to inflict on this beautiful face, full of hope in the future? You could see that the young lady was in love, quite simply in love and not giving it a second thought. She explained to Madé that her fiancé was preparing to return to Europe because he had been a volunteer and wanted to take her back with him. She asked Madé to intervene on her behalf. *You'll see, Auntie* (she called her "Auntie" and not "big sister," immediately choosing the word that, to her mind, best expressed their sorority as much as their age difference), *he's sincere, he's intelligent. He, too, is going against his parents' will. Help me; help us. At least you can understand . . .*

Madé had a flashback to the many years ago when the preparations for her own wedding had made it almost difficult for her to breathe. At night, as she lay waiting for the wedding day, she had had pins and needles in her legs. And while she had submitted in advance to the decisions made at the family meeting, she had been more than ready to defy whoever would have stood in her way. She would have done it, as timid and well-behaved as she was, she would have been capable of going all the way, to fight and elope, if she had to. Because she had known intuitively, in the depth of her heart, that Francis was meant for her. She looked at Épiphanie. The way she carried herself showed a similar determination. Why should she intervene? How long would it last? Who could possibly guess? Who would dare to doubt that it could last? Let these two people get on with their lives, let them take off and tie the knot as they wish to, let them take a gamble on marriage. It didn't matter what the family said. She would not be the one to stand in their way.

Meanwhile, Francis got a visit from his sister.

– You were born after me, she insisted, but you are the most educated in our family. We're expecting a lot from you.

She lived in another town with her husband and her in-laws, but the issue she had come to see him about was so serious that she had had to make the trip.

– I have to talk to you about this woman, she continued in a serious tone. She showed up with her eight-year-old daughter, already a big girl. She says the girl is Marcel's daughter, in other words, our niece, our very own niece, you understand me? What can we do? She says she doesn't have the means to properly raise his child. Isn't it up to you to take responsibility for the little one? Hmm? Yes, you, you have to do it. The child may as well live with the one person, among us all, who has a sound financial situation. And, more-over, the little girl looks like our brother, like two peas in a pod . . .

So there it was. His brother, reincarnated in a child born after his death of which we knew nothing until her mother, short on funds, had looked to the family. *These vacations back home*, Francis said to himself, *they never turn out the way I imagine them*. They take on another form, but the essence of them is always the same: you have to take care of things, you have to pay; this is what everybody always expects from him. That he puts the child in school, that he takes her back with him to Europe, why not, so that she can live with his family under a solid roof, so that she can get a good education by going to school over there . . . Of course, his brother would not have wished for more, but Francis was wavering. He tried to hide his reservation from those around him. So this is what it was all about, the endless phone calls, so effusive to the point where they felt strange: *It's good that you're coming, we're really happy. We miss you, you know? We really need you. When you come with your wife and kids, we're going to sit down and talk. It's important to take the time to talk. Oh, we're all excited to see you. We can't really talk on the phone. You know very well that the most important things can't be said by phone.* Those calls with no motive, for the pleasure of speaking, he should have listened in greater detail, he might have picked up some clues. And now this: the future of a child whose existence he had been completely unaware of. *His own niece!* He wanted to think about it, but what they were asking of him seemed to be a plan that they had already put in place. His point of view was just a matter of form. He felt he was being cornered. He was left to examine the proposed solutions, whereas, on their end, they had already planned it all out. They were already prepared to bring him the little girl, and he refused to meet her. He was afraid that the sight of the little girl might overwhelm him. As far as he was concerned, what he really needed to do was to steel himself, *émbè nyolo*, to make the best possible decision, according to him . . .

That discussion with his sister reinforced the disappointment he had experienced last evening when he had organized a film session. Back in Paris, he had been excited at the prospect, while packing up the huge projector that had weighed down the luggage so much.

On the taut, white sheet that served as a screen in the courtyard, he first showed the film he had shot the previous spring with great enthusiasm. An African street sweeper finds a wallet filled with bank notes on the streets of Paris. He begins to dream about all that he might be able to do with this unexpected good fortune: go back to his country, marry his beloved, have children, return to France with his new family and show them where he used to live. The street sweeper spends sleepless nights considering the different scenarios, but the guilt causes him to suffer. In the end, he decides to turn the wallet in at the police station . . .

There had been about forty or more people glued to the screen in silence in the crowded courtyard. What did they think of this moralizing fable? At that time, there were no national television channels in Cameroon and few people were used to seeing cinematic images. At the end of the viewing, the lights were turned on. Everybody was silent. A bit surprised, Francis tried all the same to interpret the silence as a sign of fascination.

He had also decided to project a film in Super 8 that showed our family. My brothers and sisters and I, we nudged each other, and snickered among ourselves, enjoying seeing these images again that we knew by heart. They showed my younger brother with his brows furrowed in anger. He had just been pushed by Junior, our older brother, who accidentally hit a sensitive part of his arm. You see him crying out in pain and all of us repeating while teasing him—Ouch, my injection—and with absolutely no compassion. The images also showed our family riding our brand-new bicycles for the first time in the Bois de Vincennes. Finally, I particularly enjoyed the images of me making a jump with my feet together before the opening electric doors at the newly built Montparnasse train station. During the projection, we were once again the only ones to react, as if the images only concerned us and therefore could only be understood by us. The family and neighbors who were gathered remained silent, hesitating as to how best to respond.

Only once, when Francis played a Charlie Chaplin episode, did the audience begin to relax. Suddenly before our eyes, there appeared a White man, poor, wearing a bowler hat, and otherwise badly dressed who aimed to improve his lot by means of a thousand gimmicks. Not only was his situation difficult to imagine, his comical demeanor finally released laughter in the theater. The anticipated reactions were finally awarded to this singular film and not the others, of which no one even hazarded to voice a remark.

As I was helping my father put away the projection equipment, his older sister came up to him and, holding her chin with her thumb and index finger, asked:

– I know you left that important position you had over there . . . That's why I would like to know something. Explain to me, now that you are going to have a sixth child, have you thought that maybe you ought to get back to doing something serious? You can't keep on like this, carrying on like a crazy person.

I don't know what followed in the dialogue between my aunt and my father. The seniority of the older sibling must have weighed heavily on her brother's mind. Feelings of guilt gnawed at him. I would like to imagine that he had had the audacity to look her in the eye and push back, just to give things a fresh perspective.

– And what about you, he might very well have retorted, when are you going to give me back the guitar I asked you to keep for me when I left all those years ago to go study abroad? Marcel's guitar, do you remember? I entrusted it to you . . . Why don't you go and fetch it so I can take it back with me when I return to *mbènguè*.

And just what might she have replied?

I was sullen on the return flight. My sister and I were particularly sad because we had not been able to visit with our cousins, Cricri and Fanfan, before leaving. We looked forward to sharing so much with them, especially as two years had already gone by since we had last seen them. But just as we were about to head to the back of the family courtyard to visit with them, a sudden formal ban was imposed, preventing us from going any further. The hodge-podge of allusions and innuendos didn't take too long to sort out: Cricri was going to become a mother in a few months without the accompanying etiquette of "Mrs."—a total embarrassment for the whole family. My sister and I were literally dumbfounded when we figured out what had happened. There we were barely able to imagine ourselves as young ladies and my cousin had grown up so much so that she'd already gotten involved with a boy and done the thing with him! Our stay in Douala had been too short, and we had had no opportunity to transgress the ban and get all the details from our cousin. Fanta and I were left no choice but to bring it up between us in whispers at night. We eventually passed on the dark secret to our older brother, who was also fairly surprised. And once we got to Yaoundé, we couldn't hold it in anymore, so we let the Markhoff sisters in on it as well.

While I was picking at the meal the flight attendant had just served, my thoughts immediately returned to my cousin and our childhood memories, carefree, when we would play at *dibo n'doko*, tea parties, imagining ourselves as grown-ups. Questions kept coming to me in an almost obsessive manner. Why had the adults thought it was such a good idea to keep us away from our cousin? What kind of absurd risk did they imagine was so contagious and against which we needed to be protected? Why hadn't I dared to defy them and go and see my cousin, even if for a short while? She had known I was there. At least I might have been able to express my solidarity with her . . . Why had, all of a sudden, from one day to the next, our dear cousin become *bad company*?

While the vacation had been essentially synonymous with games, this visit had nevertheless been an eye opener. It seemed to me that the ambiance was beginning to lose the feeling of transparency and lightness. Entrance into the adult world was proving to be marked with disturbing pitfalls, where the conditions for girls and women were filled with many unspoken concerns of a disconcerting gravity. For example, the visible affection within the community of the family could, in fact, operate as a veil for a veritable bitterness that was cruel and ice-cold for whoever dared to diverge, even unwillingly, from the initially mapped out trajectory. As for my parents, equally quiet in their seats in front of me, perhaps they, too, felt more than ever the oppressive responsibility that came with a sense of duty, as an additional concentric circle tightening up around them as a couple? So much so that, paradoxically, they experienced the return to Paris with a strange sigh of relief.

As for the rest—the passport for the little one, her visa, the heartbreak at having to say goodbye to her mother before getting on the flight, her departure for an unknown country and its customs with a family she didn't know at all, at eight years old, she was going to have to learn and come to understand all of it—all of that comes back to me in flashes from my memory and imagination. In the end, we are six brothers and sisters and there is love. The little one would adapt, like the little girl she was, and prove more capable than the adults in facing life head-on. She was registered with the first name Marie-Brigitte, which only existed for administrative purposes and surprised me each time I heard it. Because for me, just like for all of us, my cousin's name was Bibiche.

Our mother said:

– I have six children.

A Super 8 film shows us in the Jardin du Trocadéro, playing a game of cloak-and-dagger with Bibiche. There was also a third bed in the girls' room that balanced things out nicely with the boys' room. There is a photo of the six of us standing in front of a monument that I can't identify. Bibiche is in the middle. That photo must date back to at least two years after her arrival, because later on, our "little" cousin would stand at least a head taller than all of us. A hand, our mother's hand, also enters into the frame of the shot as she tries to turn my little brother's face toward the lens.

–15–

September in Paris that year reflected a warm luminosity. Joe Dassin was singing *Là-bas, on l'appelle l'été indien*. Friends gathered in the thirteenth arrondissement when Francis, Madé, and the kids returned. They dropped in unannounced, for the pleasure of sitting around and hearing how the country they had not been back to for some time was doing. No one was fooled: the pleasure was also about partaking in the *ndolè*, the *miondos*, the *ngondo*, the *foufou* and the *ékoki*, all freshly delivered by plane.

Madé explained to the women who had come to help out in the kitchen how the bottle of palm oil had opened up in the suitcase and spilled all over the boys' tunics! She then turned on the new Krups electric coffee maker, plugged in her Moulinex electric knife, and firmly held the chocolate swirl yogurt cake she proceeded to slice into servings.

In the living room, while the men wiped their mouths and fingers with Kleenex, questions kept coming:

– So tell us, Douala must have changed quite a bit, no?

Francis described some of the places and the general ambiance, remaining hushed about the parts that had really affected him. A chorus of exclamations burst forth.

– Oh really? It's finished! The building was destroyed? The house was re-placed by a modern clinic? Is that right? They placed a roundabout at Deïdo? Printania closed down in Yaoundé? The owner died? That's Bata now? Unbelievable. They're going to be sending us all the unwanted shoes, you'll see . . .

– You mean their oversized shoes, guffawed another.

They went as far as wanting to know if the drainpipes in the city were blocked.

– With all the things people are throwing down there these days.

The men all nodded in agreement.

– When the White man was there, all said and done, they would never have let the drains get blocked like that. With all the rain that falls on our city. They had had to find a way to redirect the used water. Nowadays, our leaders prefer to take the money and hide it away in a secret safe. Keep it all for themselves and their family. What are you gonna do? Sometimes you have to fall really low before you can get a grip on yourself . . .

The women entered the living room carrying a tray filled with cups, spoons, and sugar. Madé proudly held her new coffee maker. Someone concluded with a sigh:

– I wouldn't be able to recognize anything . . .

. . . Without it being absolutely clear as to whether he was speaking hypothetically or alluding to the future.

For the back-to-school season, six little rascals, whose bodies had shot up arbitrarily such that they were totally out of whack with the Dalton brothers, were all in need of new clothes. And to top it all off, they also needed to get new school items. Madé planned to buy no fewer than six school bags, six well-stocked pencil cases, and just as many notebooks and protective covers, as well as blotting paper as needed. The list extended to include six coats, six pairs of shoes, six pullovers, six thin polo-neck shirts, six trousers, eighteen undershirts, forty-two underwear, and forty-eight woolen socks. And that was just to get started.

In October, following the customary visits to Trigano and Galeries Lafayette, a blast of cold air swept over the city, anticipating what was to come for the season. The realization hit Francis as brutally as a straight right to the jugular vein, and he could hardly manage to bundle up with a scarf and gloves.

What did you do when the temperatures were high in your country, so far away, over there?, asked the banker, who rarely had a kind word for him. Admittedly, the disc sales were not doing so well, even if the music itself was widely played. Francis had been counting on royalties, which were not coming in. He didn't have the means to use what he had to set things right in Africa, nor to pay the accountants and lawyers to take action against those who had defaulted. And now he was indebted to artists for amounts he had not received and that, he was beginning to realize, might never be transferred to him. He also discovered the cumbersome red tape within the tax administration, ready to make demands but otherwise indifferent to explanations and feelings. Entangled in a tight mesh, the man wanted to resume his artistic endeavors, but reality was relentlessly despairing his creative impulse.

Yet another uppercut would come to hit him really hard when a decree was imposed on all foreign residents to justify their presence on French territory. Three of his children constituted a statutory offence to this new legislation. *You will lose your benefits if you leave UNESCO, friends had warned. The diplomatic passports for you and your family, you'll see, you won't have access to them anymore . . . Subsidies for vacation, all of that, it'll all come to an end . . .* All those remarks had seemed mean-spirited to him at the time. He now realized that some of the things they had said were actually true. Still, he was not angry with himself: he didn't wish to live off anyone's aid, much less benefits. He had no intention of submitting himself to a job for the sole purpose of aid and benefits. One day, Madé and he were surprised when the social welfare office summoned them but were relieved when it turned out it was to inform them they were eligible for special allowances for families with three or more children, including discounts on public transport. To think they might have had the family discount card ages ago! But they weren't raised like that, *back home, you didn't ask for things.* Maybe that kind of thinking seemed a little rigid or even stupid, but they were not looking to get special privileges.

Because I was fourteen years old, it was my turn to stand in line at the local prefecture.

– That's how it is, my father, the philosopher, explained, it's required by law.

You had to get up at the crack of dawn and cross the city to get to these dismal-looking premises, close to the Calberson warehouses at Porte de la Chapelle. You wanted to be sure to be among the first to arrive. You had to take a ticket number and the lucky ones got to present their file to one of the employees. At 1 p.m., it was all over: the employees closed the service windows and headed into the back offices with opaque walls where they handled the requests. My father armed himself with an arsenal of documents that he had gathered and organized into his briefcase. Ever prudent, he decided to wear one of the suits he used to wear as an international civil servant. I had to dress like him, which meant putting my best foot forward, so that together we distinguished ourselves from all the other people present, notably from the weathered faces, marked by fatigue that the foreign workers of North Africa origins displayed. His thinking was that our elegant appearance would some-how endear us to the employees and that we would be issued those precious documents faster. We sat for a long time, staring at the clock on the wall and watching the minute turn, waiting for our number to be called. Some windows remained closed. Sometimes, an employee who was present for one hour would suddenly disappear after having stuck a piece of paper against the window that read "Back in 5 minutes" or "See you tomorrow." When I wasn't annoyed by the spelling mistakes, I would be agitated because of the hidden meaning behind the text. "See you tomorrow." Seriously? As you might say to someone, while showing a sign of affection with your hand. "See you tomorrow, I miss you already"?

While he was waiting to get past the hurdle, my father immersed himself in his reading—*Jeune Afrique* or *Nouvel Observateur*—and handed me *Le Courrier de l'UNESCO*. I didn't dare admit to him that I was dying to get a subscription to the magazine *Quinze Ans*, which I had recently discovered thanks to a friend. So I pretended to read while I kept looking around in the waiting room. I don't think I saw one Japanese, English, or American foreigner. Did they send them to another location? Finally an employee called our number. We hurried up to the window. My father pointed at me, then handed over the file as he launched into a detailed explanation that the woman promptly interrupted with a gesture of the hand, indicating *stop*.

– The photocopy of the school certificate needed to be certified by the school, she decreed coldly after getting to the third document in the file.

Without even bothering to take a look through the rest of the file, she re-turned the documents to my father and wrote on a scratch of paper the next appointment date. You had to be available on that date and bring the document requested before you might find out if you might or might not be missing one or two other documents. *I know, I know, sir, but the legislation has changed in the meantime and I'm not the one who makes these laws, believe me.* Oh, the hours spent proving that you were living an honest life, by the book, and that you were paying for your right to be here with taxes and employee contributions for the benefit of everyone, as does every good citizen. I was raised here, born in Baudelocque-Port Royal Hospital, and there it was after all these years: I had to prove, with an accumulation of school reports and school certificates, that I was, in fact, the person I claimed to be, to have the right to stay here.

They should never have created borders, my father grumbled. Anywhere. Never. This is one of those inventions man was wrong to have imagined!

As we walked away, I could hear in his remark and see in his averted gaze the sadness that came from needing to prove his legitimacy after all those years in France. Was he afraid that the vicious circle of the administration might actually turn against him and that we wouldn't be authorized to *stay*? I cleared my throat, in my own way. I was embarrassed for him, for me, unable to find the words to say to him that this all means far less to me than to him, for sure. Shuffling between appointments and reports, I wound up getting the precious residence permit at the end of a long process. Relieved, my father exclaimed in a tone of complicity:

– We succeeded in proving we're one of the good guys, isn't that right, Madame Kidi? So they placed the stamp on the corner of your mouth? Didn't they see how beautiful you are? What about if we make another appointment and get them to make you a new card?

But I just didn't get his compliment or his sense of humor. I was at an age where I was riddled with insecurities, so for me, my own physique was questionable. I frowned when I noticed in the photo not so much the smudged ink but that my face was excessively shiny and my forehead a constellation of acne. And now I was going to have to show this pathetic picture everywhere I went when they asked for ID!

The family ship advances in the middle of a gray sea weighted down by ice. Walls of water as high as thirty feet thrash against the rigging, wearing at the cords that tighten and rip the sails. Despite the conditions, you have to try to cleave through the waves, somehow or other. The captain stands firmly at the helm. He has but one idea in mind: to get through the worst of the bad weather, after which he would have to descend on the other side of the globe, sloping gently beneath the azure celestial vault. Oh, Good Hope! The ship tilts to one side then recovers. It has been like this ever since the ship first set sail. What's important is that we can maintain the smoothness in the lower decks and cabins. So that passengers don't notice that the ocean liner on which they embarked is no more than a schooner, which if confronted by a menacing iceberg would only be able to count on the maneuverability of its breakneck speed and the talent of its captain. As it turns out, the passengers are having a good time. Bach is playing in the ballroom, and the choir knows how to hold the complicated notes of the polyphonic pygmies. The bread and butter on the dining tables hint at other delights. The service can now begin. From time to time, the apprentice climbs up the ladder and sticks his head out, holding on to his cap as he asks:

– Is everything okay? Do you need anything?

The apprentice has a female voice. The captain knows it quite well.

– Nothing, not to worry, I am steering the helm. It'll get better. Who hasn't experienced some rain and divine storms on his path? The gods are making manifest their concerns. They're like us, that way. They don't always see everything.

The apprentice agrees and spurs him on with a loving glance, which goes, as always, right to Francis's heart. That glance has the effect of reassuring and encouraging him to keep on going. He is confident. This night will come to an end. Daylight will open her arms widely to him.

Stepping back from his pride, he confided to a close friend:

– I must be a terrible manager. All that money I got from UNESCO when I left has vanished, just like that. That's what you call going from the frying pan into the fire.

He burst out laughing. He preferred to laugh it all off, thus reducing the fear of what might happen. He wouldn't have his children want for anything.

Madé suggested she could get a job, but he was not having it. It was up to him to handle the situation. Up until now, he had been in charge of this aspect of their life: to make a living while his wife devoted her time to making sure everybody was taken care of.

His friend laughed with him.

– You know that pretty soon women will be in charge! Haven't you noticed? There's a female minister in the government now in charge of their rights. No, I'm telling you! Can you believe this is happening? No one will ever let something like that take place *back home*. Sometimes, all you can do is laugh.

His friend wasn't wrong. Francis thought about how things were back home, all that rigidity that had exasperated him on his last journey. The absolute incomprehension on the part of everyone when all he was trying to do, in the absence of encouragement, was at least generate a budding interest. Marcel, he would have understood him. But Marcel was no longer here. Almost fifteen years had gone by since he had had to accept that his brother was gone. Sometimes, all you can do is laugh. An idea came to Francis while worries were bickering with his heart and keeping his eyes open at night. He got up and went into the living room and wrote a few lines. He loved the magic that delivered him from fear: so long as the gods kept visiting him, took hold of his voice, took hold of his hand to trace the words, he knew he was not wrong about his path. *Émbè nyolo*, Marcel used to say. No, on the contrary, in order to create he must let his body relax so that his heart can speak, open up, and blossom. He took a deep breath, exhaled and sighed.

At the crack of dawn, he was back at it with his tape recorder and his instruments and began to play in his pajamas, pressed by a sense of urgency. *You don't know Sizana? Sizana is my wife. She's my wife because we've been married now for seventeen years. Sizana used to be very kind. I would say to her: "Sizana, I'm hungry", and she would bring me something to eat. "Sizana, give me some water," and she would bring me water to drink, clear water, okay? Great. Only, for the last few days, people over there, they've been bringing up talk about the status of women. Apparently, over there where they live, they've placed a woman in an office so that she can give orders to men. Aye, Aye, Aye! Have you ever heard of such a thing? Now when I say to Sizana: "Sizana, bring me something to eat, I'm hungry!" Her sole response is . . . Hey, women's status . . . Hmm . . . I have got to go get the water myself . . . So I say to Sizana: "Listen to me, I only know one female position: the woman obeys her husband, she feeds him, she gives him children, there you go." Wouldn't you know, Sizana got angry? She came and raised her voice at me, as if she were a man . . .*

Francis kept on laughing as he recorded his song. Were the men in the family going to realize he was poking fun at them? To him, they were so sad, stuck in ways he sometimes disapproved of. He had always wanted to be like his elders later on, become just as wise or at least approximate their wisdom. How wrong he was! They had withered, become so rigid as to seem, at times, laughable. Because sometimes, all you can really do is laugh.

Francis had his family listen to his song after dinner one night. His wife burst out laughing as did as his older son. His other children, on the other hand, looked at each other, hesitant. They had certainly heard of the new French minister for women's affairs and they were not exactly sure that their father should be mocking such a prestigious French institution . . . Francis took the time to explain what he was trying to do: not poke fun at France but at the men from his country, like the men of all the countries, who have a hard time imagining women evolving. The children listened to him but still gave him a strange look. Madé laughed even more intensely, realizing that the children were seemingly dubious about their father's general mental health. She tried to explain:

– Children, don't you know the difference between reading literally and figuratively, with irony, for example? You haven't been taught that at school?

But the children still didn't understand. One in particular wondered how she was going to go about explaining to her friends her father's imagination, which had no regard for limits, a father who pretended to be doing his job while he kept on crossing the line. So long as no one ever hears this song and if by chance they should, so long as no one makes the connection between her and this madcap singer, who, up until that moment, she had introduced as a great concert guitar player.

Francis insisted:

– Madame Kidi, you know how important it is to be serious in life. With this song, I'm trying to get people to think about what's going on, what's changing in the world, and to ask themselves whether or not they think these changes might actually be worth adopting, at least some of them. Can't we try to do things seriously without always taking ourselves so seriously all the time? What do you say?

Francis was going all the way with his project. He produced the record himself, *La Condition Masculine*, which his distributor then dispatched to Africa. He also sent it out to nightclubs and other music venues, as well as to a few curious program planners. Hooked by the title, they began to play the song on their radio programs. The record started spinning from one station to the next, eventually attracting more and more Francophone listeners. In time, success would come. One day a phone call came in from Canada.

– Sir, my students are studying your novel in a class on African literature and we have also had the opportunity to listen to your records here in Quebec. We would be delighted if you would accept our invitation to come and speak, and eventually perform in the university's amphitheater . . .

With a guitar, a book, some records, and a *gandoura* in his luggage, Francis crossed the Atlantic. During the flight, he looked out at the azure sky above the clouds. He would have loved to open the window and feel the cool air on his face. It had been months of constantly working, during which he hid his anxiety—he had even kept the sordid negotiations with the banker from his wife. *I am taking a risk in agreeing to this loan on your behalf. Nothing guarantees that . . . Had you sought out my counsel, I would never have encouraged you to pursue such an adventure. It is unreasonable to imagine that you can play at being an artist when you have a family and you're a foreigner. You're lucky I really like you. But seriously, you need to know that I'm in this, too, I'm taking the risk with you.* After months of waking up in the middle of the night, distraught, drowning in doubt, this invitation felt like the promise of a return to some peace of mind. Francis began to pray.

– Dear God, you to whom I pray so infrequently, I am putting my soul in your care on this day.

The honorarium should take care of the rent the following month. Let's see what happens. He saw this invitation as a sign of change. He hoped this first invitation might set off a chain reaction that would lead him higher up and farther along toward what he couldn't even begin to imagine. He explained all of this to God, speaking plainly to him, and then he dozed off into colorless dreams. The future would look like nothing he had known.

In Montreal, he was at first groggy from the jet lag and awestruck by the amount of snow. He had never in his life seen so much of it. His hosts warmed him up by equipping him with thick gloves and snow boots. He did the rounds with them by car and through the underground passageways of the university campus. He bought a postcard for Madé: *The airport here is called Mirabel. Snow blankets everything: every last bit of the sidewalk and every tiny branch of the trees. The First Nations people have a thousand different names for snow. But I would quite simply say: beautiful, white, and cold. Kiss the children for me. I love you. Don't forget.* The meeting with the students was followed by a discussion session, a conference, and, finally, the recital. He had put together an unbelievable program: classical guitar, humorous ballads, Bach, Villa-Lobos, and his very own compositions. He experienced an insurmountable case of stage fright. The president of the university was seated, surrounded by a learned assembly of colleagues and noteworthy personalities, each more distinguished than the other, in the first rows of the amphitheater. Back stage, Francis had a hard time swallowing. Had all these people in high places come out to see him? Had they really sent a plane ticket and a detailed contract to him? Had they prepared for him a sufficiently tidy sum that would allow him to go back to his banker and teach him a thing or two with a bit of flare? His whole body was suddenly shaking, ready to make a run for it. Looking around for the exit, his eyes came across the friendly man who had been the first to get in touch with him.

> – You know, he had told him on the night of his arrival, we are similar, you and I, do you know why? Like you, I don't live in my ancestral country. My people left European territory back in the fifteenth century to settle down here in Canada. It is said in my family that they were originally from Porto. That's why all the boys in the family have Portuguese-sounding first names, like me, Fernando . . .

The man had made him feel so comfortable that the conversation had ended with him using the familiar *tu*. Francis observed the confident air of his new friend.

> – You're on. It's going to go well.

Francis advanced toward the stage, entered, walked into the spotlight, sat, and began to play. From the moment he played the first chords, the stage fright disappeared into the upper balconies. The theater was all his. The concert went on for what felt like an eternity. And when the coda of the evening had faded, for a few moments, no one moved, enraptured. Finally, the crescendo of the applause filled the whole room. Francis blinked his eyes as if he were coming out of a dream. From the back stage, Fernando gave him a wonderstruck smile. What Francis was doing interested other people and they even enjoyed it. He was not crazy after all.

The gods listened to Francis. They had given him courage, patience, imagination, and the fervor to work. In time, it was not enough to pluck the strings of the guitar. Curious about other sounds, he took on the metal tines of the sanza. This instrument introduced into his compositions those celestial warm showers and times spent prancing around with the boys of his neighborhood back in Douala. He also layered in the unique monotonous chant of the flute with Pygmy musical tones, evoking the flutes of his childhood, so skillfully crafted from papaya tree branches.

Success followed. By way of the phone, by post, by word of mouth, and from journey to journey, Francis was appreciated everywhere he went. For his children, the crazy man he almost became had transformed into a perfectly normal father who, instead of a briefcase, took a suitcase and a musical instrument to go to work. The home country had, in the meanwhile, expanded to encompass France and the world.

Cameroon weighed in, notably the family and especially his older sister, who tried to warn her younger brother:

– We keep hearing your song on the radio. Why do you have to embarrass us like this, with these lyrics that make everybody laugh? You of all people, you worked as an international civil servant, you were an international employee!

Francis shook his head. And to add insult to injury, they were calling him collect to give him a lecture! So what if his Cameroonian peers thought he was an imbecile. Other listeners said nothing of the sort. The Belgians, the Swiss, the Germans all invited him to perform in their respective countries. The Venezuelans asked him to come and participate as a juror in an international guitar competition. The Americans and the Swedes were now studying his books at their universities. Ivoirians, Togolese, and Congolese sang the refrain to his new song in chorus, *Agatha ne me mens pas*! Francis thought about the Cameroon of his childhood. That country, he was never going to let the picture of it become discolored in some photo album. Every day from afar, he cleaned the frame and oriented its angle so that dust never gathered. Although he had not been able to own a home there, not even the smallest parcel of land, regardless of all of that he had reconnected with his foundation. He turned out to be the one who had listened. He would continue to "do things seriously without taking himself too seriously," especially if it worked. Marcel would have understood. *Émbè muléma*, he used to say. But Francis had found his own words to live by: *senga muléma*, listen to the voice of your heart. That's precisely what Marcel used to do, he had listened to the voice in the depth of his being, which had propelled him to act according to his heart. His older brother had tended to people's bodies, and Francis was now playing his music and, in so doing, sharing with his brother in taking caring of the souls of those who listened to him. Francis had liberated himself, yet these brothers were forever connected in the dream that they shared—that of a changed world. Most certainly Marcel would have understood.

Francis stood up, barefoot on the carpet in his hotel room in Manhattan. From the bay window, he could see the yellow taxis and pedestrians below frenetically going about in the streets. He stretched his arms out wide, as far as the tips of his fingers, to make them more agile. In a few minutes they would come to get him for the rehearsal and sound check at Carnegie Hall. Tonight he was performing in this prestigious concert hall. An African, alone, before an immense public. An African, alone, with his world in a guitar. To chase away the stage fright, he found himself laughing.

Me, little Francis, a truant in my early school days, I am going to be playing in this incredible place . . .

Epilogue

The story could end this way: certain returns linger eternally.

Francis didn't take Madé by the hand to have her sit down. He didn't take a seat before her and look her straight in the eyes and solemnly declare:

– In the end, my love, let's be honest, we won't be *going back home*.

But he did go on living and taking pleasure in this life and this space that had allowed him to become the man he could never have imagined. Neither of them ever formalized the fact that they had renounced, because there was probably no such official renunciation. Of the life they had had to create, much in the same way a painter brings life to a painting on a canvas, they had done what they could, what they believed they had to do: have a family, raise their children, and live in a comfortable home. They framed the painting with music, of a very particular kind. Of this life they had created, of this unbelievable life of estrangement, they had learned how to make it meaningful: they had learned that the exile they had feared had, in fact, allowed them to grow. From the distance, Francis had created a springboard, thanks to which he had dared to discover the frontiers of his freedom. And in the process, he had invented something else: his life, another life.

His older sister stopped calling. She no longer wanted to hear about the instrument her brother had entrusted to her to keep safe and that she had lost. She was afraid to say it out loud. Even more, she was afraid of provoking the gods' wrath. One never knew: Francis seemed to have changed. He reminded her of the medicine man he had been forbidden to go near when he was a boy. When she had gone to look in the dark corner where she thought she had placed the guitar, there was nothing but an old scrap of fabric that had stiffened over time, covered in mold. Not even a hint of the smallest bit of varnished wood. Not a string. Even worse, no one in the family besides her could recall ever seeing anything set in that corner. A musical instrument? Why would it have been kept hidden in a corner where no one goes? Who would have benefited from an instrument no one plays? At times, Francis's sister wondered if she was slowly losing her mind. She had since become an elder, who was called on not so much for her wisdom but rather out of concern for her well-being, as you would a child. *Maa Frida . . . É mala ndé neni?* Grandma Frida, how are you doing?

In the courtyard, one of her daughters-in-law sat with her children, a book resting on her knees. She was telling them a story:

It is said that when the sea is beautiful and the waves calm, the sky gazes into its own reflection in this never-ending expanse, and the rays of the sun try to pierce the secrets of the deep sea, and the surface of the water shimmers as if the sky and the stars had fallen in. On these days, it is said, an object of a rare form can be seen floating between the waves with rays of sunlight reflecting off its glistening, varnished wood. The object has round curves and a fierce heart—some call it the rosette—decorated with what looks like a pompon made from tulle that has faded over time. This stretch of fabric prevents it from becoming heavy and sinking to the bottom. Sailors claim they've seen this strange instrument when sailing off the French coast on the open sea toward La Rochelle. Sightings have also been made in the Americas, in the New York Bay, and even further down by the Brazilian coast, where it apparently made Christ the Redeemer wink. But the most enduring legend can be heard off the Atlantic coast of Africa. Our ancestors, the Bantus, report that thanks to this instrument, it was possible to found the First City. From its strings were born men and women who today make up all of humanity.

> – Oh yes, my dear children, the young lady concluded, according to this legend, all the people in the world, Black, White, men, women, they all originate from this unique source—the guitar.

KIDI BEBEY is a French journalist and writer. She is the author of several children's books. *My Kingdom for a Guitar* is her first novel, originally published in French in 2016 by Michel Lafon.

KAREN LINDO is a scholar of French and Francophone Studies, currently teaching and translating in Paris. She is the translator of three other books in the Global African Voices series: *The Heart of the Leopard Children*, *The Silence of the Spirits*, and *Concrete Flowers*, all by Wilfried N'Sondé.

CPSIA information can be obtained
at www.ICGtesting.com
Printed in the USA
JSHW022245200721
17094JS00001B/41